REBEL

GERAINT JONES

First published in the United Kingdom in 2021 by Canelo

This edition published in the United Kingdom in 2022 by

Canelo
Unit 9, 5th Floor
Cargo Works, 1-2 Hatfields
London, SE1 9PG
United Kingdom

A CIP catalogue record for this book is available from the British Library.

Print ISBN 978 1 80032 413 8
Ebook ISBN 978 1 80032 412 1

Look for more great books at www.canelo.co

Printed and bound in Great Britain by Clays Ltd, Elcograf S.p.A.

1

Part One

Chapter 1

In the final seconds of my life I tasted blood and felt cold steel.

The blood was not my own. It belonged to my friend, King Pinnes, rebel leader of the Pannonians, who had surrendered his people to Rome. For that he had died, but not at the Empire's hands – it was his former allies, the Dalmatians, who had robbed the world of one of its brightest sons, and now my neck rested on the same chopping block where the king had been put to death. There was a spike waiting for my head, and an impatient crowd waiting to see it put there.

Ziva was amongst them. The reptile. The snake. Known for his cruelty, he had served Pinnes as a trusted commander, but the young man had turned on his lord to gain power for himself. He had whispered words of treason to Bato, the Dalmatian war master, spreading rumours that Pinnes had agreed to do the Romans' fighting for them, and attack those who had stood beside him in this brutal rebellion.

They were lies. All lies. Peace was all that King Pinnes desired. He had ridden with his royal bodyguard to Bato not to shed blood but to spare it, and so Ziva and his men had fallen on them in a trap. Vuk, one of my few friends in the world, was killed along with the king he had sworn to defend. To further inflame the enmity between the tribes,

Ziva had left soldiers to kill the Dalmatian hostages held by the Pannonian army. These women and children were the families of Dalmatian nobility, and they had been put to the sword so that Bato's rage against King Pinnes's people would be complete.

Only two hostages had survived. A fierce mother, and her young son. She was Miran, he was Borna, and I loved them both.

Their freedom had been bought with the life of my friend Thumper. It was he who had led me to the rebel army, and service with Pinnes. I had once been a hero of Rome, the man who saved an eagle, but all that had changed when I deserted my legion. So it was that I came to fight the Empire instead, and so it was that I came to believe wholeheartedly in the rebel cause:

Freedom from Rome.

With Miran and Borna, I had struggled to reach Bato's camp in the mountains before the king was put to death, but I was too late. Ziva's treacherous poison had already seeped into the mind of Bato, and King Pinnes's head was taken from his shoulders.

And now I was to join him. It did not matter that I had saved two of the Dalmatian hostages from slaughter. It did not matter that I had proven myself in battle against Rome. All that mattered was that Bato believed Ziva.

'He is the agent of Rome that turned Pinnes against you,' he hissed to Bato. 'He must die, lord.'

And die I would. There was a blade against the back of my neck. I could feel the hunger of it against my spine. The executioner stood beside me, and soon he would swing, and I would die, and Ziva would win. *Rome* would win.

I wanted to spit, but I had nothing to give. My life had been nothing if not brutal. I had killed more men than I cared to remember, and lost so many that I didn't dare to forget. I would see them when I died, and I would meet them with pride. At the end of my life, I had done something right. Something honourable. The lives of Miran and Borna were worth far more than my own, and I had smiled at the thought.

Ziva hadn't liked that. He didn't like that I was heading to my death with anything other than dread, and so he had knelt beside me, and whispered the names of the four Roman soldiers that had murdered my father. Names that he had extracted under torture from Roman prisoners. Only one of them mattered to me.

Marcus.

My oldest friend. My most painful betrayer. Now there was no hiding from the truth. The only escape was in death.

'Do it!' I tried to roar at the executioner, but my tongue was so dry it stuck to the top of my mouth. 'Do it!'

The crowd wanted blood. The crowd wanted steel.

'Kill him!'

'Kill the Roman!'

'Kill the traitor!'

There was violence in their voice, and violence in their ranks. I only saw a ripple of it, my eyes blurred by blood and dirt, but I could *feel it*. The buzz of confrontation. Raised voices. *Hard* voices.

'Get it over with!' I knew who those words belonged to. Bato, the warrior, chieftain of the Dalmatians. He was a mountain made of flesh and muscle, but in that moment I could not see him, and it did not matter. That the executioner could hear him was all that did, and I felt the steel move from my neck as he lifted the blade to swing, and sever.

I was ready to die.

Ready for death.

But it was not ready for me.

There was a scuffle. There were curses. Men swore, grunted and spat. I heard swords being drawn. Orders being shouted.

I was hauled to my feet.

I was at the centre of a knot of men who faced away from me, with blades in their hands. I was being held by the arm, and looking into the face of their leader. His thick beard was shot through with white, his face as lined and scarred as the land where the rebellion raged. I was taller than most, but he was taller again, though he was without the boulder-like muscle of Bato. The man was appraising me, as one does a newborn lamb.

'Just kill me,' I told him. I had no humour for entertaining Dalmatian warriors, and from his shining armour, and the quality of his helmet, there was no doubt that he was that.

'You won't die that easily.'

I knew what was coming, then. I knew what my end would be. No quick death by the sword. That was a fate for kings, not traitors.

I would be tortured.

How would they do it? Ziva had once wanted to crucify me – would he get his wish? Perhaps I would be boiled alive, or pulled apart by horses. There is no end to man's imagination – at least not when it comes to creating suffering for others – and it was only the fact that I had already resigned myself to death that stopped my stomach from lifting out of my mouth, and my hands from shaking.

But the eyes could not lie. The nobleman saw the thoughts behind mine, and laughed at me.

Bastard. I would not show him weakness.

'What will it be?' I demanded in a tone that I hoped showed defiance. If Miran was watching, I wanted her to see me die well.

A sly grin crept over the man's face. He was enjoying this. Every moment.

'The most painful torture of all, lad,' he whispered in my ear.

'*Marriage.*'

Chapter 2

I didn't have time to think about what the nobleman had said to me.

My head span as I was pushed away from the chopping block. The heads of my friend Vuk and King Pinnes were grisly trophies atop their spikes, and anger surged through me as I saw the flies dancing over their dead eyes.

'Take them down!' I ordered. 'Take them down!'

No one listened. Instead, surrounded by the knot of armed and grim men, I was being half-dragged by the warrior with the greying beard. He wasn't manhandling me, but he didn't have to – I was weak from fatigue. To get to this camp and save Miran and Borna I had pushed myself beyond exhaustion. Beyond limits. It was a miracle I was still on my feet, but imminent death has a way of holding your attention.

I could hear someone shouting. Bato, I realised. His words were like claps of thunder.

'Stop! Agron! *Stop!*'

'Just keep walking,' the man beside me said.

I kept walking.

Bato's hall was at our backs. It was the biggest building in the camp, but not the only one. Constructions of stone and timber showed evidence of weathering at least one winter, and into one of these dwellings I was now led.

'Wait outside,' the nobleman told his men. He let go of my arm. Looked at me. 'We don't have long.'

I said nothing.

'My name is Agron.' He didn't offer me his hand. 'Miran says that she owes you her life.'

Again, I stayed silent. He saw the question on my face.

'When Bato ordered you killed, she went into the crowd to look for someone to help you,' Agron explained.

Ziva had delayed my death by trying to convince me to 'confess' my crimes to Bato, and so cement Ziva's lies, but evidently that time had bought Miran the chance to find what she was looking for.

'Who are you to her?' I asked him.

'We are of the same tribe. Her father was a dear cousin of mine, and her husband was a brave warrior. If what she says is true, then we were about to kill the wrong man. Is that so?'

I nodded. 'Ziva's men ambushed King Pinnes, and he ordered the hostages in the Pannonian camp to be killed.'

The man looked grave. 'That's what Miran said.'

I said nothing.

'She also said that you saved her, and the boy.'

I didn't deny it. 'They deserved saving.'

'And King Pinnes, it seems, did not deserve death.' He looked pained.

'Neither did his men.' Vuk had been a loyal friend. One of the only ones I had left.

Agron met my eye, then nodded in grim agreement. 'You are right.' he said. 'There were those of us who opposed the execution – at least one so hastily carried out – but we were voted down. Ziva's announcement that the hostages had been butchered was all the tribal leaders needed to hear. Those people were dear to us, and we wanted blood to pay for blood.' He let out a breath. 'Were we tricked into killing a good man…?'

'Pinnes wanted to end the war for all sides. He didn't plot any harm against you. He just wanted Bato to come to the same agreement with Rome as he had.' That agreement was a stop to the war, tribute paid, and soldiers provided for the Empire's never-ending desire to conquer new lands.

The nobleman opened his mouth to ask more, but then there was a roar from outside.

'*Agron!*'

Something of a smile played at his lips. It was dry, and humourless.

'It appears that Lord Bato would like to join our conversation.'

–

When we stepped outside I saw that we, and Agron's dozen men, were surrounded by a thick ring of more than a hundred warriors, three ranks deep. These were Bato's household troops, hard men all – every one had the eyes of a killer.

Bato was standing alone in the space between the two groups. He did not have a weapon drawn, and neither did his men, but their looks were enough for me to know that violence was only a word away.

'Agron…' Bato tried to speak calmly. 'Hand over the Roman.'

I bristled at that. I may have been tired to the marrow of my bones, but I had pride, and I was no bastard Roman. Bato and Ziva had long enjoyed needling me over the Empire that I had deserted, and now I saw that shit was standing with Bato's men at the edge of the crowd. His eyes burned into mine with hate.

'Kill him, Lord Bato,' Ziva beseeched the rebel commander. 'He is a traitor.'

'This is a conversation for Dalmatians,' Agron silenced the Pannonian. 'I believe you'll want to hear what Corvus has to say, Bato.' He said it politely, but without grovelling deference. 'It makes for good listening.'

'I've already listened to this turd,' Bato snorted, and that was true enough. I had tried pleading my case when the two hostages and I had been brought into the camp, but my words had fallen on deaf ears. Miran's, too.

I broke my eyes from Ziva's hateful stare, and looked to the rebel leader instead. Bato and fewer than a hundred thousand Dalmatians were all that stood against Rome now.

'You have been deceived, lord.'

Bato spat. 'Yes, by you, Roman. You and Pinnes have conspired against me, and the sooner your head is beside his the better. Agron, stop this nonsense.'

'I'm afraid that I can't do that.'

A scar on Bato's skull pulsed like a bright red worm. 'What do you mean, can't? You can, and you will! I am the leader of this army, and if I say the Roman dies, then that is the end of it!'

Bato's boiling rage was something to behold, but if it bothered Agron then he showed no sign. 'You are indeed commander of this army, Lord Bato,' he replied evenly, 'and my people make up a *willing* part of it.'

Agron let the implication hang. When Bato said nothing, he made his intention clear.

'Corvus is under the protection of my tribe,' Agron announced to the rebel leader, 'and any harm done to him will mean the end of our alliance.'

For a second, nothing happened. The entire mountain seemed to hold its breath… and then it erupted.

Bato roared and raged, spit flying from his mouth and veins bulging in his neck.

But Agron did not flinch. Agron did not back down.

'I take it you accept what I am saying, lord?' he asked in a rare breath between Bato's curses.

'Accept? ACCEPT? You would threaten our alliance, our war, *for a Roman?*'

The calm nobleman shook his head. 'For a Dalmatian, lord.'

At this Bato snorted. 'He is as Dalmatian as Julius Caesar!'

'He was born and raised in Iadar.'

'He is a Roman.'

'He is Dalmatian,' Agron corrected gently, then firmed his tone, 'and he will *marry* a Dalmatian.'

Bato's eyes burned into me, but I was not looking at him. I was looking at the ranks of Bato's men. I was looking at Miran, pushing her way through the circle of killers as though they were merely petulant children.

My heart leapt to see her. Her slender frame. Her jet black hair. Her nose, perfectly crooked and bumped. She had broken it while risking her life for her son, and Miran showed that same courage now as she shoved past another of Bato's men.

Her face was tight with anger. She'd looked that way when we'd first met. Her eyes had been ablaze, and they were that way now, the set of her jaw was as proud as ever.

Miran's look to me was quick, but said it all – 'don't make this worse.'

And so I kept my mouth shut.

'I will marry Corvus,' she declared to Bato.

His eyes popped. Words failed him. Agron spoke before Bato could cough out his anger.

'Corvus will marry into my tribe, Lord Bato. He will *be* of my tribe, and as such,' he looked at the assembly of Bato's killers, 'any attack against him will be considered an attack against us all.'

'Madness,' Bato was mumbling, 'madness...'

I expected that at any moment he would give the order to seize me, and men would draw blades and fight, and we would surely die. I did not want that for Miran, and opened my mouth to speak.

She shut it for me with a look, and then everything changed.

Bato was laughing.

'Ha!' The rebel rumbled once, twice, and soon there was no stopping it, his huge frame shaking with the convulsions of his humour. He was the only one privy to the joke, and the rest of the assembly watched on in silence until Bato wore himself out, and rubbed a thick hand across his face. 'The gods eh, Agron? How they love their drama! How they love their comedy!'

A moment ago every man's hand had been ready to draw their blade, but now men shared befuddled looks at the laughter of the rebel leader. I was as confused as any of them, and tried to read what was truly behind the humour – was Bato claiming to embrace the idea because he knew that to do otherwise would risk losing him part of his alliance? At any other time I would dismiss the thought, but days ago a hundred thousand Pannonian rebels had surrendered to Rome. Without doubt there would be leaders in Bato's camp considering the same path. At a time of tribal friction, perhaps taking my head was not worth the potential cost to Bato.

'You are betrothed, eh?' he asked of Miran.

'We are,' she answered defiantly.

This was news to me.

'As of when?' the warlord demanded.

'As of now,' Agron replied for her, and from his tone there was no doubt that he, and his tribe, stood armed and ready behind that decision.

Bato nodded to Agron, then smiled at me. It was a scary thing to see. I had never seen a lion, but I had heard stories of predators with hungry eyes and long teeth. I felt myself being devoured by his gaze.

'Are you wed to anyone else, Roman?'

This bastard. '*I am not a Roman,*' I said firmly.

'Answer the question,' he snapped back.

I felt Miran's stare. The unspoken words – *don't make things worse.*

I swallowed my pride. Part of it, at least. 'No, *lord,*' I told him, burying the word in contempt. I could feel Miran's look growing hotter: I was making things worse.

'No, I am not married, lord.'

Bato snorted again. 'Then this will be a new experience for you.' He turned to his soldiers. 'No doubt he will be begging for me to kill him before the year is out, eh?'

His fighters laughed. This time it was Miran who tensed, and needed to be calmed.

'Don't...' I heard Agron say quietly.

Bato turned his eyes back to me for a long, terrible moment. In my life I had known fear, and I had known killers – Bato was a man who instilled one, and was a master of the other.

I did not want him as my enemy.

He turned to Agron. 'I accept, my good friend, but on one condition.'

We waited for it.

'Corvus must fight the Romans.'

'I swear to it,' I said quickly, but Bato eyed me with disdain.

'You have already shown that your word means nothing, deserter.'

Angry heat built inside me, but I stayed silent for Miran.

'Lady,' Bato grinned at her, 'if you marry Corvus, and he betrays us to the Romans, then your life, and your son's, will be forfeit. These are the only terms on which I can accept this marriage. Do you agree?'

I was stunned by the demand, but Miran did not falter.

'I agree, lord.'

I didn't know what to say. What to do.

Agron spoke before I could undo his work with a careless word or prideful sneer.

'Now that that is settled, my friend,' he said to Bato, 'I believe we have something to discuss with the lord Ziva.' All eyes turned to where the snake had been standing.

Bato was the first to curse, and spit.

Ziva was gone.

Chapter 3

In the course of a morning I had gone from the executioner's block to the promise of the altar. When the news reached us that Ziva had ridden out of camp at the head of his men, the last reserves of my strength left with him. I would live, for now, and such a revelation robbed me of the nervous excitement that had kept me upright.

'I have to lie down,' I told Miran.

She nodded, but said no more. She was almost cold to me, and I knew why.

To escape the net of Ziva's men and their massacre, I had ambushed a small patrol to steal a horse. She had seen then who I truly was.

A killer.

Agron led me back inside of his dwelling. 'You can sleep here,' he told me, and I collapsed onto the pile of furs that was his campaign bed.

—

When I woke neither he nor Miran were anywhere to be seen. I groaned at the pain in my head, and then the door opened: Agron, holding cups, and wineskins. He said something to one of his men that I didn't hear, then stepped inside, leaving the makeshift door open.

'You stink,' he told me.

'I don't suppose there's a bathhouse on this mountain?' I asked, thinking about the times where I had slipped into hot waters in the past. I had my issues with Rome, but the baths were not one of them.

I groaned again as I sat up. Every part of my body felt like it had been trampled in a cavalry charge. My shoulder – the most painful part of all – had been kicked out of its socket by a dying horse during our flight from Ziva. Miran had put it back in, but the joint was tight with swelling.

'Do you feel as bad as you look?' Agron asked.

'Worse.' I felt no need for bravado with this man. He handed me some water, and I thanked him.

He watched me drink. 'Miran says you have a habit of almost getting killed.'

'It's a war.' I wiped my lips. 'And I'm a soldier.'

He liked that.

'Thank you for saving Miran and Borna,' he said. Sadness passed over his strong features, then. 'I thought all of the hostages from my tribe had been lost. When I saw her again...'

He said no more. He didn't have to.

'The hostages died quickly,' I lied, hoping it would give him some ease. The truth was that they had been hunted down and butchered as they screamed and begged for mercy.

None had been given.

A warrior appeared in the open doorway. He was carrying a plate of meat, and biscuits.

'Set it down here, Danek,' Agron told him.

I gave the fighter an appraising look. He was about my own age and build, though my skin was darker, and I boasted a lot more scars and a broken nose.

'I have heard you fight well,' he said, apparently making his own assessment of me.

I didn't deny it. My reputation was known to the rebels well before I joined their ranks. I was the man who had stopped an eagle from falling into their hands. And then, while serving King Pinnes, I was one of the men who broke into my old legion's home and stole the pay chests that were supposed to pay Rome's soldiers. Instead, that money had gone towards supporting the rebels' war.

'Maybe we can practise together,' he said, but there was as much challenge behind the words as camaraderie. I recognised him as the kind of young soldier who thirsts for reputation and glory. Every army has them. Every army relies on them. They are the men you need to lead a charge. To volunteer for certain death. To push, pull and exhort their comrades. Without them, an army is stagnant.

Agron smiled. 'You can go, Danek.'

'Yes, lord.' His eyes stayed on me for a moment longer than they needed to, and then he obeyed his tribal leader.

'Please,' Agron told me, gesturing to the food, 'eat.'

I tried not to fall on the meat like a hungry wolf. I didn't know if I had ever tasted anything more divine, though in truth the game was tough and charred almost to blackness. Any food turns a hungry man into a grateful one, though, no matter the skill of the cook.

I gestured towards the open door through which Danek had left. 'Your son?'

He shook his head. 'Alas, the gods have taken all my children from me.'

'War?'

'Sickness.'

I said no more. Life could be cruel.

'I owe you a debt for the lives of two of my tribe,' Agron said firmly. 'Name it.'

There was nothing to name. 'You already saved my life.'

'That was Miran. Well, Borna, actually. He was the one that found me in the crowd.'

I laughed at that. Saved by a child. Maybe I should take Danek up on his offer of practice.

'There is one thing…' I began, sparked by the thought of children. 'I had a friend in the camp. He died helping to save Miran and Borna.' The thought of Thumper's death held me for a moment. 'His sons are in Seretium – could you get word to them?'

'Of course. Leave it with me,' the nobleman promised. 'I'll see that word gets to the right place. It's the least I can do for him. What would you like me to say?'

I began to ramble about who Thumper was, and what he had done. It was painful. Raw. Agron could see that I was struggling to give words to my feelings, and he silenced me with a paternal smile. 'Don't worry, Corvus,' he assured me, 'I'll take care of it.'

We drifted into silence for a moment as Agron filled our cups. This time, it was not water that he poured.

'You looked like you needed a drink. Tell me, what will the Pannonians do now that Pinnes is dead?'

'I have no idea,' I said honestly. I had not been party to tribal councils. I knew that the king held his tribes together through skilled diplomacy and the strength of his character, but the nature of how he had woven those bonds, and what would happen to them now that he was gone, were beyond me.

'I was just there to fight,' I told him honestly. And we had done plenty of that. A near-victory at the Volcae Marshes. A doomed cavalry charge weeks later. The first had been lost when the Roman legions rallied around their eagles. The second had been over before we even arrived, but we had been driven into that fight by the thirst for revenge, as the Mazaei tribe were put to the sword by Roman auxiliary units.

Ziva had ridden away from that fight and not been seen again until my near execution. My heart sank as I remembered those moments, and what he'd whispered into my ear. Though his plan to kill me had failed, Ziva had murdered any hope I had that the man who had killed my father and my first love had not been Marcus, my oldest friend.

Agron recognised the dark clouds forming on my features, and why. 'What will Ziva do?'

I didn't need long to think about it. 'He wants the Pannonian crown, and there is no one wearing it. Then, I believe he will try and lead the tribes back into war.'

Agron considered that. 'He will tell the Pannonians that King Pinnes was dealing with the Romans to betray us, and that he was caught and brought to justice by Bato. What if they want war against the Dalmatian tribes?'

'To avenge Pinnes? Ziva wouldn't allow it.' I shook my head. 'His fight is against Rome. He is a lying shit, but if there is one thing he is honest about, it is his hate of the Empire.' I had seen that hate first-hand. Ziva was well known in the war for what he did to Roman prisoners, even going so far as to offer bounties on their heads so that he could have more captives to torture.

'I won't begrudge him that,' Agron said. 'But if he was truly behind the death of our hostages, then I will have his blood.' There was steel behind his promise. I accepted it with a look.

'Will Bato kill him?' I asked. 'I can't imagine that he is taking it well, knowing that he was played by Ziva.'

Agron shook his head. 'I spoke with him and the other tribal leaders while you were asleep. Bato won't admit that killing Pinnes was a mistake. He even said that he'd sent Ziva away himself.'

I snorted. 'He's trying to save face.'

'He is, and for good reason. If Ziva really can bring the Pannonians back into the war, then we need him.'

I could see that pained Agron.

'I want him dead,' the nobleman confirmed, 'but what's most important is the war. If Ziva can bring us men, then he must be allowed to live, for now at least.'

There was a warning in his tone. I understood it but said nothing, and so Agron was forced to spell it out. 'Corvus, you can't do anything that would threaten Pannonians fighting for our cause, do you understand? You can't do anything that would threaten the rebellion.'

The thought of Ziva living made me sick, and I told Agron as much. 'Besides, didn't you risk as much when you took me under your tribe's protection?'

A sly grin crept over the older man's face. 'I was bluffing,' he admitted. 'If Bato had drawn his sword I would have backed down, and you'd be a dead man.'

I gave a single dry laugh, and thanked him for his honesty.

'You were dead either way.' Agron shrugged. 'But now Miran is happy, and that means a lot to me.'

I reached for more wine. Agron took hold of my wrist. His gaze was firm. 'I'm still waiting for your word on Ziva.'

I looked from his hand to his face. 'I didn't think the word of a traitor meant anything around here?'

'It means something to me.' He let go of my wrist, and poured the wine himself. 'You turned your back on the Empire, Corvus. How can I hold that against a man, when our entire army has done the same?'

I said nothing. The rebels had been raised to fight for Rome before Bato and Pinnes had led them into rebellion against their masters. They had no interest in dying for the Empire that had conquered their lands and enslaved the generation of their fathers. Nonetheless, it was rare for a traitor to come from the ranks of Rome's legions, and I was viewed with suspicion that was not given to the Germans, Thracians and other auxiliaries who had chosen to leave Rome's service to fight against, and not for, her.

'A lot of people still think I'm a Roman,' I said at last.

'True,' Agron agreed, 'but not a lot of people *think*. So, do we have an understanding?'

I said nothing.

'Then how about this?' Agron held out his cup. 'Once we win the war, Corvus, I will help you kill Ziva. We will skin him alive together.'

I liked the sound of that. Nothing would give me greater pleasure than seeing that bastard die slowly for the deaths of Thumper, Vuk and King Pinnes.

I met his toast. 'We have an understanding.'

Agron drained his cup in one, then got to his feet. 'I need to see to my men. We'll be marching out, soon.'

'To where?'

'Bato has decided that we will pull the rebellion further south, to stretch the Roman supply lines. There are walled towns in the mountains, and they will be our home.' The nobleman looked around at his hovel. 'I'll miss this place, though. Winter builds a strong bond between a man and a roof, no matter how humble.'

He walked to the door, then turned back to look at me. He was a handsome man, Agron, made more handsome when he smiled.

'The gods favour you, Corvus. To have survived all that you have, and now be about to take Miran as your wife?' the old warrior laughed softly to himself. 'You really are a lucky one.'

Chapter 4

I slept through the night and the next morning. There were times when I woke and filled my mouth with what food was left on the plate, but I was slipping back into slumber before I had even finished chewing. It would have been some way to die, choking to death on biscuits after all that I had endured, but a hungry, tired man will risk his life just as readily as one who is heartsick and in love.

Miran. I was to marry her.

That was the first thought I had whenever I woke up. Since the days where my first love Beatha had been murdered, and my father after her, I often woke to my own screams. Nightmares filled my head, but not this night. This night I had been dreaming of Miran.

Our life.

Our new beginning.

I could not have imagined this. Well, that was a lie. I *could* imagine it, and had done so often when I was in the Pannonian camp, and Miran was a hostage, but imagining was all that it had been – a dream.

That Miran was a hostage was no great thing in itself. It was normal practice that allies took them from each other's noble families to bind their promises with flesh. I had served in King Pinnes's army, and Miran and her son had been his hostages sent from the Dalmatian army, but it was not this that had kept me from spilling my feelings to her; Miran had been married.

Her husband served with Lord Bato and, though we had never talked at length about the nobleman, I knew enough: he was a good man, and Miran was faithful to him.

And so I had never given voice to what was in my heart, and Miran had never spoken about what I believed was in hers, but we both knew. Why else were we so quick to argue? Why else could we not walk away after those fights?

We had made a peace, of sorts. We knew what we wanted. Knew what we couldn't have. No words had been spoken. Not of love, at least. Instead, I had promised to protect her and Borna, though the truth was that Thumper's blood had paid for their escape.

I grimaced as I remembered my friend's end. Pannonian blades had brought him to death's threshold, but I was the one to carry him across it. It was a mercy blow, I knew that. I couldn't allow my friend to fall into the hands of those who were so fond of torture, but still...

There was no forgetting his eyes, as the life fled out of them.

And Thumper's suffering did not end in death. During my life on the coast, and around the port of Iadar, I had seen live bodies sink in water, and dead ones float. Miran had been aghast when I threw the slain Thumper into a river, and her after him, but the last deep breath in his lungs had kept us alive and together long enough, and we were carried away from the slaughter by the river's strong current.

Miran had hit me for what I had done to him. I had not fought back. Then, nature had been our battle. The river had been swollen by snowmelt from the mountains, and I

25

remembered how Miran and Borna's teeth had chattered. I remembered how she'd looked at me when I told them to strip out of their wet clothes. I'd had to shout to have my order followed, but follow it they had, and despite the imminence of death I'd felt my eyes pulled to her.

In action I had found distraction. I led us across meadows, and into woods. The sun dried our clothes. We dressed, and again Miran's body lured my eyes. So, too, did the movement of four horsemen. They were part of a net, sent out by Ziva to catch survivors of the massacre before they could reach Bato, and tell of his treachery.

With the help of Miran and Borna I laid my own ambush. It was a short but brutal fight. An awful fight. It was not the glorious combat that young men talk of, but a scrap for survival on an unknown track, in an unknown forest, in a little-known war. Still, it was the end of four men, and the last one left the world screaming as I tortured him for answers about Ziva's plans. It took the loss of a few fingers for him to realise that talking was in his best interest. After I had what I needed, I gave him a quick end, but Miran had heard the screams, and she'd seen what I'd done to Thumper. Perhaps at one time she had loved the man that she thought I was, but there were no such feelings for the heartless brute she now knew me to be.

And yet here we were, soon to be married.

Why was she doing this? Guilt? Pride? Was Miran repaying me with my own life, for saving her son's? Surely there could be no other reason. She had seen the killer in me, but Miran was a woman of honour. My life was a reward. She would suffer me, because I had spared her the most insufferable pain of all – the loss of Borna.

I heard the rickety door open. Agron entered. His arms were full with weaponry and armour that he set gently onto a chest.

'Sleep well?'

'Like the dead.'

I saw his eyes go to the empty plate. 'I'll have someone fetch you more food. Can't get married on an empty stomach, can you?'

I stood and felt my tight muscles stretch. Everything was painful. Looking down at my body, I saw that I was filthy with dirt and dried blood.

'I can't get married like this.'

Agron laughed. 'Come on. We don't have a baths here, but we do have the next best thing.'

–

With Danek and a dozen men in tow Agron led me across the camp, where I saw rebels preparing to move out. There were thousands of people spread through this mountainside, men, women and children. I was witnessing the mobilisation of a large village as much as that of an army.

The sky above us was empty blue and the air was warm. In the summer, the heat of these lands beat an armoured soldier down, but today it was pleasant and friendly. Good weather for farming. Better weather to sit with friends, and drink, and eat and laugh.

I had such friends once. Brothers of my legion. Brutus, Priscus, Varo and Octavius. As far as I knew Brutus still lived, though he had one leg less than he was born with. The others had been lost to the war. I had seen Priscus die in battle. Octavius had fallen without me. I had buried him but the rebels had dug him up and desecrated his body. So it was that I took him to Iadar, and interred him beside Beatha.

There was no such funeral for Varo. He had simply vanished. That happened to soldiers in the mountains, and their ends were the worst of all men's.

I shook my head to clear it of such thoughts. I could hear it then. Rushing water.

'Here,' Agron said.

Water burst forth from a mountain spring. There were young children filling buckets from it, but they soon moved away as the warriors approached. The Dalmatian tribes were a martial society; there was a hierarchy, with warriors at the top of it, and noblemen like Agron atop of them.

'Throw that tunic away,' Agron said to me. I pulled it off, grimacing as scabs came with it. I was naked and no doubt made a wretched sight. The corded muscles of my limbs were already dark from the spring sun, but the only colouring to my torso was deep bruising and stained blood.

'The mountain will heal you,' Agron said.

I walked into the cold waters. It shocked my skin and stole the breath from my lungs. Within seconds my heart was beating faster, and my mind told me to step away, back into the warm sunshine.

I looked at Agron. Saw the faces of his men. They might call me a Dalmatian, and I might be under their protection, but I was not one of them, not truly, and they were appraising me to see how I behaved.

Fine. Let them watch.

I let a smile creep onto my face as I embraced the pain of the cold, and began to scrub myself with my hands.

Agron took a step forwards. 'Here. Use it up.' It was a pumice stone and a small sliver of soap. 'Can't have you marrying Miran smelling like a goat. A dead one at that.'

I scrubbed at the blood on my skin.

'Have I missed any?'

'You look like you bathed in it,' Agron laughed. 'Keep scrubbing.'

When the nobleman was satisfied that I was clean – or clean enough, at least – I walked out into the sun. It was a beautiful feeling, a kiss on my skin. I was almost disappointed to have to put on the clean tunic that was handed to me.

Agron scooped a handful of water from the spring, and drank from his palm. 'I love these mountains.'

For a moment he surveyed me. The smile had gone. He was thinking. Of what, I had no clue.

'Let's go.' He said at last. 'It's time.'

–

When I was a young man I had dreamed of marriage. The bride in my heart and mind had been Beatha, my father's slave. We dreamed that we would run away together to Rome, and there we would start a life as husband and wife.

Rome thought differently.

So did my father. At the time, I believed that he'd put a stop to our eloping because he did not want me to make a mockery of Rome's traditions, and our family name.

I had been wrong. He and my childhood tutor Cynbel – himself a slave, and a friend of my father – simply did not want their children to flee their homes. They planned on separating Beatha and I long enough that we could see sense, and would not stray from our town of Iadar. My father had intended to manumit Cynbel and his daughter, but not until he was sure that I would not vanish with her. In time we could have married, and inherited my father's home and land. There, we would have raised our own children.

Part of the older men's plan had involved Marcus. He had offered to buy Beatha so that she could be separated from me, but kept with a family that cared for her. It was a temporary measure. A rope to tether us to our town and family just long enough for two young lovers to see sense, and abandon plans to flee for Rome.

Instead, once he owned her, Marcus acted within his legal rights, and raped and killed his property.

I'd found her body on the hillside at our secret place. I blamed my father. I beat him. I tried to kill him but Cynbel intervened, and so I did what many young men do when they find themselves in trouble, and ran away to the army. I turned my back on my family, and on the thought of ever being married.

Of ever being happy.

Much had changed since then. My father's murder had denied me the chance to make peace with him, but at least I had been able to atone with Cynbel. My old tutor had accompanied me to King Pinnes's rebels before leaving for his homeland of Britannia, a place of white cliffs beyond the Empire. Cynbel was a good man, a friend and mentor, and I knew that it would please him to see me now.

Having washed in the spring, I dressed myself in brightly polished armour. The chainmail was well made, a gift from Agron, as was the sword I belted at my hip. In the crook of my arm was a helmet engraved with two fighting wolves.

'This looks expensive,' I told Agron.

'It was. It belonged to a fine man.'

I saw the pride in his eyes. Sadness, too. 'What was his name?'

Agron hesitated. 'Alban,' he said at last. I sensed there was more, but he didn't say it.

'I will wear it with honour,' I promised, feeling the connection that all soldiers have to the dead. 'I will do right by Alban.'

Something passed over Agron's face. 'You already have,' he smiled sadly. 'Come, Corvus. It is time.'

–

I was standing on the same ground where Agron had faced down Bato and saved my life. Thanks to his bluff I now awaited the arrival of the woman that I loved. Agron stood close by me; some fifty men and women of his tribe had gathered to bear witness to what I hoped would be a short ceremony. I loved Miran but despised attention, and I did not enjoy the searching eyes of dozens of strangers who were no doubt casting judgement on Corvus the Traitor, as I had been known since I abandoned Rome's eagles.

I saw Borna first. The young lad was just shy of ten years, but he was noble-born, and expected to carry himself accordingly. The boy looked at me and smiled, and for that I was grateful. His life was precious to me. Indeed, we were similar in many ways. Neither of us talked a great deal, though we both enjoyed being in each other's silent company.

I saw a cloud on Agron's face. He felt my look, and spoke quietly. 'He still doesn't understand that his father will not be coming back.'

My heart sank a little at that. Borna had been witness to terrible death, but not that of his own father. Like all young children who lose a parent out of sight, he must still have been harbouring great hope that the man would reappear.

He never would. Borna's father had been killed days before we reached the camp, and Bato had broken the news to Miran when we arrived. He had taken no pleasure in it. Evidently her late husband was held in high esteem, though not by all – it was my belief that Ziva had killed him.

I had no more time to think about it. Heads were turning, and mine with them. Someone was coming from behind the small crowd.

The first time I had seen her, Miran's eyes had burned with defiance. She carried herself with that same confidence now, but none of the heat. She was beautiful. She was strong. She was everything a man could ever ask for in a wife.

Agron was right.

I really was a lucky one.

Miran knelt before her son, and kissed his forehead.

She put her arms around Agron, and hugged him.

Then she took one look at me, and burst into tears.

Chapter 5

When I had imagined my bride on our wedding day, I had not pictured her weeping silently at the sight of me.

'This is my fault,' I heard Agron say quietly. 'Miran agreed that you should have Alban's armour, but...'

Alban. Miran had never given name to the man that she thought she would return to. The man who she had vowed to love unto death.

That I knew his name now made the man even more real. I felt the weight of his presence on my shoulders. I was wearing his armour, and it suddenly felt ten times as heavy.

I walked forwards and placed my hand on Miran's arm. 'I'm sorry,'

Miran wiped the tears from her eyes. She was a strong woman, and as she heard the muttering of gossip behind her she turned viciously. 'None of you have ever grieved for a loved one?'

That shut them up.

'Come,' she said to me. 'Let's be done with this.'

I wasn't offended at her words. Her husband was fresh in the ground, I was a killer, and Miran was saving my life to repay me for saving hers, and more importantly, her son's.

'You don't have to do this.'

'Agron,' she ignored me, 'you will do the ceremony?'

'I will.'

'Then let us proceed, please.'

Agron looked from her to me. 'Take her hands, Corvus.'

I took her hands. They were softer than mine, but they had known a hard winter. Miran did not recoil from my touch, but neither did she look up into my eyes.

Agron began speaking to his deities. I heard about gods of mountains, gods of farms, gods of warriors, and gods of fertility, but I paid them little mind.

I was looking down. I knew that I held not only Miran's hands in my own, but her life, and Borna's. I was wedding myself to Bato and the Dalmatian rebellion as much as I was to Miran. There could be no escape from this army, or her life would be forfeit. I would either survive the rebellion in victory, or die trying to win freedom from Rome.

'Corvus,' Agron looked at me, 'pay attention.' I had missed something. 'Do you consent to this marriage, Corvus?' he said again.

My mouth was dry. 'I do.'

'Do you consent to this marriage, Miran?'

She did not look up from my hands. 'I do.'

'Repeat after me. When and where you are, when and where I will be.'

I followed on, fumbling over my words.

Miran would still not look at me in the eye.

'Bring forth the horse,' Agron said then.

Danek led the animal out from behind the crowd. I recognised it at once. It was the mount I had taken from Ziva's men. The one that had carried Miran and Borna to safety.

I knew what the animal's service would cost it. A wedding demands sacrifice. Life demands it. The gods demand it. There is no escaping sacrifice.

The horse that saved Miran was a worthy one, and that the animal must die saddened me. He had done more for me than most people ever had.

Somehow, the beast knew what was coming. Agron pulled his sword as the horse's nostrils flared and its eyes bulged. He swung the blade through its throat and the animal staggered to its knees, bright red blood pulsing out onto the dirt of the mountain. I took no pleasure in its death. I had never been one for gods and tradition, but Agron was, and his people were, and so it was important for Miran's sake that I appeared to be of the same mind.

We watched the beast as it kicked, bled, and heaved its flanks one final time. Agron appeared satisfied, and cleaned his blade against its mane.

'May the gods continue to bless you,' he told us both. He sheathed his blade then, and put his hands on ours. 'You are married, now.'

Agron was smiling.

I was not.

And Miran would still not look at me.

'Corvus,' he said, quietly enough that only Miran and I could hear him. 'Take her inside, now.'

I let go of one of Miran's hands. With the other, I led her towards Agron's dwelling, and the pile of furs that served as his bed.

I opened the door. Miran would not look at me, but she walked through.

I followed, and closed the door.

Our life of bliss was about to begin.

'Miran,' I told my wife. 'Miran, please stop crying.'

'Alban is dead,' she said softly. They were the first words she had spoken since the ceremony.

I touched the armour that I still wore. 'I should give these back to Agron.'

'That won't bring him back,' she snapped, and there was some heat to her words. It was directed at me, or the cruelty of life. Perhaps both.

'Miran, how can I help?'

She said nothing. At some point before or during the ceremony, one of Agron's tribe had placed food and drink on a campaign chest. I opened a skin, and smelled wine. Miran snatched it from my hand before I could offer it, and guzzled.

'Careful,' I said.

She drank more.

'Here.' She held it out. 'I expect you could use it too.'

That was no lie. I took a deep draught of the wine.

Miran wiped at her eyes. She'd stopped crying. I felt hollow. As if her grief wasn't enough, I had burdened her further.

'I'm sorry,' I said.

'For what?'

'For this,' I told her. 'For dragging you into it.'

'Dragging me?' Something of a smile played at her face. 'Corvus, when I met you I was a hostage. The region is at war. A war that has taken Alban's life, and nearly Borna's. You can't drag someone into a lake if they're already swimming in it.'

I lay beside my wife on a pile of furs. We were naked. We were spent.

'I thought that you hated me,' I told her.

'Part of me does.' She said nothing for a moment. 'What you did to Thumper...' We both knew it had to be done, and yet... 'I see it whenever I close my eyes. Would you do it to me?'

The words stunned me to silence.

'Of course not!' I managed at last.

'And what if I asked you to do it?'

'Miran!'

This woman – my wife – considered me for a long moment. 'You don't kill to kill, do you, Corvus?'

I said nothing.

'Do you enjoy it?'

I thought of lying. 'Killing? No. But victory... yes, yes, I enjoy victory.'

We fell back into silence. I looked at my wife. Thought of what must be in her mind.

'Your life has changed for ever,' I tried to put words to her feelings, 'and you have had no control over it.'

Miran lifted her chin and looked at me. I had chosen my words badly. 'No choice? *I'm* the one who chose this for us, Corvus.'

I had offended her. 'I'm sorry.'

She softened. 'Don't be. I owe you Borna's life.'

'How is he?'

'He doesn't understand, yet,' she said sadly. 'What we've been through. What is to come.'

And neither of us knew exactly what that would be. Only that it would be hard, and dangerous, and likely the end of us all.

'I couldn't look at you,' Miran told me. She was talking about the wedding.

'Why?'

For a long moment she said nothing. 'You looked so much like him, I... I couldn't help but think back to that time, and my first wedding. I thought then that Rome was done with Dalmatia, and that he and I would live in a hall, and raise children in peace.'

War had come instead.

I thought I understood, then. 'You couldn't look at me because it reminds you of what you've lost.'

But I was wrong. Miran turned, and put a hand on my face.

Her eyes were wet. 'I couldn't look at you because of *shame*, Corvus.'

'Miran.' She was crying again. I wiped the tear that ran over her cheek. 'Why would you be ashamed?'

More tears. More than I could catch.

Her voice faltered as she said it. 'Because my husband is dead, my tribe is at war, and... and I think I could be *happy*, Corvus. I think I could be happy, because I have *you*.'

She looked away.

Words failed me.

I kissed her instead.

-

I woke before dawn.

Miran was naked, and cradled in my arms. We had spent our first night as husband and wife. As man and woman. I could lie with her for ever, but the war would not allow us to be idle. Today we were to leave this place and go south. Bato intended to occupy fortresses in the mountains there, and so the rebellion would drag on.

A rebellion that I would fight for, and willingly. I could no longer allow myself to be carried along by the tides of war and fate. The lives of Miran and Borna were precious to me, and I would not fail them.

I felt the warmth of the woman that I loved against my body, and shuddered as a memory came to me. Of Beatha, and her end. Of my father, and his. It was all clear to me now. What I must do. Who I must face. There was no doubt.

Rome was my enemy.

Ziva was my enemy.

Marcus was my enemy.

Marcus had killed the people that I loved. What would he do to Miran, and Borna? What would *I* do to protect them?

Everything, I realised.

For the people that I loved, *I would kill them all.*

Part Two

Chapter 6

Summer had come to Dalmatia. I stood on battlements with Agron, and surveyed mountains that raised their heads like waking titans from beneath the blanket of dawn's haze.

We were in the walled town of Raetinum. The air was hot, and often heavy. There was not a whisper of cloud in the sky, and in the weeks since we had left Bato's camp, my skin had grown darker by the day.

Not so my temperament. In the weeks following my marriage I was happy. I was in love, and among loved ones. Life was good.

The empire had laid siege to Seretium, a walled town on the Sava. That river was to our north, and Bato evaded the Roman column sent south to engage him. The Romans were wary, and feared traps, and so they followed at a distance. I didn't even see their scouts, let alone the main body of their force.

And they were right to be cautious. Bato's host was large. More than thirty thousand marched behind the rebel leader, many with family in tow. The rest of Bato's followers had been sent to other towns, or on raiding parties to the east.

If there was panic when we marched, I saw none of it. The tribes had faith in their leader, and hate for Rome.

They still held hope that the Pannonians would reconsider their truce, and come back into the fight on the rebel side.

Borna had been sticking close to me. As we had done in the Pannonian camp at Mons Alma, I practised and played swords with him, though this time I was a willing participant. He was a quiet lad, but a happy one. It had been a long time since he had seen his father, and he still did not understand that he would never see him again. Miran had told him, and Agron had talked to him, but he was a child, and children have an unquenchable source of hope.

'Are we almost there?' he would ask his mother as we walked every valley, and climbed every hill.

'No.'

'Oh… are we almost there?' the child would begin anew.

It made me smile. It made Agron smile. He was a good man to walk beside through the valleys of Dalmatia. He had a horse, but the older warrior chose to lead it by the reins. He seemed to know every bit of country, and which tribe owned what, who had fought where. He told stories of gods, and the strife they created.

Agron reminded me of Cynbel in that he enjoyed tales, and teaching. Where they differed was that Agron wore his love of the warrior life openly. Cynbel and my father had tried to shield me from soldiering but, following my father's death, I had learned that he had been a warrior, and a proven one at that. The proof of his courage was a golden disc that hung by a leather thong around my neck. It was an award for valour, given to my father for saving the lives of his comrades in a war that I knew nothing about.

Cynbel would not talk about his own battles, either, save that one had resulted in the enslavement that had taken him from his beloved Britannia.

I worried about him. Men from King Pinnes's guard had seen Cynbel safe for the first part of his journey, but the road to his island stretched across a hostile empire. The last I knew of him was that he was joining a trade caravan bound for northern Gaul. From there, I imagined that he would take ship to the white cliffs he talked of so fondly.

I would have liked Cynbel to see me now. He had asked that I allow him to carry the burden of Beatha's death with him to their homeland. Though she would be forever in my heart, I had tried to honour his wish. Beatha would want me to live, I knew, and she would want me to live happily.

And so I was. The region was at war, but Miran was by my side. Life had been cruel to me, but now it was kind. I was married to a woman that I loved, and though she grieved for her husband, I knew that she cared for me, flaws and all. With each mile that we had put between ourselves and Bato's camp, and the death that had lingered there, the more her spirit had returned. There were no more tears, but Miran was often quiet for long periods of time. Agron advised that I should let her be in these moments.

'She is strong, Corvus,' he had told me. 'Miran doesn't need you to solve her problems, or to carry her grief. There will be times she wants to share, and times that she does not. Your job is to listen when she does, and not push when she doesn't.'

The man had experience.

'Two wives,' he confirmed. 'I made my mistakes with the first one. The second, we had bliss.'

I did not need to ask to know that both women had passed from his life. The sad smile on his face told me that. 'I loved them both.'

And he loved Dalmatia. 'You'll enjoy Raetinum,' he had promised me in the days after we departed the rebel camp to the north.

'Why?'

He'd clapped me on my healing shoulder. 'It has a bathhouse!'

The thought of those hot waters and steam-filled rooms had motivated me as I had walked my aching body south. When we finally caught sight of our destination relief had flooded through me – though the Romans were not in sight they were never far from my mind, my eyes always drawn to the horizon, and the expectation that the enemy might fill it. Now, without doubt, there would be sturdy walls between us and them.

'It's impressive,' I'd told Agron. And it was. The town of Raetinum was surrounded by thick walls, and the approach to them for an attacking enemy was steep in most places. It was a formidable position.

'It's been here a long time,' he had told me.

'Has it ever fallen?'

Agron had shaken his head. 'We considered occupying it as soon as the rebellion began, but we would have been besieged. The town is well provisioned and has springs, but a war must be won through offensive action.'

I'd agreed with him. At the beginning of the rebellion Bato and King Pinnes had a hundred thousand men each under their command. There had been a very real chance to defeat the Romans – even invade Italia – but in that they had failed.

I had been part of the legion that had stopped them. Barely at half strength, we had faced ten times our number. Bato had pushed us aside during the day, but we followed his victorious army through the night, and fell on them in a surprise attack the following dawn. Our losses had been grievous, but it had bought Tiberius the time to position his forces on the road to Rome. Bato had retreated, and Italia was saved.

I held no official rank in the rebel army, but I was recognised as an officer of sorts. My place was by Agron's side, and once I had seen Miran and Borna into the small townhouse that would be our home, I'd walked with the nobleman to inspect the town's defences more closely.

High walls. Thick walls. We could put a lot of men on them. There was a ditch on the outside, and a rampart beyond that. Any attacking force would have a hard time getting siege engines up the slopes, and across the ditch, but...

'The legions could do it,' I told Agron as the mountains climbed out of the haze. 'They'll come up in testudo formation, with shields interlocked above their heads. Men on their hands and knees will dig away the rampart. They'll fill the ditch with bundles of wood.'

Agron nodded. 'They build as well as they kill.'

'Yes. Even in battle.' The legions were Rome's blade, but they were also her saw, her spade, and her hammer. They built roads, bridges, aqueducts. They would not be stopped by a ditch.

I turned to face the old warrior. 'Any news of Ziva?' It was something I asked him every day. I had heard nothing of him since his disappearance from Bato's camp, and I did not believe for one moment that Bato's scouts and spies would not have word of the Pannonian's actions, but if they knew anything, they had so far refused to share such knowledge with me.

'I'm sure we'll know in good time,' Agron said.

I spat over the battlement. 'Unlikely. Ziva is a snake.'

I was surprised to see Agron shake his head. 'Ziva is a turd, Corvus, but he is no snake. Snakes are protectors. Snakes are a symbol of virility! You want children, don't you?'

I didn't know what to say to that. I had always wanted a family with Beatha. After her I had given up hope, but now that I was married, could children be a part of my future?

'We have a war to win first,' I said, failing to tamp down the hope that suddenly flared inside of me.

Both of us fell into silence after my words, as we imagined the battles that must surely come. The enemy on the hillsides. The blood on the battlements. Screams, cries and death in the air.

'Bato has command,' Agron said at last, 'but you will go where *I* send you, Corvus, and that will be to where the fighting is thickest.'

I said nothing.

'Some men lead with words, and others by deed. I just need you to kill the enemy. Can you do that?'

I met the man's eyes. 'I can do that.' And I would – Miran and Borna depended on it.

Agron knew as much. 'You really do love them, don't you?' He smiled. 'At first, I thought that maybe you had just used them, manipulated Miran's emotions for your own ends. But, these last few weeks... I've seen it. She loves you, too. So does the boy.'

I didn't know what to say, and so I said nothing.

'They are happy in the house that was allocated to them?'

I nodded. My first home with a family was a small dwelling, but it had beds, a table, four walls and a roof. After a winter on a mountainside, it was a palace.

Agron saw that something was on my mind. 'Speak,' he encouraged with a smile.

'I'm not used to it,' I admitted. 'Having a family.'

The older man saw what was truly on my mind. 'You've been thinking about Alban?'

I nodded. Miran's late husband was often in my thoughts.

'What is it that troubles you?' Agron asked. 'Speak openly, my friend.'

'I'm not Borna's father,' I said at last. 'I don't know how to raise a child.'

'Just act like a father,' Agron shrugged, patting me on the shoulder when he saw my look. 'A parent plants a seed. A father nurtures that seed into an oak. I've seen you with him, Corvus. You care for that boy.'

'I love him,' I said honestly.

'And is there anything you would not do for him?'

I shook my head again. 'No.'

'Then you are a father, Corvus,' Agron declared. 'Congratulations.'

I said nothing. I was too overwhelmed with the thought of my family. The joy of it.

Agron took one last look about the walls, then placed a fatherly hand on my shoulder. 'Come on,' he grinned, 'let's go and visit those baths.'

We were walking along one of the town's paved and guttered streets when I heard it.

'Corvus!' someone was shouting. 'Corvus, is that you?'

There was humour in the tone, not challenge, and I turned with Agron to see two young men chasing after us.

They were smiling.

So was I.

'Ranko! Zoran!'

They hit me at speed and pulled me into an embrace. We laughed, and shouted, and talked over each other.

'Agron, this is Ranko and Zoran,' I said at last. 'We were friends in Iadar!'

As the brothers nodded in respect to the noblemen, and exchanged pleasantries, I studied my old friends. The boys had not taken after their father Milos. They were both slender lads with dark hair and bright eyes. They could have passed for twins, though the truth was that they were separated by a couple of years.

The Dalmatian friends of my youth had been caught up in Rome's recruiting surge. Levies had been made for a war against Germania, but the men who were supposed to fight as auxiliaries for Rome had instead fought for their own freedom.

Thousands were dead. Their eldest brother was one of them.

'I was sorry to hear about Mytilus,' I told them.

The brothers looked at the floor in grief. 'How did you hear about him?' Zoran asked me.

'I saw your father in Iadar.' Milos, the man who had secured the passage for Beatha and me to Rome. At the mention of the gregarious man, happiness returned to the faces of his sons.

'You did? When? How was he?'

'He was well. Very well.' I did not have to tell them that I had been in Iadar because I had deserted the legions. Every man in both armies knew of Corvus the Traitor.

Sure enough, Ranko squeezed my shoulder. 'So this is what a deserter looks like, eh?'

'We thought it must have been another Corvus!' Zoran chuckled 'Since when do you like fighting?'

His brother grinned and playfully punched me. 'You always used to be a soppy arse, Corvus, but now look at you! Look at all the scars!'

'He can't be that good a fighter if he gets cut so much!'

We joked, we laughed, and my childhood friends brought something of the old me to the surface. Agron slipped away, and left us to our happy reunion. For a while, I forgot that there was even a war going on.

And then they said it.

'What of Marcus?'

My smile drowned.

The war returned.

'Marcus is dead.'

Chapter 7

I was not a man of possessions. When I deserted the Eighth Legion I took nothing with me but a tiny toy wooden horse. It had belonged to one of my section, a young lad named Gums, and he had died in battle. There had been so much fear in his one remaining eye, so much pity as he tried to hold his guts in. He had begged for his mother, but death had come for him instead. I should have been a better leader back then. To Gums. To the others. Instead I had ruled with my fists, and my temper. It was only after I'd lost the boys of my section that I realised I'd had them. They had been my responsibility, and I had failed them all.

The toy horse was lost, now. When I had escaped the slaughter of the hostages I had left with the clothes on my back, a sword and Thumper's axe. The wooden horse, and the chest of scrolls gifted to me by my old friend and tutor Cynbel, had been lost to the war.

That saddened me. I would have liked to place them here, on a shelf, in the first home that I ever had with a family. I would have liked to have shown the scrolls to Borna, and told him about the man who had given them to me. I could still do that, at least.

'Have you heard of the island of Britannia?' I asked him, as I sat down to eat with him and Miran. There were bakeries in town, and Miran tore me a thick piece of bread, and handed me a pot of honey. There was not an unlimited supply of rations in Raetinum, but after a hard winter and a successful march south, Bato had been generous with his followers.

Borna shook his head. 'Is it far away?'

'It is. Very far away.'

'Have you been there?'

'I have not.'

'Then how do you know where it is?'

Miran shot me a smile. I met it with my own, then turned back to the child.

'I have a great friend from there, Cynbel. He was taken from his land as a slave,' I told him. 'Eventually he came to my own family, and became my tutor. You met him.'

'I did?'

'When you came to practise fighting with me,' I reminded him. Borna had come looking to clash wooden swords with the Roman in the Pannonian camp. Instead, I had hit him over the head with a tent peg and sent him running away. That was how I had first met his mother, her eyes full of fire. She had repaid me with interest for the hit I had landed on her son.

I laughed at the memory.

'What?' she asked me.

Before I could answer, Borna spoke up. 'Where is he now?'

'Cynbel? He's gone back to Britannia.'

'Why?'

'Because Britannia is his home.'

'Why?'

'What do you mean, why?'

'Why is Britannia his home?'

'Because that's where he was born,' I answered with a soft laugh, wondering how many more 'why's' rested inside his little skull. 'Britannia has white cliffs taller than the biggest buildings in Rome,' I said grandly.

'He's never been to Rome, Corvus,' Miran smiled. 'None of us have.'

That was true. I had never so much as set foot in Italia, but I had talked and heard so much about the city that it had become a reality in my mind. I could picture the place as well as if I had been born there.

'And we have cliffs here,' Miran teased.

'We don't have white ones.'

'What makes white ones so special?'

I chewed on my bread and honey as I considered this. It was deliciously sweet, and it was a while before I answered. 'They're special because they mark the end of the Empire,' I said honestly. I hadn't expected my answer to be a philosophical one, but in the weeks since our wedding, I had become comfortable speaking truth to my wife in almost all things. 'The white cliffs mark freedom from Rome.'

'I'd like to see them,' she smiled.

'Why are they white?' Borna said through a mouthful of food.

I shrugged. 'I don't know.'

'You eat like a pig,' Borna's mother told him gently. 'Slow down. You too, Corvus.'

I shared a guilty look with Borna. The child laughed, strands of honey stretching between his lips.

My eyes moved to Miran. She smiled.

We were happy.

Once our food had settled, Miran told Borna that he should go and play with his friends.

'I don't know anyone here,' he shrugged.

'Then go and meet them.'

'There are children out in the street,' I put in, which was the truth. As the rebellion wore on, more and more families had joined their men on the campaign trail.

Borna walked out into the sunlight. I closed the door as Miran put her hands on me. 'Lock the door,' she ordered.

'I can't give you what I want,' I teased. 'I have a headache.'

Miran's hands fumbled for my belt. 'You'll have a headache if you *don't* give me what I want.'

I grinned and kissed her, but no sooner had I done so than a knock rapped on the other side of the wood, and we both cursed at one – the knock had an authority to it, and I was not surprised to find one of Bato's elite guard waiting on the other side.

'Yes?'

'You're to come with me to Lord Bato.'

I looked back to Miran, let my smile say that I loved her, then followed the soldier out into the street. I was not worried about any tricks, or foul play. The soldier had come alone, and in truth I had no fear of Bato – or at least, I had as little fear of him as it was rational to have for someone so fond of violence. I had seen very little of him since he had accepted that I would marry Miran. Agron was, without doubt, a key part to the Dalmatian alliance of tribes, and he liked me, and vouched for me, and so I considered myself to be relatively safe within Raetinum's walls.

I didn't talk to the soldier as we walked through the town. Instead I watched the children playing in the streets, and adults trading gossip and jokes in the sun. It was the closest thing I had seen to normality in a long time, and I allowed myself to dream – what if this could be life, for ever?

I was interrupted from such thoughts as we entered the town square. There were more than a hundred soldiers here, armed and armoured. They sat in groups, some playing dice, some telling stories, and some snoring against their shields; others stood watch on the walls. These were the ready reserve, who could be thrown immediately at any crisis, fire or foe.

The soldier led me up a set of steps and into a powerful stone building that reeked of governance. Sure enough, the rebel leader was there, though not as I had ever seen him before.

'What?' Bato grunted at me from behind a desk, looking up from a sheaf of papers in his massive hands. 'You didn't think the barbarian could read?'

He didn't call me a Roman, at least, but there was no doubt from his grim eyes that he still considered me to be one.

'You summoned me, lord?'

'I did,' he said, then looked me over. After a moment he waved my escort away, then set his papers back down onto the desk before stepping out from behind it. There was a sword on his hip, and the man-mountain walked forwards until he was looking down on me. 'You're hard to kill,' the rebel leader said. There was some admiration in his words. Curiosity too.

'I could say the same for you, lord.'

He snorted at that, but did not deny it. Bato had suffered a head wound at the beginning of the rebellion, but that had not stopped him from leading his men straight back into battle. He had fought many times since. He had failed to break Rome's legions, but that he possessed great courage was beyond question.

'Do you drink?' he asked then, surprising me.

'Drink? Yes, I do.'

He snorted again. 'Really? I always thought you'd be too much of a tight arse. *Wine!*' he shouted over his shoulder, and a servant appeared instantly with jugs and cups.

'We don't need those,' Bato said, taking the jug and sending the cups away with the servant. He took a long pull straight from the vessel, then handed it to me.

I met his eyes, then drank deeply. It was good wine, and I was thirsty.

Bato laughed. 'From standard-bearer of the Eighth Legion to sharing wine with a barbarian. Oh, your poor emperor.'

I didn't rise to the bait. In Bato, I recognised a man who lived for conflict of any kind. To deny him that satisfaction gave me a great deal of my own.

I wiped my lips with the back of my hand. 'You sent for me, lord?' I said again.

'Pass me that wine back, you greedy bastard. Yes, I sent for you. I want to talk about battle.'

I handed the rebel leader the jug, and shrugged. 'This town has excellent walls, and we have a—'

'No, not about this place,' Bato cut me off. '*The* battle, where we beat you in the valley.'

I understood, then. I knew what he really wanted to know. What he couldn't say. Bato wanted to know how, and why, he had lost a battle that had seemed so clearly to belong to him. The battle against my legion, where I had saved the eagle.

'Very well,' I said, and I thought back to the early days of the rebellion. The days when I had led a section of men in the Second Century, of the Second Cohort of the Eighth Legion. When I had fought beside my comrades Priscus, Varo and Octavius.

'We were half a legion,' I told him. 'The other half had marched north with Tiberius for his planned campaign.' It was a campaign that had ended before it began, and the reason for that aborted conquest stood in front of me now.

'Continue,' Bato urged me impatiently.

'You had us,' I admitted, 'in the valley. We couldn't hold, so our commander pivoted our ranks to open the valley to you.'

I could see the memory of it play over Bato's face. 'The road to Italia was open before us...' he said wistfully.

But it had not remained that way. 'We left our wounded to form a shield wall at the edge of a wood. They were there to mislead the scouts you had no doubt left to watch us. Then, after dark, any man who could still fight was led up into the mountains. We used goat trails, and came out behind where your army had set its camp.'

I could see Bato grinding his teeth. He wouldn't speak, and so I spoke for him. 'Your army thought we were defeated. You hadn't set a proper watch. I imagine your soldiers were exhausted. They were still sleeping when we attacked.'

I saw the big man's nostrils flair. The scar on his head burned bright. 'You came like cowards,' he snarled, but I could see that his true frustration was at his own failings. We had no right to win that battle. If they had made camp with more discipline, they would have repulsed us with ease, then marched on Rome.

'It was a hard fight,' I remembered. 'We were winning at first, but you had the numbers, and once you began to rally, it was all we could do to hold on. Another hour and you would have had us.'

But the rebels hadn't had that time.

Bato spat on the floor as he remembered it. 'My scouts told me that Tiberius had come from the north and closed the way to Italia,' he growled. 'I could have wiped out your legion and taken your eagle, but...'

But he would have handed it straight back to Tiberius's cavalry later that day, and the lives of his men with it.

I decided to chance my own question. 'Why didn't you fight Tiberius?'

He eyed me a moment before answering. 'I didn't know how much of his army he was bringing, but I knew it would be at least equal to my own force, and we had already fought for a day and more. It was the first action for most of my men. They would not have stood up to more.'

I agreed with him, but decided it was best to keep that opinion to myself.

'I had to break away, reform and deter Tiberius from attacking. That was my only option.'

'Then you were successful,' I said honestly – a large number of rebels had escaped to continue the war with Bato at their head.

The warrior looked at me for a long moment. I saw frustration in his eyes, but grudging respect, too. A true warrior has love for his enemy, for who else can know the life of a soldier except those who have stood in the ranks? The fighting men of wars have more in common with the men they kill than the men who send them.

Bato handed the wine back to me. 'I could be fat and drunk in Rome today if it hadn't been for you and your friends,' he grunted. 'Did you lose many?'

I drank, and passed the jug back to him. 'I did.'

'As did I. That's war, eh?'

'Yes.' What else could I say? 'That's war.'

Bato drank deeply, then cast the empty vessel aside. It smashed, and I saw something in his eyes – a wicked thing – and it did not surprise me when he drew his sword.

'Let's fight,' he grinned. There was no malice there. Bato had the look of a child who was in love with a game. 'Draw your sword, man. Come on! Let's fight!'

I hesitated, and that was a mistake. Bato lunged and swung the blade towards my head in a mighty sweep. I ducked and stepped back as he bellowed out a laugh. 'Come on, Lord Hard to Kill, draw your sword!'

He stepped again. Swung. Missed. I drew my own blade just in time to catch his second blow in a ringing clash of steel.

I smelled the wine on his breath before he pushed me back and sent me stumbling. There was great humour in his eyes. I did not believe the rebel was trying to kill me, but his sword did not understand the difference between a game and war, and Bato's blade was singing through the air with deadly intent.

'Let's see what you've got, Corvus!' He launched another attack. The strength of the warrior was brutal. I was skilled with a blade but I felt as though I were facing a landslide, not a man. Drawn by the sounds, worried-looking servants and soldiers were appearing in the door-ways.

'Leave!' Bato yelled at them. 'This is a private council!'

They left as though their lives depended on it, and then he was slashing and stabbing as I stepped and swerved.

'You dance like a woman!' he cackled. 'Stand your ground!'

Impossible. The man's strength was too great. When we met blade on blade, I felt my shoulder throb with angry heat. I could not hold him like this. I would tire. He would strike. Game or not, I would bleed.

And so I went on the attack.

He was stronger. I was faster. There was sweat in my eyes, and the wine wanted to come back up from my stomach.

'Hard to kill!' he cackled.

Step, clash, step, clash, and then—

Bato pulled away. Sweat was pouring down his smiling face as he sheathed his sword in one easy movement.

'Thank you,' the rebel grinned. 'I haven't been tested like that in a while. Hard to find someone who'll go the distance against you when you're in charge.'

I said nothing. Bato's smile dropped.

I had not sheathed my blade, and he had ordered the death of King Pinnes and Vuk.

My friends.

Bato laughed when he saw what was on my face and in my mind. It was a short, single bark of laughter directed as much at the world as at myself.

He'd seen how fast I was. Could he redraw his blade in time to save himself?

If he felt any worry at this, he showed none. 'You were fond of him,' Bato stated simply. 'The king.'

I did not deny it. The fact that I still held the blade in my hand spoke loudly enough.

'Why?'

'He was a good man,' I said. 'A good leader who wanted an end to the killing.'

Bato shrugged. 'He wanted peace? Well, he has that now, does he not?' The words were cruel, and I felt my hand tighten on the sword's hilt.

Bato's lip pulled up when he saw it. 'The dead know peace, Corvus, and the Pannonian army that he led has surrendered. The peace that Pinnes wanted for his people has become a reality, and so tell me...' He took a step forwards, and grinned. 'Now that peace exists, have the Romans left Pannonia?'

I said nothing, and so he spoke for me.

'No, they have not. Pinnes wanted something that you can only find in the grave.'

'You killed him.'

'I did.'

'You did not like him.'

'I did not. He was too much of a dreamer, and the rebellion needs warriors.'

'That's why you killed him?'

For a moment, Bato said nothing. 'We could have beaten the Romans at the Volcae Marshes,' he spoke at last. 'We could have beaten that bastard Severus, and wiped out his five legions.'

'You were late to the battle,' I reminded him, and there was an accusation in my words. Bato made no reply. 'Why?' I pressed.

It was a long moment before he answered me.

'I didn't trust him,' he growled. 'Not fully. I worried that he would make a deal with Severus, and ambush us at the agreed meeting place, and so I came from the opposite direction.'

'He was there to kill Romans,' I said, and I saw that Bato knew that truth now. Behind his eyes was the haunted look of a man who knew he had guessed wrong, and lost much.

He spat on the floor, then sighed. 'I see that battle in my sleep,' he said.

'Is that why you killed him?' I asked. 'Because you didn't trust him?'

'What other reason is there to kill a man?'

Revenge, of course, and we both knew it.

Bato looked at the blade in my hand, and leered.

'Either kill me, or call for more wine.' The bastard grinned. 'Now, which will it be?'

–

I leaned against the town's wall. The second jug of wine hadn't seemed to touch the massive Bato, but my balance wasn't what it usually was. The rebel leader noticed my drunkenness, and laughed.

'You grow up soft on the coast.'

After I had sheathed my sword Bato had called for more wine, and then bade me follow him to the walls. He wanted to talk tactics.

'You should have asked me this before you got me drunk,' I told him.

'Nonsense,' he snorted. 'Have you ever tried talking to sober Corvus? You're insufferable. You've got a mighty stick up your arse. I should use you as my standard. Ha! My own Roman eagle...'

I laughed at that. I had been laughing a lot since marrying Miran. Bato cackled at his own joke, slapped the wall, then looked out over the sun-drenched slopes that surrounded his town. Some were smooth, while the lower reaches of others were broken by jagged rock.

'What happens when the Romans get here?' he asked me.

I shook my head. 'I don't know.'

'Then take a guess, you stubborn bastard.'

I rubbed at my eyes to try and see straight before I answered. 'It depends on who leads them. If Tiberius comes from Seretium he may be willing to make a truce, or starve us out.'

'We're well supplied here,' Bato answered. 'Why might he be willing to make a truce?'

'Because he's already won prestige in this campaign. Tiberius got a king to surrender a massive army, and he might not want to risk tarnishing that victory with a failed assault on a walled town.'

Bato grunted as he considered that. 'Honour is important,' he acknowledged. I knew that he was a believer in such virtues himself. Bato may have hated Rome, but he was just as hungry for glory as the leaders of the Empire.

'I'm only guessing, you understand?' I told him.

'Yes, yes.'

'Tiberius will be emperor one day,' I went on, recalling the conversations I had shared with comrades, soldiers ever keen to talk about the politics that governed their lives, and deaths, 'and an emperor would not want failures to haunt him. The Roman nobles are sharks; failure is blood in the water to them.' I wiped sweat from my brow. 'Germanicus, on the other hand...'

'What about him?'

'He's a young commander, and a favourite of the mob in Rome. He defeated the Mazaei tribe, but that was no great battle.'

In fact it had been a massacre, and my stomach soured as I recalled the screams of the women and children as they were raped and put to death.

I spat in an attempt to clear the image. 'Germanicus will have a thirst for glory,' I reckoned. 'If it's his army that arrives here, I expect he will press the attack.'

Bato nodded at that. 'Do you think it is wrong of me to wait for them here?'

I shook my head – at some point, the rebels had to stop running. 'These are strong walls, and you say the place is well provisioned? It is as good a place as any to make a stand.'

Bato could see that I had more to say. 'What else?' he pressed me.

I looked back to the streets, where the people seemed to have forgotten that there was a war to be fought. Bato read my meaning. He almost smiled.

'It's good for them to be living like people, instead of hunted animals,' he agreed with my unspoken sentiment. 'Before, they were fleeing and fighting for their lives. On these walls, they will fight for their *home*.'

The rebel leader's words made me look at him in a new light. I had known him to be a fierce warrior, but here was a canniness that had been unknown to me. Bato saw my recognition of it and grinned.

'Let me give you a piece of advice, Lord Hard to Kill. Never let anyone see all of your true faces.'

Bato turned and looked out over the lands of his people. There was a smile on his lips. Pride in his heart. He was a warrior at peace.

'They will come here,' he told me, 'and we will kill them.'

There was nothing else to say.

Chapter 8

Beneath a hot sun, we waited.

Sweating soldiers stood guard on the walls, children played in the streets, and adults sought pleasure in their own games. For the first time since the beginning of the rebellion there was some semblance of normality to our lives, but the knowledge that the Romans would come was never far from the minds of the warriors, or from the hearts of the women who loved them.

And so, we waited.

Agron. I drank wine with Ranko and Zoran. I played games with Borna, and loved my wife.

She sat with me in the narrow street that trapped the sun. After a winter of misery in the snow I wanted to feel the warmth on my skin as much as possible, and so I had brought stools into the street to clean my armour. It had belonged to her late husband, Alban, and Miran handled it with reverence.

'I miss him,' she said honestly. 'He was a good man.' My wife's words were sad, but she was not drowning in grief. She looked up at me.

'Please,' I encouraged her to speak.

Miran sighed. 'I feel guilty that because of his death, I can be with you.'

I leaned across and kissed her forehead. 'You shouldn't feel guilt over something that was out of your control.'

Miran grinned at that, and poked me in the ribs. 'And when will you be taking your own advice?'

She had me there. Long had I tortured myself over the death of others. 'That's different,' I shrugged. 'I could have done something.'

'Spoken like a true man,' my wife teased, but she let it go at that.

I was glad of it. I wouldn't have been able to explain to her *how* it was different. I just knew that it was.

I leaned forwards to dab my rag into water, then into wood ash, and worked it in small circles against the chain-mail that might save my life. I was never much for spit and polish as a soldier, but I wanted to look good for my family, and when fighting came, I wanted to be recognisable on the walls. Bato had not called me into his presence again and, despite the thaw in his attitude towards me, his warning still rang hot in my ears: Miran and Borna's lives depended on me fighting and killing Romans. With that being so, I would see to it that I was as conspicuous on the battlefield as a Roman eagle.

Borna appeared along the street and came to stand beside me, ruddy-cheeked and smiling coyly. 'Been playing with the girls?' I asked him.

The lad said nothing. His wide eyes were on my armour and sword.

'They'll be yours one day,' I told him, which was the wrong thing to say: though she fought to save it, Miran's smile slipped away.

I could understand why. As a noble-born male, Borna's fate was to fight. Miran knew that and accepted it, but she would not be a mother had she not wanted to spare her son from that violence.

Of course, we would have to survive this war first.

I lifted my sword to work the edge. Borna's eyes went a little wider still. What was it that drew boys so irresistibly to war?

'Here,' I said. 'Why don't you help me clean it?' I looked to his mother, but she made no objections. It must have been hard for her, seeing him on the path from child to killer, but life was hard, and Borna would not have the strength to stand against it if he was shielded from its realities.

Miran got to her feet. 'I have things to attend to,' she said tactfully, though she needn't have bothered – the lad was fully absorbed in the beauty of the blade that his father had carried.

Should I speak with Borna about Alban? Would Borna accept that? Would Miran? I could speak openly with her, but she was my wife. I loved Borna, but he was not my son, and I did not want to cross a line that would see the lad upset needlessly. I had lost enough of my own loved ones to know that, sometimes, the best way to cope is to think about anything else but them, and their memories.

'Here. Put this on.' I placed the helmet on Borna's head. It was too big of course, but he grinned beneath the lopsided metal.

'How many men have you killed?' he asked abruptly.

If there is one question that a soldier will always hear, it is that one. 'As many as I had to,' I told him honestly.

'Did you enjoy it?'

I settled the blade across my lap as I answered. 'No.'

'You hated it?'

The lad looked up at me. He deserved the truth. 'I neither hated it nor loved it, Borna. Battle is battle. It is not something you should wish for, but it is not something you should hide from, either. I do not kill for sport. I kill because it is my duty to protect the people that I love.'

The boy nodded, though the truth was that he would never really understand my words – not until he had stood on a battlefield himself. I could fill his ears, but he would learn more in a few seconds of combat than he could ever learn from listening to another man's war.

Sure enough, Borna grinned. 'What was your favourite time that you killed someone?'

My words had gone over his head. He was a child, and saw nothing but glory in war.

What else could I do but laugh?

'What's that noise?' Borna asked, cocking his head. His young ears were sharper than mine, and he caught it a second before I did.

'Horses,' I told him. *A lot of them.*

I stood quickly, pulled my armour over my head, and took my helmet from Borna's young head and placed it on my own. I considered shoving the lad into the house, but at the end of the street I could see a couple of soldiers leaning back against the wall. They were looking in the direction of the gate, and the town's main thoroughfare, and neither seemed concerned by the cause of the noise that was coming from there. 'Come on,' I told Borna. 'Let's go and look.'

The boy didn't need telling twice, and followed me at a jog-trot down the street, a grin plastered across his face.

'What's going on?' I asked as we reached the two soldiers.

They nodded respectfully to me before answering. Word spread quickly in armies and walled towns, and everyone had heard about how I had clashed blades with

Bato. That I lived was enough for them to know that I could fight, and that I was in their leader's good graces.

'Cavalry's coming in, sir,' they told me.

I could see that. Dozens of mounted men were riding beneath the gatehouse and into the town. 'What tribe?' I asked.

'Don't know, sir.'

Was Bato gathering more forces here? Why?

'Come on.'

I led Borna down the street to get answers. The cavalry came in their hundreds, an unbroken stream. As we got closer to them I saw that many of the men and beasts carried wounds. They had been in combat, and recently. Borna's jaw hung slack in awe, resembling the severed heads that were tied to the top of the troopers' spears.

Civilians were watching the procession from their doorways. 'Who are they?' I asked, but no one had an answer for me.

They had been let inside for a purpose. There were a lot of mouths to feed here. If Bato had brought these soldiers inside the town, then he had done so with a reason.

It wasn't until the last rider entered the town that I saw it.

Ziva.

–

The first thing I thought when I saw Ziva was that I should kill him. The second was that I should see Borna to safety, and *then* kill him.

Nowhere in my mind was there mercy.

'Come.' I grabbed Borna by the hand and ran back towards the small house that had become our home.

Someone was waiting for me there, relief on his face when he saw me.

'You haven't done anything stupid, have you?' Agron asked me.

I said nothing. My face said everything.

'Corvus,' the old warrior tried gently, 'now is not the time, nor the place.' He looked to Miran and Borna, back to me, and lowered his voice. 'Not if you want them to be safe.'

Anger gnawed at my stomach and closed my throat. Having seen Ziva, it was all I could do not to fly into a fit of rage. '*He killed King Pinnes*,' I said through gritted teeth. 'He killed Vuk, and Thumper, and the rest of the hostages. People of your *tribe*, Agron. Don't you want his head?'

'Of course I do,' the nobleman assured me. 'But first and foremost, I must see to the safety of this army, and those of my tribe who are still living.'

I spat on the stone. 'Ziva brings death, not safety.'

'No,' Agron shook his head and placed a gentle hand on my shoulder. 'Ziva brings two thousand mounted soldiers, Corvus. He brings them to the rebellion.'

'Two thousand?' I narrowed my eyes. 'King Pinnes commanded a hundred thousand soldiers between the tribes, Agron. Where are the rest of them?'

'They're not coming,' the warrior said sadly, and I could see that the knowledge weighed heavily on him. 'The Pannonian tribes will honour the peace that King Pinnes made with Rome.'

For a moment I said nothing. That Ziva had failed to usurp the king's crown should have pleased me, but now the weight of his failure would be carried by us all: 'Dalmatia stands alone…'

Agron nodded gravely. 'We stand alone, and as such, Corvus, we must not do anything that would threaten what Ziva is about to do.'

I scowled and looked at him in question.

Agron squeezed my shoulder. 'He has come to pledge an oath to Bato.'

'*What?* Bato would build an alliance with that shit?'

'No alliance.' Agron shook his head. 'Ziva will offer himself, and his men, as subjects.'

I couldn't believe it. '*And Bato would trust him?*'

'We need them, Corvus. We need every man. Even Ziva.'

I went to spit again, but my mouth was dry with hate. 'The thought of him drawing breath makes me sick.'

'Then don't think about *that*.' Agron tried. 'Instead, think about how the lives of Miran and Borna give you *happiness*.' The old warrior squeezed my shoulder again. '*Two thousand men*, Corvus. Perhaps two thousand of the most seasoned soldiers we can muster against Rome! *That* is what Ziva has brought us.'

My stomach turned. Fire burned through me. I wanted to punch the wall.

I was angry because Agron was right, and I hated it. I hated that revenge for my friends must come second to preserving the lives of the ones that I still had. Ziva was a treacherous shit, but he was a treacherous shit who had fought Rome since the first day of the rebellion. His men had been blooded. They were savage dogs and ruthless killers, but such men were what we needed if we were to outlast Rome in this war.

Agron read my thoughts. 'This war has dragged on long enough for Rome's enemies to smell weakness, Corvus. We must hold on until they strike at the Empire's borders, and then Tiberius will be forced into making a peace that favours us. He will grant us freedoms, and when that happens, you and I will take our revenge on Ziva, I promise you.'

I wanted to tell the nobleman that his words were dreams. I had no doubt that Rome's enemies would be stirring as the Empire sought to put down this rebellion, but Rome granting freedom to rebels? No. That was not the Roman way. Rome sought vengeance on a continental scale. The terms that King Pinnes had secured for the Pannonian tribes were as lenient as could be hoped for, and now that large force had been taken out of the campaign, Tiberius could afford to be more demanding of the Dalmatians.

'I won't harm him,' I told Agron quickly. For the good of the rebellion, for the good of my family, I would not harm Ziva. 'But I do not trust him.'

Agron patted my shoulder. 'Neither do I, lad.' He gestured to a house on the opposite side of the street. 'You've seen the four soldiers living in there?'

I had. Lacking large barracks in the town, the army was billeted throughout Raetinum. 'They're four of my best,' Agron told me. 'I wasn't going to worry you with it, but I put them in there to watch your home. They have no other duties except that, so don't worry about Ziva, Corvus. You're one of us now.'

I could see that he meant it, and I thanked the noble soul with a weary smile. There had been a time when I felt like I belonged nowhere, and was alone everywhere, but I had found a home and a family in the chaos of rebellion.

'Thank you,' I told him. The words were heartfelt. Agron looked at me for a long moment, and I felt fatherly pride in his eyes. His own family had been lost to life's tragedies, and I did not doubt that in me he saw a son that he wished was still with him. 'You're a good man, Agron.'

He liked that, and I changed the subject quickly so that two men would not have to suffer through an acknowledgement that they had feelings. 'Ziva's men looked like they'd seen recent fighting,' I said, leading us to the comfortable conversation of war.

Agron nodded. 'They've been harassing a Roman force for two weeks now.'

'What force?'

A smile crept onto the old warrior's face. There was no humour in it. Only the promise of death.

'You'll see soon enough.'

—

That evening, I stood on the walls beside Agron and the other noblemen of Dalmatia. Bato was in their centre. I saw no sign of Ziva, but Agron had told me that the other Dalmatian nobles had accepted his presence. The death of the hostages had been blamed on men loyal to King Pinnes, and if anyone doubted that story then they did not doubt that Ziva's veteran troops would help in the battles to come. A lot of water can be let under the bridge if it ensures your own survival, or the lives of those that you love.

The summer sun was setting to the west. The sky was gold and red and purple. The air was hot, and breathless.

'Here they come,' Agron said.

As though a mirror of the sky's canvas, a red tide began to creep up the hillsides. We saw them before we heard them, but then it came, the tramp of thousands of men.

'Gods, but there's a lot of them...'

They filled the valleys like bloody water. I turned my eyes in every direction, and there were more of them. North, south, east and west – no point was safe from the scraping touch of Rome's blade.

'How many?' Agron asked me.

'Three legions at least,' I guessed. 'At least twenty auxiliary cohorts.'

'What's that in men?'

'Fifteen thousand heavy infantry. Ten thousand light, and cavalry.'

It was the heavy mob that worried me. They were the jaws of conquest. The machinery of death. The men that Bato led were the match of the auxiliary cohorts, but the legions?

They were peerless.

'It will be a fight,' Agron understated. 'It will be a real fight.'

I said nothing. The wings of the Roman force halted on the slopes beneath Raetinum. Further along the battlement, Bato had seen enough.

'We will make a beautiful slaughter on these walls!' he promised us all. 'Seal the gates!'

Wood and iron slammed shut. Carts of stone were pushed against the gate, and their wheels smashed to prevent treachery from within.

Beneath us on the slopes, out of range of everything but the loudest insults, the Romans began to dig their camps.

'So it begins,' Agron said quietly.

We were under siege.

Chapter 9

Little happened at first.

The summer evening was long, and after the sun had set the Romans began to dig their defences in the twilight. Bato was wary, and a strong guard was on the walls, but I did not expect the Romans to attack in the dark. Attacking uphill, and against walls, was a difficult proposition at the best of times.

That did not mean that scouts did not come close, of course. They would be engineers looking for weak points, and centurions looking for fame. 'Where should we attack?' was the question that both would be asking themselves.

The occasional arrow flew out at those who ventured too close, but mostly it was insults that came from the town's walls. Romans replied in kind. If the soldiers' taunts were to be believed, then many a man had knowledge of the other side's mothers.

I checked the guards with Agron, but found none wanting. Danek, the young warrior of Agron's tribe, seemed competent and eager. As he had wished, we had practised together often, though our conversation had never drifted beyond swordsmanship. The young fighter had skill, and now he looked for glory.

'I hope they attack soon,' he told his lord, and I believed that Agron did too, but for different reasons – a warrior knows that the wait is the worst.

After checking the guards, I walked with Agron through Raetinum's streets. The mood of the town had understandably shifted. The gossip was now nervous, and hurried. Children played in the street, but under watchful eyes. No one wanted their child venturing too far, should the Romans come.

A few who knew Agron called out to him. 'Lord, will they attack?'

'Lord, how long can we survive a siege?'

Agron's replies were short, and sure:

'If they do, we will kill them.' 'Fear not, we are well supplied.'

His words worked as a salve. He was trusted, proven.

'How long have you led your tribe?' I asked him.

'More than two decades. I was about your own age when my father died.'

'In battle?'

Agron shook his head. 'Sickness. We die young in my family, Corvus. For whatever reason, the gods chose to make an exception of me.'

'It was for this fight,' I told him. My own faith in gods and their ways was not certain, but Agron's was as solid as rock, and so I gave him words that he would like to hear. A man needs steel in his heart as well as in his hands.

'Yes,' he liked my answer, 'maybe that is why.'

The town square was thick with Ziva's men and horses. I stepped over dung that bore a remarkable resemblance to their leader, and followed Agron into Bato's headquarters. It bustled with his assembled commanders, and one of them was looking straight at me.

'Ziva,' I greeted him with a scowl. 'I almost stepped in you.'

I heard Agron sigh heavily at my words, and that was warning enough to stop me speaking further. I expected a return insult from Ziva, but he said nothing. Instead, he looked away.

'Come,' Agron said, leading me to the opposite side of the room from the man I yearned to kill. It put distance between us, and allowed me to study the face of the man that I hated above almost all others. My eyes burned into him, but Ziva wouldn't meet my gaze.

Something had changed in him. He was still the dangerous-looking soldier he had ever been, but something about Ziva's presence had… gone. Where was the fire? The hate?

I wanted to say as much to Agron, but at that moment a door crashed open and Bato entered the room like a chariot.

'Who's ready to kill Romans?' he asked of his assembly. They cheered, and the rebel lord licked his lips.

'The enemy have delivered themselves to us,' he said confidently. 'Rather good of them, don't you think?'

Bato's commanders laughed dutifully. The Dalmatian leader was a brute of a man and oozed confidence. He was built so much like a god that it was almost possible to believe he could beat a legion single-handedly, but as much as I would have liked to, I could not buy into that dream. More than anyone in this room, I knew the legions for what they truly were: *unbeatable.*

'Have we got the count?' Bato asked one of his younger commanders.

'Yes, lord. Thirty thousand Roman bastards.'

'Then we are a match for them in numbers,' Bato clapped like thunder, '*and* we have the walls.'

His men chorused approval of that. I did not. The numbers may have been equal, but the quality of the fighting men was not. The legionaries were worth two of the rebels apiece, if not more. The town's defences would help to even those odds, but if the Romans could take the walls, and form ranks in the town, the battle would be over.

'Who leads the Romans?' Bato asked the assembly. 'What legions have they brought? I want to know which eagles will decorate my hall!'

There was more laughter at that, and I felt a few pairs of eyes on me – I was the man credited with thwarting Bato's first attempt at capturing an eagle, after all.

'Lord Bato,' someone spoke up, 'if I may?'

The words had come from the opposite side of the room, and it took me a moment to realise that they belonged to Ziva. The words had been dull, almost plaintive.

Where was his bluster?

A sullen murmur spread through the room, and I could not help but smile: Ziva's actions might have been overlooked for the good of the continued rebellion, but they had not been forgotten.

I looked at Bato. Did he believe that Ziva had tricked him into killing King Pinnes? I had been on the end of Bato's rage. What effort was it taking for him to be cordial to the leader of the reinforcements?

'Speak, Ziva.' There was a hardness to his words, an edge that led me to believe he wanted to say more.

'I believe we should raid the Roman camp to take prisoners, Lord Bato.'

The rebel leader couldn't help a snort. 'Your love of killing prisoners is well known, Ziva.'

A ripple of angry murmurs suggested agreement with Bato's statement. Ziva was dark from a life in the saddle beneath the sun, but I thought I saw him colour.

'We need a tongue, sir,' he told Bato.

'A tongue?' this was Agron.

'A prisoner that will speak.'

A greying Dalmatian nobleman spoke up. 'The enemy are at the gates, Pannonian. What else do you want to know?'

'The answer to Lord Bato's questions,' Ziva replied. 'Who leads the enemy, and what are their intentions?'

'Their intention is to kill us, you idiot.' Many men laughed, but not Bato. I saw him consider the suggestion. So did everyone else. The laughter ended.

'There would be value in knowing if they plan on attacking, or continuing a siege.' Bato scratched at his chin, then looked at me, no doubt recalling our conversation on the walls. 'And the identity of their leader may give us insight into those plans. The Roman soldiers will know who commands them, even if they don't know what those commands will be.'

'I agree, lord,' Ziva said.

'You couldn't find this out when you were trailing their army?'

'My men were… overeager, lord.'

'You mean you killed the bastards before they could talk?' Bato grunted, then shrugged. 'Understandable enough.' He hated the Romans as much as any man.

'I would like your permission to go over the walls, lord,' Ziva tried again.

'Running already?' someone shouted. More laughter. More colour in Ziva's cheeks. He was a proud bastard. How long until he drew his sword?

'Enough.' Bato waved his hand as though to petulant children. He looked at me then. 'Corvus…' I knew what he would say before he said it. 'You will go with him.'

I said nothing.

Ziva said nothing.

'Each of you is to leave two runners from your units outside this building at all times,' Bato told his nobles. 'Now, go and see to your men.'

The rebel leaders began to file out. Agron stayed by my side. 'You can go, Agron,' Bato told him.

'I will stay a moment, lord.'

At first Bato's nostrils flared like a bull's, then he shook his massive skull. 'Very well, Agron. You can bear witness to this warning.'

The mountain of a man stepped forwards and towered over me. 'You and Ziva will retrieve me a prisoner, Corvus. Betray the rebellion, and I will flay your wife alive on the walls, do you understand me?'

I said nothing.

'Lord,' Ziva tried, 'I can't take him with me, I don't—'

'Enough!' Bato boomed. 'I do not want to hear another word from either of you until you have put a legionary in front of me.'

His flaming eyes dared us to speak.

We said nothing.

'Now, go,' Bato growled. 'Night is falling.'

—

I returned to Miran alone. Agron could see that I wanted my own company, and gave it to me.

As I walked back to my wife and Borna I tried not to think about the very real possibility that this could be the last time that I saw them. I told myself to push such thoughts aside, and enjoy my time with them free of worry, but Miran was not fooled.

'What's wrong?'

Borna was in another room, and my wife was deserving of honesty. 'I'm going out,' I said calmly. 'Tonight.'

She took it well. I was not the kind of soldier who would stand watch on the walls. Doubtless she had prepared herself for this moment, as I had done myself, but...

'There's something else, isn't there?' There was no hiding anything from her. 'Is it Ziva?'

I nodded. After promising Agron that I would not compromise the service of the Pannonians, and before attending Bato's headquarters, I had told Miran of Ziva's arrival. She had taken the news pragmatically – more soldiers now stood between the Romans, and her son.

'Ziva wants to snatch a prisoner to interrogate,' I told her, 'and Bato ordered that I should go with him.'

Miran frowned. 'You think that they're doing this to kill you?'

'I don't know,' I admitted. In truth, I thought I had seen shock in Ziva's eyes when Bato had decreed that I join him.

'Let's think about this, Corvus,' Miran said, placing her hands on mine. 'If Ziva wanted to kill you, why would he need to do it outside of the town?'

'To blame the Romans,' I shrugged.

'But no one will believe that.'

I shrugged again. 'It doesn't matter what they believe, Miran, just what they *say* they believe. Everyone knows

83

Ziva's men killed the hostages, but they overlook it because he brought men. They would no doubt overlook it if he killed me, too.'

My wife's brow knitted as she thought on it. 'And what would Bato gain from seeing you dead?'

'He will never forgive me for being part of the army that beat him.'

Miran shook her head. 'He wouldn't throw away a warrior.'

I said nothing.

'No,' my wife decided. 'He's sending you with Ziva because he wants you to be successful, Corvus. *I know it.*' And the certainty in her eyes did something to convince me too. Perhaps she was right. As much as I hated him, Ziva was a proven warrior, and so was I.

'You're both outsiders,' Miran continued, sure of herself now. 'If you...' she stopped before forcing out the painful words that had been on her tongue, 'if you didn't... *come back*, then Bato loses two warriors, yes, but he does not lose two Dalmatians. He does not lose noblemen.'

'He could send ordinary soldiers,' I said, but Miran dismissed that notion with a shake of her head.

'Who in the ranks is the match for you and Ziva? Any Dalmatian who has proven himself a great warrior has already been given a position of command.'

'Perhaps...'

But Miran was certain. 'It's no secret that you're here on Bato's sufferance, my love, but so is Ziva. You've seen what Bato is like. No doubt he's enjoying this, sending you out together, but I do not believe that he wants you to fail.'

I wanted to agree. There was something more, too, but I wouldn't say it to my wife, and hurt her: I believed that Bato had seen the chance to make a bet where he could not lose. Either Ziva and I returned with information, and Bato could better plan Raetinum's defence, or we did not return at all, and the rebel leader would be rid of two men who had damaged his pride: Ziva with his trickery, and myself when I had fought for the legion that defeated him.

I raised my wife's hands in mine and kissed them. It was hard for me to meet her eyes. If I died, would Bato believe that I had deserted him? Would he follow through on his promise, and flay my wife alive?

'Corvus… what's wrong?'

I stood, pulled my beloved tight to me, and said nothing. Miran's head was pressed against my chest, where I wished I could hold her for ever.

'I will wait for you,' she promised me. But the war would not.

As darkness gripped the mountains, I slipped away into black night.

There was an enemy to kill.

Chapter 10

We gathered at Bato's headquarters. I had left my armour with my wife. I wore a dark tunic and had covered my exposed skin in soot. I had a sword on one hip, a dagger on the other. Short loops of rope were coiled on my crossed belts.

Agron was there. He had gathered four local soldiers to lead us out.

'We can find our way over a wall well enough,' Ziva told him, but Agron shook his head.

'You'll see why you need them soon enough, Lord Ziva.' To anyone else, Agron's words would sound neutral, but to one who knew him, they were heavy with threat – this pleasant man had not forgotten what Ziva had done.

The four local soldiers introduced themselves. I nodded greetings, but deliberately forgot their identities. Tonight would be deadly. I did not need to be adding more names to the scrolls of comrades lost. They had each other, and could carry the weight of comradeship without me.

'Follow me.' Agron lead on.

'We need ropes,' Ziva spoke after him. There was scorn in his voice.

Agron did not rise to it. 'You will not,' he said calmly.

Were it any other man speaking, I would smell a trap, but my trust in Agron was absolute. Such confidence had failed me before, of course, and so there was no helping the worm of doubt that squirmed in my gut when I saw that we were not walking to the town's walls. Rather, we were heading to the baths.

'Is this some kind of joke, Agron?' Ziva tutted. For the first time since I had known him, we were of the same mind.

'No joke, Ziva. If you want your Roman prisoners, this is the way to get them.'

Agron let the four local soldiers go ahead as we entered the building. I looked at Ziva's silhouette. Neither of us wanted the other at our back.

'Come on,' Agron insisted. 'You're on the same side, remember.'

I snorted at that, but it gave Ziva a chance to upstage me.

'Very well, Corvus. Hide behind me.'

Bastard.

The interior of the baths was lit with a few torches that cast long shadows. As we walked within, I could not think of anything I'd rather do than drive a blade between Ziva's shoulders, except maybe take my time in drowning him instead.

Pride and hate got the better of me, and I opened my mouth to tell him what was on my mind, but the words died as I realised that the four local soldiers and Agron had vanished. For a second I suspected treachery, but then the elder warrior appeared from behind a false wall – a narrow door disguised with tiles and set into the stone of the building's structure.

'Down here,' he said, before vanishing again.

I followed behind Ziva, and saw steps leading down, lit by torches.

'What is this?' I asked Agron.

He closed the door behind me before answering. 'This mountain is littered with caves and tunnels, Corvus. Some of them come all the way up into the town.'

'*What?*' I asked, aghast, picturing thousands of Romans pouring up from the ground like lava.

Agron recognised my worry. 'Most of the tunnels are no wider than a man,' he assured me. 'They are guarded and can be easily held.'

My expression said that I doubted that, and Agron laughed. 'We're not idiots, my friend. We wouldn't leave a road to our beds. We have local men holding every tunnel, and each can be closed off.'

'How?'

Agron showed me. At the bottom of the steps, an alcove had been cut into the tunnel's side. A metal gate had been set across the cut, behind which pressed a mass of rock.

'You pull the gate back across the tunnel, and that's one barrier,' Agron explained. 'The rocks falling out would be another. It wouldn't hold them for ever, of course, but it would buy more than enough time to backfill the top of the tunnel.'

'Backfill? How?'

'How do you think?' Ziva asked. 'By bringing the building down on top of it, you idiot.'

That the bastard had worked that out before me made my pride burn. 'Maybe you could fill these tunnels with the shit you talk, Ziva.'

The Pannonian snarled, but Agron quickly stepped between us. 'Try and remember why you are here,' he told us both, as though to children. 'I will step away, and if you want to kill each other then so be it, but that will leave two fewer swords for the rebellion, and more Romans alive outside this wall. Is that what you want? Would you put your own pride before your army? Your people?'

I said nothing.

Ziva also said nothing. He turned and walked away, down into the tunnel.

I met Agron's eye in the torchlight. 'For the gods' sakes Corvus, please don't kill each other. We need *you*, and as much as I hate to say it, I believe we need that bastard too.'

'Fine, Agron.' But my blood was up, my pride was burning, and I wanted to fight. 'Then show me to the Romans.'

The tunnel mouth was hidden in the sharp rocks of the mountain. We had been led here through the labyrinth beneath Raetinum, and as we descended further I did not doubt Agron's promise that the tunnels could be held against the Romans. At points, I had to turn sideways to push through the narrow gaps.

'There are wider passages,' Agron told me. 'There were natural caves here, then mines. You could lose yourself easily, so stay close.'

I did as he said, and gladly. There are many ways a man can die, but alone inside a mountain ranked high on the list of most miserable.

The flames of our guide's torch were extinguished inside the tunnel before we closed on the mouth, and now we waited in silence for our eyes to adjust to the darkness. I had expected moonlight, but thick cloud had rolled over from the coast.

'Are we past the Roman lines?' I whispered to Agron.

He repeated the question to one of the locals.

'No.' The man was just a dark shape in the night. 'They're another two hundred yards down after the rocks.' Too far to hear our whispers, but I felt the gnawing teeth of fear all the same.

The wait. The wait is always the worst.

'They'll have pickets out in front of their lines,' I said. 'That's what we need to find.'

'How many men in a picket?' Agron asked.

'The Eighth Legion used two,' I replied, careful to avoid saying *my* legion, and giving Ziva an opening to insult me.

'Do all legions do the same?' Agron spoke quietly.

'We'll soon find out, won't we? Come on. Let's get this done.'

Ziva and two of the local soldiers stood up from the shadows. The other two would remain here, with Agron. He gripped my shoulder before I left. He said nothing, but his firm hand said everything. I had to put my faith in him. If I did not come back, I hoped that he could convince Bato that my absence was due to death, and not desertion.

'We won't be long,' I promised.

'Take your time,' he said. 'So long as we are gone by dawn.'

I said nothing. Instead I looked to the sky and saw a carpet of clouds tinged yellow by the moon that they hid. It was not pitch dark, but close to it. It would be hard work to find our way, let alone to find the pickets. I wanted to curse Ziva for putting this idea into Bato's head. Instead I spoke the two words that every leader must know:

'Follow me.'

It took us a long time to find the Romans. I had two local men who knew the ground, but I didn't need them to tell me that the Romans lay further down the slope. We picked our way through the larger stones before emerging onto the open hillside. As much as I wanted to see Ziva die, the soldier in me had a grudging admiration for the way that he moved silently in the darkness. The locals were good too. They were hunters, I guessed, before they'd been pressed into service for the war. Of course, we were all hunters this night, and it was as we waited in still silence that we caught the first sign of our prey.

It was just a few words, carried on a light breeze. It wasn't much, but it was enough, and the killer in me latched on to the scent of a man who had been careless with his life.

I didn't speak to give my orders. I put a hand on the shoulder of the two local men in turn. A little downward pressure was enough to communicate to them that they were to stay there. When I moved, I felt the presence of Ziva beside me.

So poised, we inched our way down the black hillside. I heard it again. A few words. Careless talk. The third time, I could hear the nerves in the Latin. A soldier and his comrade were standing watch in the dark night, and darkness draws out men's fear, and fear draws out men's words.

I didn't need to say a word to Ziva. Like me, he had a natural instinct for killing. We crept upon the two Roman sentries by inches. The night was dark, but their silhouettes were darker still, and by being lower than them we could see their shapes against the night sky.

I struck first. I was there for prisoners, but men do not come tamely into captivity, and so I attacked with vital violence. Before the soldier even knew of my presence the air had been knocked from his lungs, the helmet from his head, and he had been driven face first into the hard dirt. Beside me I heard the wet sound of butchery as Ziva killed the other soldier, but I did not break from my own task as I pinned the Roman beneath my weight with one hand, and beat him viciously with the other.

I heard Ziva move from the body of his man. Nervous excitement was already running through my limbs, but now it surged – if there was a moment that he would try and kill me, then this would be it, and I prepared myself to defend a blow that I would never see coming.

'Let's go,' he said instead.

Relief washed through me. 'Hold him down while I tie him.'

I took a loop of leather lace from my belt and worked it onto the prisoner's wrists. I needn't have worried about him struggling. Any flight in him had fled. There was only the shock of capture.

'He's pissing himself,' Ziva whispered in delight.

I pulled the man to his feet and felt his hot piss. I paid it no mind. Getting back inside the town was all that mattered. 'Stay silent or you die,' I said, cursing myself for not bringing something to gag him. 'Let's go.'

I began pushing him up the slope. With a lead on the Roman forces behind us, we could risk a little noise. Even if they heard us and gave chase we would be back in the sanctuary of rocks by the time that they caught up.

Ziva began making a clicking noise with his tongue. It was mimicked in the darkness. Our two locals joined us.

'Come on,' Ziva growled. At me or the prisoner, I couldn't tell. We kept going up the hillside. We were close – so close – when I felt everything change.

The moon.

My head snapped up at the sky.

The clouds were breaking, and the light of Luna was pouring through them.

No matter. We were almost back at the rocky outcrops. The big stones were only yards away. We would be safe.

'Come on,' Ziva said again.

And then my heart stopped.

'Corvus…'

Because rocks don't move.

'Corvus!'

Stones don't stand.

'Corvus!'

And then they struck.

Chapter 11

One of the local soldiers was the first to die.

I heard his death more than I saw it. A wet sound as the blade pierced his flesh. A sucking noise as it was pulled free. Dark shapes had risen from the ground, and now they raged in Latin:

'Kill them!'

Blurred movement all around. Charging. Screaming. My senses told me there were at least a half dozen of them, and my intuition told me that I would die. The Roman ambush had been positioned between us and the rocks. Between us and the caves. We were outnumbered, and I had a prisoner in my hands.

I thought about killing him. Instead, when the young lad made no attempt to escape, I decided that he'd serve me better as a shield than as a body. I held my sword with my right hand, and pulled him to my front to cover my left side, and just in time.

The shapes of soldiers were charging towards me. Death was yards away.

'I'm Roman!' the lad suddenly screamed, and the second of confusion was all I needed to drive my sword forwards, and through a man's throat. I felt blood spurt across my face, and then I was driving my 'shield' forwards, and into the fray.

All around me was the clash of steel on steel. The grunting and cursing and breathing of men trying to prolong their lives by ending others'.

'Stop!' I roared in Latin. 'We are Roman! Stop!'

Perhaps my ruse would have worked, but there was one man on the mountainside who would not break from the fray – I saw him in the moonlight, stepping and spinning in a dance of death.

Ziva. Gods, he was good.

I saw one Roman fall to his blade, then another. So furious was his violence that he drew the eyes of all, and I thrust my sword through a legionary's unguarded back. The blade pushed out through his chest, and as the bastard collapsed, his ribs took my weapon with him.

'No!' someone was shouting. 'Please! Don't kill me!'

It was my prisoner. A pair of Romans were running at us across the moon-kissed mountainside. I had seen them too late, but as my captive ducked the blade that came towards us, the violence of his action pulled me down with him. Then I was down in the dirt with a soldier on top of me. I let go of the prisoner and reached around for my blade, a stone, *anything* to hit the Roman who had missed his chance to stab me…

I found nothing, but I still had my teeth. I gripped the back of the Roman's head and pulled him down towards me, feeling blood run into my mouth as I clamped onto his face like a dog. The soldier was screaming, shaking, hitting me, and I shook my head violently and spat away the meat that came free in my mouth.

Blood was pouring over me now, but the wound did not slow him. It only made him fight harder. We were two animals, clawing for survival. It was a battle between beasts, and I can only thank the gods that it was too dark for me to see into the man's eyes before my thumbs found them, and pressed the orbs into pulp.

I will never forget his screams. I will never forget the feeling of digging my nails into the wet tissue behind a man's eyes. He rolled off me then and howled like a gutted dog. I scrambled to my feet, wet with blood and shaking with nerves.

Two of them were waiting for me.

'Kill the bastard!' one said, but they did not rush me. Instead they split apart as I drew my dagger. They would attack me from two sides, and I knew then that I would die.

'Come on!' I roared. 'Come on!'

The blade of the first man seemed to shine like silver as it swung through the moonlight. I took a step back on my left leg, and twisted. I dodged the blow, but I had no doubt that this second of survival had been bought at the expense of his partner's blade in my back, and I readied myself for steel in my flesh.

But it never came. Instead, I was shoved sideways, and someone met the sword with their own.

Ziva. He held our cowering prisoner in one hand, and a gladius in the other.

I looked behind me, and saw one of the Romans dead on the ground. It only took Ziva three sword strokes before the second joined his friend in death.

As the blood of that man ran into the dirt, the Pannonian turned and stood over me. He was painted in gore, but barely out of breath. I held the dagger tight in my hand, but I was on my knees, and with the shorter blade. I was a dead man if Ziva chose to make me one.

Instead, he sheathed his own blade and offered me his hand.

'Get up.'

I stared at his moonlit face, then found my feet alone. I would not take the hand of the man who had caused the death of people that I loved.

He tutted. 'Are you injured?'

'No.' My voice was hostile. Further down the slope, Romans who had heard the fight were charging up the hill.

'Come on,' he said. 'Follow me.'

The last thing I saw on Ziva's bloody face was a smile. Then, as though the moon had seen enough death this night, the clouds drew together, and the mountain was painted black.

We had survived.

I had survived.

And Ziva was the reason why.

—

Both of the locals had been killed in the ambush by the Roman patrol, and so it took some time, and a great deal of luck, before we were able to find the cave entrance where Agron waited for us.

'I owe you,' I told him, because the noblemen had put himself at risk by leaving the cover of the tunnel to look for the two bloodied men and their prisoner.

Agron didn't ask us what had happened. We stank of blood and gore and were two men down. Some stories told themselves.

As part of the Eighth Legion I had feared the mountains, but now, as we were welcomed back into the tunnel, I felt nothing but love for these bastions of the rebellion. Rome had her legions, but Dalmatia had rock and ridge, cliff and peaks. Matched against Rome's forces on an open battlefield, army against army, the rebellion would have been over in a day. That it had survived this long was testament to the will of the mountains as much as any general.

When we finally emerged from the tunnel in the bath-house, Agron held out a friendly hand to stop me from leaving.

'Take a moment,' he said. 'Wash. Relax. Bato can wait.'

I shook my head. 'No.' I wanted the rebel leader to see me this way. Let him try and doubt my loyalty when I was painted in blood, and pulling a frightened Roman captive behind me.

The prisoner had said nothing. He had the look of the damned. There is only so much shock a man can take. Courage can be drained. Fear can run over. It was possible to recover from such states, but some men never do. The prisoner was now nothing more than a pathetic passenger in his own life.

I took little pleasure at that. He was young. Very young. I doubted that his frightened face had ever needed shaving. What was *he* seeing from behind those glazed eyes? What terror must tear at a man's spirit when he finds himself visited by the enemy's best in the night? Grudgingly, I had to admit that there was no doubt that Ziva was a brilliant fighter. I had clashed with him once, and I thought I had defended myself well, but now I wondered if he had simply been toying with me that day for the sake of the crowd who had watched on. When the moment finally came for me to take vengeance for the lives of Vuk, Thumper and King Pinnes, would I have the skill to kill him?

And what was more: could I kill someone who had saved my life?

I had no more time to think of it as we left the bath-house. There were a dozen men waiting outside with picks and tools – no doubt a part of the tunnel system was about to be sealed off.

We walked into Bato's headquarters. The Dalmatian leader was waiting for us at the end of a long table. He was chewing at a piece of meat, and threw it to a hound when he saw us enter.

'You're back.' He smiled, wiping a hand across greasy lips. 'Come, sit.'

Ziva hesitated at first. It seemed an odd thing to do, joining a lord at his table when we were so gruesomely decorated, but Bato laughed. 'Sit!' he insisted. 'You too, Roman,' he said in Latin.

At first I thought Bato was talking to me, but his eyes were on the shaking prisoner. 'Sit down, or don't you Romans have any manners? Wine!' he called over his shoulder.

We took seats at the table, Ziva and Agron on one side, me and the captive on the other.

'What's your name?' Bato asked the young soldier, as though they were meeting on friendly terms.

'Gaius, sir.' The words were hollow. Numb. The lad was in another world.

'Tough night, eh, Gaius?' Bato laughed. 'Do you like wine?'

He stood and poured some for himself, then filled up Ziva's cup, Agron's, and my own. I caught the scent on his breath, then. This was not Bato's first jug.

'Drink!' And we drank. The wine was harsh in my dry throat, but I took it down in one. 'So,' Bato went on, 'I expect you know why you're here, eh, Gaius? You know who I am, don't you?'

The lad said nothing, and Bato frowned at that, his pride hurt. 'Of course you do. You ever see any action before tonight?'

'No, sir.'

'Your first fight and your last, eh?' Bato laughed. I looked to the lad to see if this confirmation of his imminent death would unmask him, but his spirit had already fled. He was a living ghost, nothing more.

'What legion are you?' I asked him. If Bato minded that I interrupted then he did not show it. Rather he leaned back in his chair, and eyed the lad expectantly.

Gaius told him.

I gripped him by his shoulder. Harder than I needed to, but my mind was on violence, and the protection of my family. 'Where are the Eighth?'

He hesitated. I slapped him. Bato enjoyed that. 'Where are the Eighth Legion?'

'With Tiberius, sir. Up north.'

'You're sure?'

He said nothing, and so I slapped him again.

'I'm sure, sir.'

Bato leaned forwards in his chair, and placed his thick arms on the table. 'And what is Tiberius doing?'

'He's laid siege, sir.'

'To where?'

'Sirmium, sir.'

This seemed to confirm what Bato already knew. He snorted. 'Pour us some wine,' he told his captive. 'Go on. Make yourself useful, and I might consider keeping you as a slave.'

Something of hope sparked in the lad's eye, but it was his undoing, as now nerves flooded into his body and his limbs began to shake. He had only held the jug of wine for a moment before Bato stood and snatched it from him. 'You shake like a shitting dog. Sit. There's a good boy.' He laughed at that. I saw Ziva smirk. Agron remained impassive.

For my own part, I was both relieved and angry that Marcus and my old legion were not outside the gates. A part of me did not want to face the man I had once called brother. A smaller part of me wanted the wait to be over, and resolution to be found.

'You look like you have something on your mind?' Bato spoke, looking at me.

'If we're done, lord, then I will return to my wife.'

'We're not done,' Bato grunted, pouring more wine. 'Are we, Gaius?'

The prisoner didn't know what to say to the rebel leader. Instead he mumbled something incomprehensible as Bato drank.

'Where are you from, Gaius?'

'Rome, sir.'

'Rome, indeed?' Bato feigned great delight. 'Tell me about the city.'

The lad didn't know what to say. I caught Agron's eye. He looked bored, but untroubled.

'Tell me about your grand games,' Bato pressed him. 'Tell me about the women.'

'My parents wouldn't let me go to the games,' the prisoner answered pathetically.

Bato tutted at that. 'Why?'

'They had a bakery, sir. There was work to be done.'

'You should have stayed and baked bread, boy.' Bato grinned. 'Then you wouldn't be here.'

'My father lost it, sir.'

'The bakery? Why?'

'Debt, sir.'

Bato chuckled. 'Liked to gamble, did he?'

Gaius nodded. The rebel leader seemed to be enjoying the conversation. I couldn't tell if he was toying with the lad, or genuinely intrigued to hear from someone who had lived in the city that sent armies against him.

'So you joined the army for a job, eh?'

The Roman shook his head. Gods, he looked pathetic. 'I was conscripted, sir. Last year.'

That made sense. When the rebellion had started, there had been a great panic in Rome. Veterans had been recalled to the standards. Levies had been raised. Even freed slaves had been armed and dispatched to the war under the command of a young general. I had heard this and more when I had visited the port of Iadar.

'Germanicus commands you?' I asked him.

'He does, sir.'

Bato tapped his knuckles on the table so that the lad turned to look at him. 'Will he attack?'

'I don't know sir.'

'There was no talk of it? No orders?'

'None that I heard, sir.'

For a moment, Bato observed the broken soldier, if he could even be called that. Pressed into service, and captured in his first action, the lad's military service would be short and tragic.

'You know Rome is in the wrong in this war, don't you?' Bato asked him, and Gaius nodded. '*Say it.*'

'Rome is in the wrong in this war, sir.'

'You shouldn't be here, should you?'

'We shouldn't be here, sir.'

Bato looked at the lad for a long moment, then his face clouded over, and he threw his cup against Gaius's head. It bounced off his young skull with a crack, wine running pathetically down his face.

The rebel leader leaned back in his chair and observed the wretched creature. 'There's not much he can tell us, is there?'

The words were for myself, Agron, Ziva. None of us spoke, which said it all – we had the name of the Roman commander. We knew that there was no immediate plan of assault. At least, none which had been passed to the troops. There was nothing else for the lad to say.

Bato gave the slightest shake of his head. 'If you had stayed in your bakery, Gaius the Roman, we could have been friends, but you came to my country with an army. What am I to do with you?'

The lad said nothing.

'Can you bake?' Bato asked.

The boy managed to nod.

'Agron,' Bato turned, 'we have a bakery here.'

'We do.'

'Could they use a slave?'

Ziva cleared his throat before Agron could speak. 'Lord, I do not think it would be wise to put a Roman somewhere where there is fire they could use to torch our stores, or set light to the town.'

Bato grunted at that. 'No, we wouldn't want that, would we?' Agron remained silent. 'Then what do you propose, Ziva?'

'Make an example of him, lord.'

Bato laughed, grim and dark. 'Of course. The Ziva special, eh?' He waved his hand then, sealing the lad's fate. 'Very well. Do as you please with him. The troops will enjoy it, I imagine. They'll be pleased to know we drew first blood.'

I looked into the young soldier's face. There was nothing in his eyes, now. Not even fear.

Bato got to his feet. There was the slightest wobble, and he steadied himself with his hand against the table.

'Good work tonight,' he said, his eyes on the blood that painted us.

The rebel general turned his look to Gaius, then. There was no hate in Bato's gaze. Simply the acceptance of a butcher taking the life of a lamb.

'Be happy, young Gaius. Not every soldier gets to spend his last night in the company of greatness.'

He departed then, leaving behind him three men, a living corpse, and a half-finished jug of wine.

I picked it up from the table, and went home to my wife.

–

As I walked through the dark streets of Raetinum I came across one of the town's fountains, from which folk would fetch their water to drink, cook and clean. I took a heavy draught from the jug of wine in my hands, then poured the rest out onto the stones as a libation. I wasn't fanatical in my religion, but I had a soldier's beliefs. I had the blood of other men on me, and though I did not regret their deaths, I would honour them. Perhaps, in a different life, we would have been friends. As it was they were dead, I was their killer, and so I would offer wine before returning to the reason I had for killing them – my wife, and her child.

The jug now empty, I filled it from the fountain and poured it over my head. It was cold and vital, and for a moment my mind flashed back to the day when I had washed in a mountain stream before marrying Miran. In the weeks following that union, war had trailed us at a distance, and we had had the space to love and to laugh. Since the sun had last set, all that had changed. Germanicus was here at the head of his legions. First blood had been spilled, and it was mere droplets compared to the flood that was sure to come.

How many lives would I take?

How many would I spare?

I was not an idiot. I knew that many of the men I had killed had their own wives. Their own children. Their own brothers in arms. In the coming siege some would fight for the love of plunder, but many would fight for love of kin. I had once believed that Rome was a light in the world, and that those who stood against it were worthy of death. No doubt the soldiers I had killed this night believed the same. If we could sit, and talk, and drink, and banter, perhaps we would become friends. As it was, they were my enemies, and I was theirs. That was war. I could not escape it any more than I could outrun the rising sun, and so I would go to my bed and my wife while we still drew breath.

At least, that was what I *should* do...

Instead I turned on my heel, and resigned myself to ending another life.

Chapter 12

I was waiting for him in shadow as the clouds turned red with an angry dawn.

I knew where he'd be, and when he would be there. Revenge is predictable. I knew that, and so did he. There was no surprise on his face when he found me waiting on the battlements above the town's gate.

'Come to beg for his life?' Ziva asked me. He held the young Roman prisoner by a rope. It was tied to Gaius's neck, and coiled about his body. The lad was a shell of a man, and followed the rebel as though he were naught but a meek lamb.

'I'm not here about him,' I told Ziva, and that was the truth. He could see it in my eyes, and his free hand moved slowly to the pommel of his sword.

I gave the slightest shake of my head. 'I'm not here for that either.'

And again I spoke the truth. I had not come to the wall seeking violence, but answers. Since he had returned to Bato's army I had seen something different in Ziva. At first that was nothing but a curiosity to me, an appraisal of an enemy, but all of that had changed in the darkness on the mountainside.

'You saved my life,' I said evenly, leaving out the question that had brought me here – *why?*

Ziva's eyes narrowed. He shoved the prisoner towards the wall. 'Sit.' He spoke to him as a dog, and the lad obeyed.

The Pannonian turned his stare back to me. When he had served King Pinnes his eyes had been brimming with confidence, and hate. Now, I believed what I saw behind them was frustration.

Ziva looked at me but said nothing. *Bastard.* He was going to make me say it.

'Why did you kill the Romans that were on me?'

Ziva sneered. 'You fight for the rebellion, don't you?'

'That didn't stop you from trying to crucify me,' I replied, willing myself to be calm. 'It didn't stop you from trying to convince Bato to take my head, and put it on a spike.'

I could see pride fighting a battle in the muscles of his face. 'Times change,' he said at last.

'They don't for King Pinnes.' I stepped forwards. 'They don't for Vuk. They don't for Thumper.'

Ziva stiffened, but he did not back away. 'Who is Thumper?'

'Who *was* Thumper.' My anger was building. 'He was my friend. Your men killed him but he died a hero, protecting the hostages.'

'Those men were acting without orders,' Ziva said with a straight face, though neither of us believed a word of it.

I took another step. 'I should gut you.'

And I should have, but...

He had saved my life.

We both knew it, and a smile played at his lips. There was no humour in it. It was the smile of a man with death in his nostrils.

'Look over the wall, Corvus. Tell me what you see.'

I didn't look. I wouldn't give him an opening. Ziva tutted grimly, and answered for me.

'Three legions, light infantry, and cavalry. Just part of the Roman armies in Dalmatia and Pannonia.' This time it was he who stepped forwards. 'You want to know why I saved your life? Look over the wall, and you'll see thirty thousand reasons why. You're a sword. You're useful to my people. *That* is why I saved your life.'

I laughed, but the sound had all the humour of scraping steel. '*Your people?* You killed your people, you treacherous shit. You killed Vuk. *You killed your own king.*'

He snapped then. It happened in an instant, but I saw it behind his eyes. Like the gates in a fort wall Ziva's defences burst apart, and regret and pain rushed forth like routed cavalry.

'Do you think that I wanted to kill him?' Ziva growled. '*Do you?*' His words were loud, then all of a sudden, quiet and pressurised as though escaping like steam. 'You fucking bastard. How long did you know him? A year? I'd served Pinnes since I was a *child*. I'd *loved* him since I was a child! I loved him as a king, and a father, and a brother, and a friend, and you *dare* look at me and tell me that I wanted to kill him? I would fucking kill you now and piss on your body, if I didn't think it would hurt the rebellion.'

Ziva's chest was heaving. His eyes were wild.

And I believed every word that he had said.

Ziva saw that. He snorted a laugh, stepped away, then spat over the wall. 'I begged the king – *begged him* – to keep fighting, but he was leading us out of the war. He was throwing away every death. Every ounce of suffering. What our people went through, it would have meant *nothing* with surrender. I tried to make him see that. I pleaded with him, I begged, but his mind was set.'

I shook my head and sneered. 'And so you decided to take his crown.'

Ziva's eyes snapped to me, and judged me an idiot. 'You think I wanted a crown, you thick-headed fool? I want to kill Romans! We *need* to kill Romans!' He stepped forwards. He was so close that I could feel the hate on his breath. '*Everything* I have done has been for Pannonia, and the people of our tribes. *A crown?* I want to kill the scum who killed my father, you bastard! The enemy who enslaved my uncle! Who raped my mother!'

Ziva jabbed his finger into my chest. His raging eyes were a hand's width from mine. I could hear his gritted teeth gnashing. '*I* did not betray, Pinnes, Corvus. *He* betrayed *me*, and every other Pannonian, when he made his peace with Rome.' Ziva stepped back. 'He betrayed *you*, you fucking idiot! What do you think would have happened to Corvus the Traitor in a world where Pannonia was a peaceful part of the Empire?'

I said nothing. Ziva said it for me.

'Eventually you would have been hunted down and killed like a dog. You have killed Romans. You are as much a part of this rebellion as anyone, Corvus, but you're too blind to see that your friend the king would have had you *killed*.'

'He would not,' I snarled.

'Not by design, no,' Ziva admitted. 'He *did* like you, Corvus. You were his friend, but a man who has made peace with Rome has shown the Empire that he is weak, and in time they would have come for you, and killed you. If the king would not make war for the thousands of his own tribes already killed by Roman blades, and starved by Roman sieges, then why would he do it for *you*?'

I said nothing.

Ziva appraised me, and saw the truth settle heavily onto my shoulders. 'It's not pleasant, is it?' he said. 'Knowing that the ones we love have failed us?'

I did not trust myself to speak. Ziva had the blood of my friends on his hands.

He knew this. I saw his killer's mask slip. 'Have you never killed against your wishes, Corvus? Can you say before the gods that everyone you have slain has been deserving of their death?'

I could not.

'Look at what I have done, Corvus, and I dare you to tell me that it was not done for the good of the rebellion.'

I felt my fists clench as my mind raced through war, and battle, and bloodshed. Ziva had tortured Roman prisoners, but if what he said was true, these were the people who had raped and murdered and enslaved his family. How many men could say they would not do the same? The greatest of them, like Cynbel, perhaps, but for the rest of us…?

Revenge was as much a part of life as breathing.

I thought back, then, to the day when Ziva had ridden from battle instead of joining our doomed charge, but in truth our Mazaei allies had already been routed: had Ziva made the right decision, and saved his men to fight another day? And the death of Vuk, the royal bodyguards, and King Pinnes: this was Ziva's most treacherous act, and yet…

'You see it, don't you?' he asked me. 'They had to die so that I had a chance to bring the Pannonian tribes back into the war. Bato's army can't stand alone and win, you know that, Corvus.'

I knew that. And I also knew that it made me sick to see myself in Ziva.

He looked at me for a long moment. The confident soldier's shoulders suddenly became heavy, and he looked more like a flogged horse than the prized champion he once was.

'I hated you,' he told me. 'Not only because you were a Roman, but...' I could see it eat at him, '...but because when I left Bato's camp to rally the tribes back to war, I heard stories about you. I heard how you had led the charge to save the Mazaei, even though there was no hope. You were willing to sell your own life to buy those of Dalmatians and Pannonians. They said you killed more of the enemy that day than any warrior of the tribes, and now, I have seen it myself.'

He breathed out.

'You are as loyal to this rebellion as anyone, Corvus, and more important to it than most.' Ziva stood up straight, and looked at me in the eye. 'Rome is my enemy. You are not.'

I wanted to tell him that he was wrong. That a man who'd had a hand in the death of my friends was forever my enemy, in this life and the next, but...

But Miran was alive. Borna was alive. They were alive because the rebellion was alive, and if Ziva's actions had truly been intended to save it...

'I have wanted nothing more than to kill you.' I spoke in words of iron, and my mind searched for a reason why this could still be so. 'Miran's husband,' I growled. 'You had him killed.'

Anger crept across Ziva's face. *Vicious* anger. 'I kill *Romans*, and those who would surrender to them, you bastard, and I will fight any man who says different.'

He stepped forwards in challenge, and I had no doubt that he meant it. Could I beat him?

'I saw her husband die,' he snarled. 'He died as a hero of the rebellion.'

His words fell heavily. I searched his face for lies, but saw none.

We stared at each other, two proud warriors, two bloody killers. We were two of the best swords in Bato's army. Two outsiders who could carry the fight to Rome.

'You don't have to like me,' Ziva spoke, and his words made it clear that the same extended to his opinion of me, 'but there's an entire army outside of these walls who want to rape and enslave your family, Corvus.'

My fingers touched the hilt of my sword. 'I can never forgive you for what you've done.'

'That's all right,' Ziva smiled darkly, 'I can never forgive myself, either.'

He put out his hand. I looked into his eyes and sought falsehoods.

'One day we will have a reckoning,' I told him.

'We will,' Ziva promised, 'but first we must win this war.'

Chapter 13

With grim eyes, I took the hand of the man responsible for the death of those I had called friends, and brothers. Ziva met my look. In his I saw death.

He let go of my hand, and looked at the prisoner who cowered against the wall.

'I suppose you want to let him go?' he tested me, but I shook my head.

'He would have killed my family. Stand up,' I told Gaius. He would not. 'It's all right,' I promised, pointing over the wall. 'Look. A herald is coming. They want to negotiate for you.'

The young soldier, who had understood nothing of the language in which Ziva and I had spoken, suddenly found his legs like a newborn lamb. There was a moment for me to see some hope in his eyes, and then he was looking out over the walls, and at an empty slope.

No one was coming for him.

My hand clamped over his mouth. I drew a dagger across his neck, then stepped back as the blood rushed forth.

The lad dropped to his knees. His wild eyes went first to Ziva, then to me. I did not look away. Blood pulsed onto the stone of the walls. Walls that would protect my family against soldiers such as him.

I made myself forget that the lad had been pressed into service, and had no more choice over his life than any other pleb or peasant. One must dehumanise an enemy in order to kill him. He wasn't Gaius, son of a baker with a gambling habit. He was a soldier of Rome. A man who would rape and kill the ones I loved.

And so, I had killed him first.

'Help me hang him over the wall,' Ziva said.

'Let him die first.'

Ziva tutted, but made no move. The lad's eyes closed. His breaths became rapid, shallow, still.

Ziva tied one end of the rope to a metal loop in the stone, then the other to the bindings on the boy's wrists. I felt hot blood as we lifted his body without a word, and dropped it over the wall. A sick crunching sound was loud against the dawn as his dead arms were pulled from their sockets.

'He will be a nice warning for the legions,' Ziva said happily.

I said nothing.

This was war, and I hated it.

I walked away.

—

Miran could see a change in me when I returned to her. I could see it on her face, her relief that I lived tempered by fear of the killer who now sat in her home.

It wasn't the first time that she'd seen me like this.

'Corvus… what have you done?'

What needed to be done. It was not her place to know what. It was not her place to understand. 'I'll take breakfast now,' I told her.

My wife's eyes went narrow. 'You think this is an inn? You come into your family's home, stinking of death, and think that I will just ignore it and feed you breakfast?'

I met her gaze with hard eyes. 'Yes, Miran, that is exactly what I think.'

For a moment there was anger on her face, then the fear returned. Only when she sat and put a hand on mine did I see that it was not worry for her safety, but my own.

'What happened?' she asked me gently.

Nothing I wanted to talk about to her, or anybody. 'I would like some breakfast, please, my love.'

She held my hand for a long moment, then squeezed it. 'Then I will get you breakfast.' She kissed my head as she stood. Despite my wash in the fountain, I was sure my hair must still stink of blood and sweat and dirt.

Miran brought bread and salted meat. 'Here,' she said then, fetching a bowl. 'Let me wash your hands, my love. I've heated water.'

Her words were gentle and her touch more gentle still. I didn't fight it as she put my hands into the warm water and began to work her fingers into the meat. I looked at my thumbs. Last night I had driven them through a man's eyes and into his skull.

'I missed you last night,' she said to me, and I heard a falter in her voice. I knew why it was there. The water in the bowl was turning red. My acts of violence had followed us to our home, and Miran was doubtless wondering how close she had come to losing her second husband.

'I wasn't in danger,' I lied to her, as soldiers do.

She squeezed my hands, leaned over, and kissed the mouth that had bitten flesh from an enemy face. 'Someday this fighting will end,' she smiled.

And in that she was right. Nothing lasts for ever. Not even war.

I could no longer see my hands in the bowl. They were lost to blood, as my life has been lost to violence; the dead men on the hillside… the young lad hanging from the walls… Cynbel had taught me about the difference between the soldier and a warrior, but what about the difference between a warrior and a killer? A butcher? What would my old friend think of my actions today?

I let out a heavy breath. I looked up and into the face of my wife. For her, I would kill a thousand Romans on these walls, if that was what it took.

'I love you,' I told her.

Miran's own eyes were full of love, and worry. She stood, put her arms around my shoulders, and nuzzled her face into my neck.

'I just want this to be over,' I told her.

I was sick of war, sick of death, but the fuel of the Empire was glory, and the ambition of Germanicus and his army cared little for the desires of one man and his family.

Later that day, the Romans launched their first attack.

Chapter 14

They came from the west. The cloud of the previous night was gone, and I had to shield my eyes from golden light as the Romans advanced beneath the dipping sun.

'How many of them?' Agron asked me.

'A legion,' I said. I stood beside him on the western wall. We were part of the curtain of flesh and bone drawn to protect Raetinum from the light of Rome.

'Why only a legion?'

We knew of at least two more in reserve. Auxiliary units, too. Those formations were readied for battle, but had not moved forwards from their siege lines. 'Germanicus is sending a blade, not a hammer,' I told him. 'It's a reconnaissance in force.'

Agron chuckled darkly. 'Bloody big force.'

And it was. Five thousand men were advancing in slow, shielded centuries.

There was no sign of siege engines. 'They'll be carrying ladders beneath the testudos,' I reckoned.

'Testudo?'

'It's the name for the formation that they're in. See how the shields overlap to their sides, and overhead?'

Agron nodded. Aside from the metal greaves of the Romans' legs, there was no sight of the legionaries that moved in the mass of shields towards us. It was a powerful formation. One that had served Rome well.

117

'I do not fear a tortoise,' Agron grunted. 'If armour was all that mattered in life, a lump of iron, not a man, would sit on the world's thrones.'

True enough, but the men who made up those formations were the most highly trained killers in the world.

Or at least, they had been...

I gave voice to my thoughts as I watched the enemy creep up the hillside. 'If this is a new legion, raised for the war, they won't have the ingrained ability of a veteran legion.'

Agron looked at me in question and I continued. 'In most legions there are men who have served twenty years or more. The experience runs deep. If Germanicus raised this army in Rome, then was forced to rush here from Italia, how much training have they had?'

'Enough to form testudo,' Agron smiled, and he was right, but...

'There's a big difference between making a formation, and holding it once the fighting begins.'

The older man recognised something in me, and grinned like a wolf. 'You're looking forward to this, aren't you?'

I shook my head. 'I'm looking forward to it being over.' And that was the truth.

The wait was the worst.

I pointed to the other Roman forces we could see, those which were not advancing from their lines. 'By remaining ready and surrounding us, Germanicus knows that Bato has to spread his forces around the town. If any area of wall looks thinly defended, I think these unit commanders will have orders to exploit it.'

Agron nodded in agreement. I set my eyes back to the legion rising towards us like a bloody tide.

'If they get a hold, he will be ready to force more men into the breach.' I turned to face my friend. 'If they get onto the walls and form solid ranks it will be over, Agron.'

The nobleman said nothing. Down the hillside, the Roman formations were slowing as they encountered the ditches and traps that had been sewn into the soil. Planks of upturned nails had been buried across the slope. Pits had been dug, and filled with sharpened stakes that were smeared in human shit. The Roman engineers and scouts had found some of these traps, but not all of them, and the summer evening became a home to screams and groans.

'Beautiful music,' Agron smiled. Along the wall, Dalmatian soldiers decided the time had come to add their own chorus, and began to shout insults at the men who approached. The wait was the worst, and if there was one proven way to battle fear, then it was to shout, and sing, and roar and rage.

Another way was to drink.

'Here,' Agron said, offering me a wineskin that a servant had presented him. I took a pull. I didn't want to be drunk, but only a madman would make himself fight while fully sober.

'The traps won't stop them getting to the wall,' I told Agron. Indeed, the Roman formations were holding well and tight despite the screams. 'They'll get into the ditch below us, Agron, but they're no danger to us there. We can't get distracted by the men in the ditch, you understand? It's the ladders that matter.'

'Yes, *sir*,' the nobleman smiled. 'Don't worry, lad, I've done this before.'

Beneath us, the Roman testudos marched on. The tramp of five thousand feet was getting louder, and the constant bump of their shields sounded like the rumble of distant thunder. Behind the formations, hobbled men grasped their wounds, and the dead lay in the pits, but they were few: the might of an entire legion was about to crash against Raetinum's walls.

Agron squeezed my shoulder, then offered me his hand. 'Wherever the fighting is thickest, that's where I'll send you,' he promised.

I shook his hand. We drew our blades.

The Romans were at the walls.

The townsfolk of Raetinum and their ancestors were the first heroes of the battle. Not only were the town's walls high and solid but, since the beginning of the rebellion, children and women had been gathering stones from the slope, and depositing the rocks to make a heavy arsenal along the wall's top. As the Roman testudos crossed the rampart, and went down into the ditch, the soldiers on the walls let loose a rain of death.

Roman shields were strong, but every man and object has its limits. The weight of some stones simply crushed the joints of the soldiers as they braced against the impacts. Other rocks, through sheer luck, happened to find a momentary gap. The more men fell, the more of these holes appeared. Beneath the shields the Romans would be tripping over dead and dying friends. Slipping in their blood. Gasping as they saw their brothers' heads split apart, and brains spilled over their faces.

These mountains had known earthquakes quieter than the noise that gripped them now. The smash of stone on shield. The screams of men. The roar of challenge.

From the Romans:

'Push on!'

'Leave him!'

'Ladders!'

From the rebels:

'For Dalmatia!'

'I got one!'

'Kill them all!'

The ditch was a slaughterhouse, but the legions had been bred for such pitiless pits. They were the masters of death's domain, and any hope I'd had that this was a freshly minted legion fled when I saw them soak up the bloody punishment like a surgeon's sponge.

I leaned over the wall long enough to see that wherever a shield buckled, another filled its place. Wherever a man went down, another stepped over him.

'They're holding,' I told the old warrior. 'They're veterans.'

Agron nodded grimly. 'With me,' he said, and I followed, though not without questions: he was heading to the steps.

'Where are we going?'

'You said it yourself, Corvus, we can't get sucked into the fight in the ditch. The wall will be chaos once they start getting their ladders up. I can't see what's happening on the wall if I'm caught up in the middle of it.'

By moving to the top of the steps that jutted back off the wall, Agron had bought himself a few feet that allowed him to better see along the walls that would soon be assaulted, but the Romans were out of sight, and that unsettled me.

Agron saw my impatience, and grinned darkly. 'They'll be here soon enough, lad.'

And in that he was right.

'Ladders!' Danek called, his eagerness now tempered with fear. 'Ladders!'

I saw one swing against the wall, and a rebel moved swiftly to push it back. He succeeded in doing so, but a Roman javelin found its mark, and the man paid for his courage with his life.

'A brave death,' Agron said, and I could see his chest swelling with martial pride as he watched his men fight along the walls. I did not see one man shrink back. Perhaps, on another day, or in another town, some would have shirked their share of danger, but having families to defend does wonders for a soldier's courage.

I looked into the town. Despite Bato's orders that they stay indoors, many civilians had left their homes to watch the battle, and who could blame them: if Romans were about to take the walls, sack my home and enslave my family, I'd want to be the first to know.

'There,' Agron pointed, bringing me back to the fight. A ladder had found purchase, and I recognised the transverse crest of a centurion as he climbed into view, leading from the front.

I felt the need to do the same, but Agron held me back. 'Not yet, Corvus. Not yet.'

I chaffed, but Agron was right to be patient. The centurion was cut down before he even set foot on the wall. His quest for glory had ended quickly, as it did for most men.

'Go on, lads!' Agron shouted. 'Kill the bastards!'

Ladders rose, ladders fell. The fight dragged on. Men tired, but steel did not. Casualties mounted as Roman javelins found their marks.

'We need to rotate fresh men,' I said.

Agron agreed. 'But how?' The men on the walls were engaged in constant fighting. There were reserves beneath us in the streets, but there wasn't enough space to have them brought up, and to pull others back. It would be chaotic, and into that chaos the legion would pour. With a sick feeling in my gut I realised that we – *I* – had missed something. We had the same raw material as the legions – brave men – but we had put ourselves at a disadvantage by not training to their level. If this had been a Roman-held wall, they would have had a well drilled system for relief in place. We did not, and now it would cost us.

'This is my fault,' I snarled at myself, and Agron looked at me, puzzled. 'We could have drilled,' I told him. 'We could have trained. We should be fighting like the legions fight, Agron.'

The man's greying beard shook as he laughed. 'If we wanted to become Romans, then we would have stayed in the Empire, lad.'

And then his humour fell in an instant. 'There, Corvus!'

A ladder was against the wall. At the head of it, a hulking legionary battered a rebel back with his shield, and for the first time, the Roman war machine found purchase on Raetinum's walls.

Agron pointed his sword. It was all that I needed to see.

'Go!'

–

I did not hesitate. I did not wait. I ran forwards along the wall, ducking a javelin that came up from below, and weaving between men who threw rocks into the ditch, and pushed ladders back from the battlements.

I did not know if I ran alone. I held no command of men, but Agron knew that I commanded *attention*. Where I fought, he believed that others would follow.

The big Roman who was the first onto the wall was being followed by others. Soon they would overlap their shields. Soon they would build a wall that we would struggle to break. There was no time to waste, and so I threw my short sword at him on the run, end over end. The big Roman saw it coming, and easily parried it away to his left with his shield.

Exactly as I had hoped he would.

His wide chest was open now. There was still his blade pointing towards me, but I took that on my own shield, then drove my helmet into his chest, using myself as a battering ram to take us both down onto the stone. We hit it hard, which was as far as my plan had extended, and I prepared myself for a feral fight to the death. Instead, I felt the big Roman convulse beneath me as a javelin was driven into his face.

I looked up at the man who had killed him. Danek was grinning as he drank deep on glory. 'For Dalmatia!'

Rebel hands hauled me to my feet. They saved me from a Roman blade that stabbed down towards me. I took it on my shield, then picked up the gladius that had fallen from the big Roman's dead hand. I parried two thrusts, then stepped back to assess my position.

More Romans had come over the ladder, and behind them, mere yards away, a second ladder struck the wall unopposed.

There was no more time to look. The nearest Roman stepped towards me. He held his shield tight to his left side, and stabbed with his sword down towards my thigh. I had seen the move so many times in training that I could counter it in my sleep. I stepped back on my left leg, brought my shield down to deflect his blade, and drove my own into the soft target below his neck, above the top of his chainmail. I felt the sword scrape against his sternum, and sever his windpipe. In the legion we had called that 'collapsing the chimney,' and the soldier crumpled as he begged for life from lungs that would no longer serve him.

And then, as is the way of battle, all sense of detail was lost to me. Where I had seen movement with the clarity of diamonds, now all was a blur. My body was present on the battlefield, but my mind was not. Training took over, the drilled moves of my shield and sword arm sharpened with the nervous excitement that flooded my limbs, tempered by the rage that a man finds when he is fighting and killing for those that he loves.

It was slaughter, now. Shield on shield. Blade on blade. Roman on rebel. This was the time when a man needed luck. Slip the wrong way, and you might evade the killing blow. Slip another, and you might find the blade that was never meant for you.

Yell, scream, cut, thrust.

Every second full of terror. Every heartbeat lived as though it were your last.

I screamed inhuman words. Killed in inhuman ways.

The maddening slaughter of the battlespace leaves no room for pity. No thought for quarter.

There is only death.

And death made flesh.

I wiped blood from my eyes and saw him, a god of war. He swung a sword that most men would struggle to lift. Cut a grown man in half as though he were game. In all my life – in all my battles – I had never seen such savagery of purpose, or one so gifted in ending the lives of others.

He had been born to kill, this mountain of steel. Mars himself had visited the battlefield, and he had come in the guise of Bato.

'Dalmatia!' he roared. 'Dalmatia!'

His shield was ragged and splintered. A Roman tried to wrestle it from him. Bato let it go, swung the sword two-handed, and sent the Roman's head clean from his shoulders.

Blood fountained into the air. '*Dalmatia!*'

The Romans were trapped between myself and others on one side, and a god of war and his bodyguard on the other. Dalmatian soldiers pressed against my back, eager to say that they had killed beside their lord, and witnessed his work. Bato was a blacksmith, the walls were his anvil, and he would hammer the Romans until they bent to his will.

'Die!' he commanded that they fall. 'Die!'

And die they did. None could stand before him, and soon the battle step was naught but a slippery mass of leaking bodies.

I shuddered as I looked into the eyes that burned through the faceholes of Bato's helmet. I saw chaos in them. Madness. The rebel leader had been lost to battle, and I quickly pushed myself back into the press of men behind me.

No sooner had I done so than his mighty blade swung through the air, missing me by mere inches.

'Lord!' his men called to him. 'We are your men, lord!'

Their words broke through. Bato checked his second stroke, and snarled.

He looked for more Romans to fight, but they had fled, or died, and so the man who had once demanded my death stepped forwards, and gripped me by the shoulder.

Never had I been more afraid of a warrior.

And then, Bato laughed.

'A good day to kill Romans, eh, Corvus the Dalmatian?'

The words struck me harder than any blow could have done.

Dalmatian?

Bato thumped me on the shoulder, roared with laughter, then thrust his sword up into a red sky.

'For Dalmatia!' he cheered. 'For victory!'

As his men picked up the calls and chanted, I looked over the wall and saw that the Roman testudos were withdrawing, leaving behind a carpet of their dead and dying.

Beyond them, the sun was bleeding across the horizon – across the country where I had been born and raised. I had been called a Roman, I had been called a deserter, I had been called a traitor.

And now, I had been called a *Dalmatian*.

'For Dalmatia!' I cheered, and I punched my blade into the air.

For I was alive.

And I was a rebel.

Chapter 15

I did not leave the walls when the Romans left the field and returned to their siege lines. I could pretend it was because I was tired, or I did not want to return to my family when I had been killing the enemy only moments ago, but the truth was that I did not want to leave the wall because I was in the company of victorious men who were celebrating their survival. Their triumph.

Their glory.

Sense and decency cried out that there was no such thing in war, but then how to describe the ecstatic emotion when Agron found me alive, and we embraced, and we cheered our victory to the skies? If there is no glory in war then tell me: how could I embrace strangers as though they were brothers? Build bridges with those who had once called for my death?

'You did well,' Bato told me. 'Very well. Come drink with me.'

'I will, lord,' I promised, watching him leave with Agron and other noblemen. But first I would stand on the wall, and drink up courage and comradeship instead for a while.

Yes, as the sun set, and pink clouds lingered as long fingers in the sky, I allowed myself to become drunk on glory.

And then the hangover. Then the cost. Then the truth of what had happened, and what had become of those who could not now stand and embrace their brothers.

I watched as Dalmatian rebels cast Roman bodies over the wall. Rebel dead and wounded were carried gently into the town. Families found their fallen. Mothers wept for sons. Children for fathers. Wives for husbands.

Where was the glory now?

Not over the wall. I looked down into the ditch, and saw a writhing carpet of red. Men had died beneath dropped stones. There were smashed heads, and broken limbs. Some were crawling away until arrows were embedded in their backs. Others simply cried out where they lay. In Latin they begged for mercy. Begged for their mothers.

They would get neither.

Then I felt the presence of someone beside me.

'Ziva.' I looked him up and down. He was as bloodied as I was. How did I feel to see him alive? Not grateful, certainly, but not angry, either. The man was a killer, and this army needed every killer that it had.

'I thought you would be drinking with Bato,' he told me. 'I hear you and he made quite a slaughter.'

'I don't really remember,' I said honestly.

We settled into the silence of two men trying to think of vicious moments that had occurred only an hour ago, but which were already lost to time and sense.

'Look,' Ziva said then.

I followed his eyes. A solitary figure was walking up the hill towards us. His features were hard to make out in the falling gloom, but his crested helmet left no doubt of his rank.

'A centurion,' I said. And a brave one. He walked within bow shot. The first arrow missed.

'Hold your fire!' the order was shouted, but not by me. 'I want to hear what he has to say,' Ziva said. 'Speak!' he shouted down in Latin.

'You fought bravely today,' the centurion replied, his voice hard and weathered. 'You must be honourable men. As such, I would request that you would allow us to retrieve our dead and wounded.'

Ziva's lip curled into an angry snarl. 'They wouldn't be dead and wounded if you had stayed at home, Roman.'

'Please,' the centurion tried again. 'I lost good men today. I beg of you, let me see to them in death.'

'If you want them, come and get them.'

For a long moment the Roman stood in silence. I wondered if he would grovel, or if he would charge. Instead he turned his back, and walked away.

I looked at Ziva. There was no pleasure on his face. Only the set look of a man condemned to violence.

'Do we have pitch?' I asked him.

For a moment he was taken aback by my question, but then he nodded. 'The town is well provisioned. I've talked with Bato's accountants.'

'Bato has accountants?'

'Of course.' Ziva almost laughed, and looked at the bodies. 'This is but one part of war, Corvus.'

I ignored that. 'Do you know where the pitch is stored?'

'Why?'

I said nothing, and looked back out over the battlement. The sun was long gone, but dusk clung to the mountains.

I heard Ziva tut. 'You still don't trust me, do you?'

'No.'

He tutted again. 'Correct me if I'm wrong, Corvus, but didn't you once fight and kill Dalmatians? If you yourself can put old battles aside, then why do you not believe that I can do the same?'

I said nothing. What *could* I say? The bastard was right.

We fell into silence. Further along the wall, rebel soldiers were jeering at the dying Romans in the ditch.

Ziva looked at them, then to me. 'You could have left the rebellion. When you escaped with Miran, and her child. You could have left.' He was almost wistful. 'Why did you come back, Corvus? Why did you seek out Bato?'

I continued to look out over the walls. 'For the king,' I told him. 'For the rebellion.'

Ziva moved his gaze from me, and turned it onto the dusk-cloaked horizon. 'I was wrong about you.' I could hear that the words caused him pain, because they were heartfelt. Then something happened that I had never expected to see.

Ziva smiled at me, and not with hate, or bloodlust, but as one smiles at a comrade. 'I'm glad that I didn't kill you.'

Now I was the one to tut. 'I won't fight you, Ziva, for the good of the rebellion, but do not mistake me for a friend.'

'Very well.' There was a moment of silence, and then Ziva signalled to someone who waited in the town's street. I watched as the young servant ran to his master, and handed him a small box wrapped in cloth.

'Leave us,' Ziva said to the boy. 'I thought you would want this,' he told me then, holding the box towards me.

I hesitated for a moment, but saw no tricks in his eyes.

I began to unwrap it.

'When I returned to the Pannonian camp I found it in the king's possessions,' he said.

I looked at what was in my hands: it was the box of scrolls, gifted to me by my old friend Cynbel. Scrolls that I had loaned to a king.

'I admit that I was angry that the king placed such value on something that belonged to you.' Ziva spoke, but I barely heard the words: I was looking at a connection to my past. A gift from a man I admired as a friend, a father and a teacher.

'Thank you,' I found myself saying. 'Thank you, Ziva.'

I hated myself for saying it, but as I breathed in the smell of the papers, it was almost as though Cynbel was beside me.

Instead, the man I had once called my enemy was my lonely company. 'Come,' Ziva said. 'I'll show you to the pitch.'

–

Dusk fell prey to darkness. The moon was yet to rise. I stood on the walls with Ziva, and we were not alone.

'Ready,' Ziva whispered.

'*Do it.*'

Suddenly the night burst into flame. Blankets soaked in pitch had been set alight, illuminating the silent Dalmatian soldiers who had crowded the fighting step. With spears and pitchforks they threw the blazing blankets over the wall, and I stood to watch.

Conflicting emotions battled within me as I saw what we had trapped.

Dozens of startled Romans looked up in shock. They had stripped their armour to come and rescue their wounded comrades, and now they would die.

By the firelight, Ziva's face was a snarling mask as he gave the order. '*Loose!*'

Arrows flew, and brave men died in the arms of their brothers.

There was no glory on those walls that night.

Chapter 16

Days passed. So too did the high of victory. We had bloodied the Romans' nose, but they did not quit the siege. Their ramparts remained as a loose noose around Raetinum. Agron and I stood on the walls, and listened to the sounds emanating from the legions' camps.

'They're building siege towers,' I told Agron for the fifth time. 'I'm sure of it.'

We had become carpenters and engineers ourselves. Agron and other nobles had convinced the rebel leader that it was better to build something we did not need than to wish for it when it was too late, and so it was that Agron, Danek, Ranko, Zoran and I hammered wood and piled stones along with the citizens of the town.

A week ago, these people had been smiling, laughing and gossiping as though the war were forgotten.

There was no forgetting it now. Men carried wounds. Some of the families had lost loved ones. Raetinum was well supplied with food, pitch and hay, but the raw material for the barricades came from people's homes. At first, Bato had decreed that the houses closest to the wall be pulled down to build defences in the centre, but I had put a loud word in Agron's ear, and he had put a quiet word in Bato's: more space by the walls meant more room for a Roman break-in to form ranks. If they got inside the walls we wanted them as chaotic as possible, and so the order was changed, and buildings closer to the centre of the town were pulled down.

'We'll put everything back when we beat the Romans,' Agron kept saying to those whose homes we stripped.

Most were stoic. 'Take everything,' they would say, 'whatever it takes to beat the bastards.'

There was tension in the town, yes, but there was a defiance, too. I did not hear the word surrender, and if any deserters attempted to flee over the walls then I did not hear of them. Considering how Bato had publicly executed King Pinnes, and how he had promised to flay my wife alive if I betrayed him, I could not believe such traitors would be allowed to die quietly, away from the public eye.

My mind wandered to my wife and Borna. I had seen little of them since the battle. I rose before dawn and worked until darkness. I would have liked to have taken my meals with them, but Agron took his with his soldiers, and so I did the same. Miran suggested that she could come with Borna and join us at those times, but I had shaken my head. A warrior must keep space between the family of his home, and the family of the battlefield. To mix the two dilutes both.

Miran understood, and we lay gratefully with each other every night. She would talk until I fell asleep, and then she would wake me to tell me that she loved me, and I would say the same, and we would sleep until my mind woke me before the dawn.

'Corvus!' Agron snapped me from my daydream. 'Pass me that piece of wood.' I was slow in doing so. 'You're not one for manual work, are you?'

I shrugged. Wasn't killing men manual work?

'It's a good distraction for the people,' I said, confident that we would not be overheard. 'It gives them something to feel good about, and it's important for them to feel like they have control over something…'

Agron eyed me. 'But?'

'But if the Romans carry the wall, it's over, Agron. Our only hope is to keep them out.'

'Don't be such a cynic, lad,' he told me gently, but I could see in his eyes that he knew the truth as much as I did.

He was about to say more, when there was a strange sound in the distance:

Thwack!

'What was that?' Agron asked, puzzled.

A few seconds later, a huge crash echoed through the town.

Outside the walls, the Romans were cheering.

My heart sank. 'Catapult…'

Thwack! Thwack!

'There!' Agron pointed to the sky.

Two stones.

He grabbed my arm and pulled me with him towards the side of the street. 'Get into cover!' he shouted. 'Get into cover!'

Some ran. Some stood.

A stone hurtled down from the sky and crushed two men's torsos into mush.

'Gods…' Agron whispered. Beside us, I heard the patter of vomit as a soldier lost his lunch at the sight of the gore. There had been no time – no warning – to brace oneself for fear, and the eyes of all turned upwards like rabbits who feared the eagle.

'To the wall,' Agron told me, and we ran to the closest section. Something like relief hit me as we reached the fighting step: there was no sign of a Roman advance.

Thwack! We heard the sound of the catapult launching another missile, and watched as the stone sailed through the sky.

'They're going to soften us up,' I said.

Agron's words were weary. 'For how long?'

I said nothing. My guess was as good as his.

There was nothing we could do but watch.

–

Day after day. Stone after stone. The town of Raetinum lived under a cloud of fear.

The Romans were good. They knew their business. No one knew how to weaken and subdue an enemy like them, and so after the first bombardment to announce the construction of their war machines, the Romans took to letting the rocks fly at random intervals. There was no pattern to it. No method, save that of terror. You could not say that the hours of darkness were safe. You could not say whether it was better to be on the walls, or in the town. They came for anything, at any time. The catapults fired people, too, or at least parts of them. Who knew who the limbs had belonged to, but they fell from the sky as though torn apart by gods.

Tempers frayed under such conditions. Before the catapults, I had not heard of a single fight between Bato's soldiers. Days after the rocks began to fall, it seemed like an hourly occurrence. Some were almost deadly. A Dalmatian cavalryman stabbed one of Ziva's Pannonians. Thankfully the man survived, and a Dalmatian did not need to die in return.

Ziva offered to lead a raid to destroy the catapults, but Bato would not be convinced.

'They're well defended, they'll be expecting it, and they'll just build more. You'll be killed, and for nothing.'

'I am not afraid of death, lord.'

'You'll get your chance to die, Ziva, but when I say so.'

And so there would be no raid to destroy the siege weapons, but fear was allayed a little when Bato listened to the worries of his soldiers, and allowed their families to move inside the sturdiest buildings and cellars. He would not let them into the tunnels, however. There was nowhere to run from a cellar, but the tunnels? Bato would not have his people streaming out of the mountain and into Roman hands.

The casualties from the hurled stones were light, but the mental toll they exacted was heavy. In battle, death is always near, but a man can take at least some control over his own destiny through the actions of his sword and shield. There was no such relief from the falling rocks. You could be the greatest soldier in the world, but that meant nothing if you were standing in the wrong spot when the stone landed.

The manner of death was frightening, too. The rocks built up such force that when they hit a human body they smashed it into a red paste of mashed bone and organs. It was a horrific thing to see, even to those accustomed to death.

I was grateful for something, at least. The house that had been given to my family was of sturdy construction, and though that was no guarantee of safety it at least gave some illusion of it.

Borna was sitting in a corner reading one of the scrolls, part of Caesar's *Gallic Wars*. The lad had read it twice already. Funny, how he seemed to be more interested in another person's war than the one that rained stones around his head.

'What are you thinking about?' Miran asked me. She was sitting between my legs, her back to me.

'Nothing,'

'Liar,' she teased. 'You're always thinking.'

True, but there was already enough war in the air. 'I was thinking about where we should go after this is all over,' I said instead.

'What do you mean? We're already home.'

And that was true, but home had become such a place of bloodshed that it was hard to picture it being anything other than a battlefield. 'I've always wanted to see the desert,' I told her.

'Why?'

'Because I've never seen a desert.'

Miran twisted so that she sat sideways across my lap, and put an arm around my neck. 'You've been to a beach,' she smiled, 'just picture that without the ocean. I think you just want to go somewhere flat, and away from the mountains.'

I laughed. There was some truth in that.

'You're getting fat,' she teased, and poked me in the ribs. Though that was far from the truth, I hadn't been so well fed since I'd deserted the Eighth. There were some in Bato's council who said that he should cut the rations, but I believed that he and I were of the same mind – the Romans would not allow this siege to drag out over years. They would come for the walls, and Bato wanted well-fed, vital men to defend them.

'We could go to Britannia,' I said to Miran.

Her smile was warm. 'You want to see Cynbel?'

'And those cliffs.'

Miran laughed. 'Sometimes I think you wish you'd married those cliffs instead of me.' She kissed me, then. 'I would like to see more of the world,' she admitted, then looked to her son, who continued to read, oblivious to the two adults discussing him. 'It would be good for him, too.'

I knew she had more to say, and kept silent.

'His future is here, in the land of his ancestors.' Miran spoke almost wistfully. 'He must be a leader, and a good leader knows more of the world than what is in front of his face.'

Her words made me think of such a man I had known myself: Arminius. He had been born a German noble, but service to Rome had brought him to battle in this war. Arminius believed that Rome was a light in the world, but that the torch was carried by the wrong people. So it was that we had sown sedition together.

Where was he now? When we had stolen the pay chests from the Eighth Legion, Arminius's men had told me that their prince had returned home to Germania. He was planning something, they'd said, but they could not tell me what.

'Who are you thinking about?' Miran asked me with a smile.

'Arminius.'

'He is a good man?'

I nodded.

'And a great friend to you?'

I wasn't sure about that. 'We are bonded, but I don't know if we are friends.'

'How do you mean?'

I thought about it. 'We have the same dream, and we are part of the same conspiracy. I admire the man, but...' I struggled for the words, 'but he has a brilliant mind and a grand vision. I don't know if it's possible for such a man to have friends from the rank and file.'

Miran snorted a laugh.

'What?'

'You and Arminius fell from the same tree. He just happened to be born a noble.'

I shook my head, but Miran wore a particular smile. I had come to recognise it as meaning: *if you say so, darling.*

I squeezed her leg.

'Ow! What was that for?'

For being right. But I wouldn't tell her that. Miran opened her mouth to speak again, but the words died as ringing bells and hurried cries rang out in the street:

'To the walls! To the walls!'

My wife slid from my lap. I stood, pulled her close, and kissed her.

'I love you,' we said together.

I left my family and ran to the walls.

Chapter 17

You had to admire the Romans. While their catapults had sapped our spirits, the legion's craftsmen had constructed two siege towers within their main camp. The best eyes on our walls had seen no sign of these because their carpenters had constructed the towers on their backs, but now the monsters were hauled up by ropes to stand as titans against the blue horizon.

Agron stood beside me on the wall, and said the only thing there was to say. 'Fuck.'

Ahead of these towers a Roman force now advanced. They came not in testudo but in extended line, three ranks deep. It was not a good formation for assaulting town walls, and I guessed what their purpose would be.

'They're protecting engineers,' I said, and sure enough their lines crossed the pits that had been dug on the slope, and then halted. The first rank went to its knees, shields in the dirt. The second rank joined their shield above the first's, and the third rank onto the second's. In moments, a brilliant line of red cut across the slope. Behind it, Roman soldiers came forwards to fill in the pits that could snag and foul their siege engines. These were the men who had built roads across an empire, and now they prepared a highway that would hurry death to our walls.

'They're timing it perfectly,' Agron snarled. If the engineers had come earlier, we'd have had time to anticipate the siege engines. As it was, the shock of the two mono-liths would still be ringing in men's hearts when they reached the wall.

The Romans had struck a blow to win the war between our ears, and in our hearts, but though we were shocked we were not cowed. There was no doubt who would be there to meet the towers: Bato strode across the wall, slapping his soldiers on the shoulders, calling men out by name.

'Prodan! Think you can beat your record? What was it, five kills in a day?'

'Six, lord.'

'Ha! Bring me seven heads then. Goran, do you think you can make it through this one without losing any more fingers?'

'I can always tie a sword to my stump, lord!'

Bato bellowed a laugh and thumped the man's back. Here was a man born to war and warriors. I could see men standing straighter as he passed. I could see pride in their faces, an unwillingness to fail their leader.

'It's a great day for killing!'

Bato's language was war, but the enemy spoke it too.

'Stone!' someone shouted, but there was no evading the missile that clipped the top of the wall, sending masonry and men in all directions.

'Stop screaming!' Bato roared at them. 'Die like men!'

And then the god of war was standing in front of me.

'Agron,' he greeted his nobleman. 'Ready for this?'

'Couldn't be more ready,' he replied, and I believed every word. Here were two purebred warriors.

Apparently, I was a third. 'I'm going to need you today,' Bato said to me, 'I'll take the right siege tower, you two take the left.'

'They'll be bringing ladders, too,' I said.

'Of course they'll be bringing ladders, but my men can handle them. Those towers can dump a shield wall right on top of us, so that's where we need to be.'

'We won't fail,' Agron said.

Bato's lips pulled back in a grimace. 'We were born for this,' he said, then fitted his battered helmet onto his head.

Bato turned his thick back on us, and thrust his sword into the sky as he walked away.

'Kill for your brothers! Kill for your wives! Kill for your children! Kill them all!'

'Kill them all!' his men screamed back. 'Kill them all.'

Agron gripped my shoulder. His eyes were ablaze. He was ready.

'Kill them all,' he told me.

'*Kill them all*,' I vowed.

The lumbering towers came up the hillside amidst a sea of red shields and shining blades. On the walls we cheered for war. We waited for violence.

The Roman ranks came. Engineers filled the ditch where the towers would cross. The engines crept onwards – massive, ghastly insects on the slopes.

'For Dalmatia!' I shouted. 'For Dalmatia!'

I focused myself on the closest engine. The one that was heading straight for me. For my friends. This would be my battle.

The leviathan lurched forwards, forwards, and hit hard against the stone of the wall.

'Ready!' Agron was shouting. 'Ready!'

We cheered.

We were ready.

The tower's ramp dropped onto the stone, and the killing began.

They came in a storm of steel.

Behind the dropped ramp of the tower was a shield wall five men wide. No doubt they were the best and bravest that their legion had to offer, and they rushed forwards as one.

'Spears!' Agron commanded. I was on his left, my shield overlapped with his. Danek stood to my friend's right. Men to our flanks began driving across at the Romans' flanks. The enemy were good, the second rank turning their shields outwards, but they could not hold back every thrust, and one of them screamed as he tumbled from the ramp and into the ditch below.

'Hold!' Agron roared. 'Kill them all!'

It was the last thing that I heard. The last thing that made sense, at least. The Roman shields clattered into ours, and I gave my thoughts over to actions. I pushed, I shoved, I stabbed, I spat. I became an animal, because only the most vicious of creatures can walk into a shield wall and live.

There was blood in the air. I could taste it. Smell it. The reek of copper was overwhelming, but so too was my desire to live.

And so I pushed. I shoved. I stabbed. I spat. Bato had asked me to lead in this fight, and I would not fail the rebellion.

'Kill!'

I would not fail my family.

'*Kill!*'

But I felt us losing all the same…

The Romans were gaining ground, step by step, inch by inch. In battle, an inch is enough. There were no better close-combat soldiers in the world than this foe, and courage counted for little in the face of such a brutally efficient machine. Rome's legionaries were serrations on a blade and, slowly but steadily, that blade was sawing across our throat.

Our only hope was to surpass them in valour, to make up for training with bravery, but these were gallant men. Hard men. They would not be cowed by blood. They would not step back from death.

When a Roman fell, others were quick to take their place. Their gaps vanished in an instant. Their sword strokes were fast, and deadly. I heard screams. I heard them end. Men were dying. Who, I did not know.

And then Agron fell.

His household soldiers were quick to fill the space, but the Romans saw their chance, pressed in, and we could not fully close our ranks.

'Get him back!' I was shouting to everyone and no one. 'Get him back!'

A blade glanced off my helmet. It was a hard hit. I tasted blood. I tasted fear.

We were losing.

With each racing heartbeat we lost another inch of ground. Soon the Romans would be on the wall. They would have their beachhead. The tower would spew more and more of the enemy through the breach in our defences.

Miran.

Borna.

'Die!' I screamed. 'Die!' I stabbed.

I drove my blade into a face. Crashed my shield against the enemy's.

'Corvus!' someone was shouting. 'Move back, now!'

I would not move back. I would stand, and I would kill.

I felt something slosh over my shoulder. Smelled a familiar stink in my nostrils. And then, as someone took hold of the neck of my chainmail and yanked me back, the Romans before me burst into flame.

I had no time to pity their horrific screams. I had no time to stab into their burning bodies as they dropped their shields and swords, and tried to douse the fire that consumed their bodies.

My shoulder was on fire.

The pain of it was eating into me, and then I was on my back, and looking into the face of Ziva. A bucket of water crashed over me, and then a blanket.

'Stop struggling!' I heard him shouting.

The blanket was pulled away.

I was yanked to my feet.

'Can you still fight?' Ziva asked me.

'Where's Agron?'

'Wounded, but alive. Can you fight?'

'I can fight.' My shoulder was singing, but I could fight.

I looked back to the ramp. Ziva's men had seen a chance and had pushed the Romans back. The Pannonians were on the ramp now, and fighting like furies. Parts of the ramp itself licked with flame, the fire biting at men's legs, but they fought on regardless – to drop their shield was to die.

'We have to burn the tower,' Ziva told me. 'My men are bringing more pitch.'

There was nothing for me to say, and so I threw myself onto the siege tower's ramp, leaning all of my weight against the men in front of me.

'Push!' I shouted, feeling the heat against my legs. 'Push them back! Kill them! *Push!*'

The reek of burning flesh from the dead made me gag, but I shoved until the man in front of me fell, and then I was in the front rank, where there was no space for thought, only death.

'Kill them! Kill them!'

Ziva's men were not legionaries, but they were the equal in bravery to any men I had ever fought alongside. One after another they fell as they threw themselves against the Roman foe. One after another they charged forwards to fill the ranks.

'For Pannonia! For Pannonia!'

I yanked my sword back and felt a man's guts come with it. We were almost inside the tower now. The blood of the Pannonians had bought back some of those precious inches.

It had bought us enough.

Behind me, from the ramp, Ziva's troops sloshed pitch across at the structure. Javelins arced up towards them, and men died, tumbling towards the Romans on the ground. But the pitch crews did not stop.

The Romans knew what was coming, and fought like wolves to force us back, to gain some relative safety on the wall tops, but we did not give. We did not yield.

'Hold them!' Ziva was yelling. '*Hold them!*'

I felt the heat before I saw the smoke and flame. A rush of it rolling towards the sky.

Fire had caught on the tower below us.

'Back!' Ziva ordered. 'Back!'

'Back!' I shouted, and with his men I fought against the desperate Romans who knew that they must escape or burn.

I heard the cracking of wood. The splintering sounds of fire. Thick sheets of flame licked up the tower, and screams rose with them, as the Romans inside burned alive.

Some threw themselves from the ramp. Others tried to fight their way through us. I saw a few scuttle out of the base of the tower like insects, inhuman in their death throes. Their tunics and equipment were ablaze, their cries of pain sounds that no man should make.

And then there was no one else to kill.

'We did it.' There was an arm over my shoulder. Ziva cried tears of pride. '*We did it.*'

The siege tower was now a funeral pyre. I looked along the wall, and saw a thick carpet of bodies lying beside and atop one another. Dalmatian. Pannonian. Roman. They had many differences in life, but in death they knew an intimacy like no other.

I breathed deeply of the foul, bloody air. The carpet of dead reminded me of Iadar's beaches after a storm, when debris had been left in the wake of an angry sea.

'We did it…' I said.

The Romans were retreating.

The rebellion would live to see another dawn.

But at what cost?

Chapter 18

Bato called an assembly in his headquarters. Most of his commanders had not washed since the battle's end, and the room stank of sweat and gore and guts.

I couldn't have cared less.

'Agron!'

I threw my arms around the old bastard and felt him shudder with pain, though he made no sound of complaint.

I stepped back. 'Where are you hurt?'

He showed me his upper right arm, which was bandaged in bloodstained linen. 'Right down to the bone,' he told me.

'You won't be able to hold a sword for a while.'

'Of course I will. I'll just use my left hand.'

I laughed in relief to see him alive, and for his spirit. You could cut four limbs from a true warrior and he'd still like his chances of beating you.

Before I could say more I saw Agron's eyes move to the door. Ziva entered quietly and took up station in the room's most shadowed corner.

'He is a born fighter,' I said grudgingly to Agron. What I could not bring myself to say was that the actions of Ziva and his men had likely saved the day.

Agron grunted and sniffed me. 'You smell like roast chicken.'

'We burned the siege towers,' I said. The 'roast chicken' he could smell was the stink of burning Romans clinging to my clothes. I left out that the architect of that destruction was the man who had killed the hostages from Agron's tribe, and my friends: Thumper. Vuk. King Pinnes.

The nobleman eyed a blackened patch at the shoulder of my chainmail, and the frayed tunic beneath, but said nothing. The burn on my flesh was not deep. I had come close to death, but that was battle. All that mattered was that we were alive. The rest was just stories.

Bato entered the room then, wearing bloodied armour, his helmet discarded. His face and hair looked wet, as though he'd dunked them in a bucket. The rebel leader's eyes were bright and fiery, full of life, and for the first time since I had joined the man's army, his assembled commanders went to a knee at first sight of him.

'Oh, get up!' Bato laughed. 'Stand as warriors! Stand as men!'

He went about the room then, pulling his commanders into tight embraces. Bato was Mars made flesh, and in the booming voice that had once called for my death, I now heard nothing but love from a man who had been born for war.

'I saw you push that ladder back, you bastard!' he said to one bloodied rebel. 'How did the Roman look when he knew he was going backwards? Gods, I would have liked to have seen his face!

'Did you hear them scream as they burned, boys?' he said to others. 'Like virgins on their first cock!'

Men laughed and smiled as Bato poured out praise for his men, and vulgar insults for the Romans. He was flushed with victory.

'Twice they have come, and twice we have shoved their heads up their arses! They can keep coming, and we'll keep sending them home carrying their dead!'

Except that they had not gone home, I thought to myself, nor would the cheers of Bato's men make it so. The Romans were still camped around the town, and we were still as trapped as we had been when the siege began. We had suffered lighter casualties than the Romans, but…

'Lord Bato,' I spoke, and all heads turned my way. The rebel leader himself seemed as surprised as anyone to hear me speak. Then a fond smile crept onto his face. Bato might have hated me at first, but a man will forgive much to one who helps bring him victory, and there was no doubt that he believed I had played my part in his.

'I heard you fought well today, Corvus the Dalmatian.' There was no joke in his words, only praise. It was a statement to his men that I was not only accepted in his army, but endorsed. Indeed, such sentiment almost shut my mouth – I didn't want to fall back on the wrong side of this man, but I feared that if I did not speak, then the ill temper of Bato would be the slightest of my concerns.

And so I said it.

'Lord, we're going to lose this fight.'

At first there was silence.

Dead silence.

Then there were laughs, and Bato looked at me as though I'd hit my head. 'You *were* on the walls today, weren't you, Corvus?'

'I was, lord.'

'And you saw their siege towers burn, and their men retreat?'

'I did, lord.'

Bato held up his massive hands. 'Then I am at a loss. Twice they have come, and twice we have beaten them. They will come again, and we will beat them again. It is as simple as that.'

'No, we won't, lord.'

At once there was fire in his eyes.

Agron saw it, and spoke up in a measured voice. 'He might not be the best-looking warrior we have, my friend, but he's been right before. Let's hear him out.'

Bato snorted and waved a hand, but by his silence I took it that I was to speak. Every eye in the room was on me. Corvus the Traitor. Corvus the Dalmatian. From the front ranks of the Eighth, to the headquarters of the rebel army. Much had changed, but some things had not.

I still didn't know when to keep my mouth shut.

'The Roman army will take this town,' I said, and the room erupted into boos, and insults, and mocking laughter.

'Let him speak!' Agron was shouting, but it was Bato's lurching steps towards me that silenced all as men held their breath in anticipation of violence.

'What is this defeatism?' he roared, and I smelled the stink of war and wine on his breath. 'We have victory! *Victory!* The Romans will come again, and I tell you they will die!'

I said nothing.

'Well? Speak, you bastard!'

His eyes were wide. His nostrils flared. I had seen smaller bulls than this man. I had no doubt that he would trample me, but my own safety was not my concern.

I spoke to save the lives of Miran and Borna.

'Germanicus did not win fame because he was inept, lord. He has changed his tactics with each try. They

153

have been probing for weaknesses. I believe that the siege towers today were a distraction.'

Bato snorted, but I *saw* it – the undeniable flicker of worry in his eyes. The doubt that I had seen something that he had not.

'Distraction?' The anger in the word trailed away.

'Yes, a distraction, lord. The Romans knew that the towers would pull our eyes and focus.'

'They did not breach the walls anywhere else!' Bato shouted. 'They barely even tried.'

I nodded. 'I walked a circuit of the walls before coming here, lord. The Romans have begun digging saps.'

This caught him. 'What?'

'Trenches, lord. While they attacked either side of the main gate, and with a few more diversionary attacks by ladders, their men have found our weak points, and moved their front line far closer to the walls in those places.'

'And what does that matter?' he snapped. 'We still have the walls between us and them.'

But it was not that simple. 'From these trenches they will dig more saps,' I told the room. 'They will pile soil on the outside to form a lip, and zig-zag the trenches so that it is near impossible to hit the men with arrows. They will creep closer, like worms, until they can close on the walls without exposing themselves.'

'They still have to come onto the walls,' a Dalmatian shouted across the room. 'And then we'll kill them!'

I shook my head. 'No, they will not,' I looked at Bato. 'They will dig out the foundations, lord. They will undermine the walls and topple them.'

'Impossible.' Bato shook his head.

'This mountain is full of mines, is it not? The Roman legions are fighters, lord, yes. But they are some of the greatest engineers in the world. The blood of Dalmatian warriors has bought us time, but I believe Germanicus has been testing us so far. Next time he will squeeze us until we burst.'

I could see it.

Bato could see it...

But he would not admit it. *Could not.* He opened his mouth to speak – no doubt to fill his men with false confidence – but another man spoke first.

'I agree with him, lord.'

All eyes turned to face Ziva.

'So do I, lord,' Agron spoke.

'Well there's a surprise.' Bato grunted. 'Three thorns in my arse.' He turned his dangerous eyes back to me. 'Well what would you have me do, Lord of War? Surrender?'

'No, lord.'

'Then *what*?' His voice was rising. 'You don't think we can hold the town, so what else is there but surrender?'

'I don't think we can hold the town, lord,' I said honestly, 'but I still believe we can win this battle.'

The rebel leader almost laughed with frustration. 'Enough of your bloody riddles, Corvus! Speak plainly!' Bato demanded.

'Yes, lord.'

And then I told him how to destroy an army.

–

The Romans did not come the next day, nor the next. A week passed, during which time we saw to our dead, and prepared to kill again.

There was no such decency for the Romans. I watched from the walls as birds pecked and fed on their fallen.

There were a few Dalmatian bodies in the ditch, too. Men who had gone over the wall to loot corpses, only to fall to the blades of wounded men.

The summer sun beat down on both the living and the dead. Those of us who drew breath breathed in the stink of those who had moved on to the next life, and whose bodies rotted in the heat.

I heard a familiar sound and looked up as two catapult stones arched into the air, then crashed into the town. I heard no screams. Instead, I could hear the sound of digging from the Roman's zig-zagging trenches, and see spoil thrown up onto the lip.

'You were right,' someone said from behind me.

Ziva. Had he come here for me?

The question must have shown on my face. 'Walking laps of the walls,' he told me. 'I feel like they won't come while I'm here. It's stupid, I know.' He shrugged. 'Besides, I like looking at their dead.'

The corpses of this legion of strangers drew no such feeling from me. My hate was reserved for those who had sent them. The rotting bodies were pawns in the games of rich men. They needed to die to save the lives of those that I loved, but I did not hate them.

I told Ziva as much. 'I'll tell that to the next Dalmatian they murder and rape,' the Pannonian tutted.

'You've never raped and killed?'

'No one that didn't deserve it.'

I snorted. 'And what was their crime?'

'They were Roman.'

I let it go. Ziva did not. 'They'll kill Miran and Borna,' he told me.

'I am aware.'

'They will rape them.'

I turned and snarled. 'Shut your mouth while you still have a working jaw.'

He grinned at that. 'There, you see? Violence for the deserving. Who ever thought that we'd be the two most like-minded men in the rebel army, Corvus?'

I said nothing. 'The two traitors,' Ziva grinned.

'You should write a play,' I mocked, annoyed that what he was saying was true. We had both betrayed those we had once loved, but could any man claim to fight harder for the rebellion than myself and Ziva?

I wished Cynbel were here. He would have some wisdom to offer about how I should deal with the guilt that I felt. Guilt because while Ziva had the blood of Vuk, King Pinnes and Thumper on his hands, he had also saved my life not once, but twice, and I was thankful for it.

The shitbag knew as much. I could see it on his face.

I was beholden to an enemy.

'You still hate me,' Ziva laughed. 'Does it make it worse knowing that I don't hate you?'

The bastard was in my head. *Yes*, yes, it made it a hundred times worse, but I would not tell him that.

'Here comes Bato,' I said instead, almost gratefully.

The hulking warrior walked alone along the wall. He patted guards on the shoulder, but he did not speak with them. He had seen the truth of what I had told him, and the inevitability of failure weighed heavily on his thick shoulders.

'Stealing away for a kiss on the walls, eh?' Bato was trying to insult us, as was his way, but there was no weight behind his jests. He was wearing a mask, and it fooled no one.

The rebel leader turned his head. I followed his eyes, and saw a Roman cavalryman riding his horse along the length of the walls.

'What's he shouting?' Bato asked me. He spoke Latin well, but the Roman's tongue was thick and clipped by an accent.

'He wants you to come out and fight him man to man,' I told him, leaving out what the soldier had insinuated about the sexual appetite of Bato's mother.

Bato tutted and shrugged his shoulders. 'There's nothing I'd love to do more,' he said, and I did not doubt a single word, 'but Romans can't be trusted. It would be a trick, and they would kill me.'

'They would, lord,' Ziva agreed.

We watched the horseman ride back and forth. It was not uncommon for a man to come forwards from their ranks and offer single combat. In theory such things were forbidden, but in practice a canny commander would turn a blind eye to such acts. They knew the rebel leaders would not leave their walls, and so the unanswered challenge built a sense of bravado within the Roman ranks. And if Bato or some other champion did come out?

Well, then that would be a fine thing too.

The cavalryman rode ever closer. 'Is he Roman?' Bato asked of me. 'He's got balls.'

'Probably Thracian or German,' I replied.

Bato knew all about Roman auxiliary soldiers. After all, he had raised a hundred thousand of them himself before deciding that they should fight against Rome, and not for her. In the first year of rebellion, when the rebels held the upper hand, hundreds of Thracians and Germans had also deserted and joined his ranks.

'You're fighting for the wrong side!' Bato called out in Latin. 'Come and fight with me, and I'll double your salary!'

The words carried to the cavalryman, and he shouted something back from the saddle.

Bato looked at me. 'I didn't catch that. Go on, Corvus, what did he say?'

'He said you can double your mother's arse, lord.'

Bato boomed out a laugh at that. 'I like you!' he cheered the solitary soldier, but the feeling was not mutual, and the horseman rode further down the wall to try his luck for single combat there.

'What's he doing now?' Bato asked himself. 'Throwing stones?'

The cavalryman had crept closer to the walls. An arrow flashed by him, but the horseman ducked it with skill. Bato clapped to see him survive. 'Ha! Brilliant!'

The auxiliary shouted something in some tongue I could not comprehend. It sounded like some long and angry vengeful curse, and then the soldier of Rome threw a stone against Raetinum's defences.

Bato laughed.

Ziva snorted.

And then the wall collapsed.

Chapter 19

Time seemed to stand still as a section of wall toppled down in a shower of brick and rock and dust. For a long moment, the sound of the falling masonry was the only noise on the mountainside, as men dared not breathe, let alone speak.

The soldier who had thrown the stone sat frozen in his saddle. Bato's eyes were fixed on him. For the first time since I had joined the rebellion, I saw its leader struck with fear.

'*Witchcraft…*'

I needed to act quickly. 'Lord Bato! Bato! Bato, listen!' The man's eyes were wide and awe struck. 'It's not witch-craft, it's luck! He must have hit something that was damaged by the catapults! It's just luck and timing Bato, there's no witchcraft!'

But there was in Bato's mind. There was in Bato's heart. He had seen an act of magic, and he was shaken to his core.

So, too, were his men.

'The bastards are running,' Ziva hissed.

The guards who had witnessed the collapse were now fleeing, shouting about Roman magic. Only fire spreads quicker than panic, and no doubt the whole town would soon lose their heads over a lucky stone.

And then I heard it. *Felt it.*

A cheer rose from the Roman camps and, with orders or not, the legions began to rush from their ramparts, and pour towards Raetinum's open wound.

My stomach was sick. I turned to Ziva. 'It's over.'

He knew as much. 'Good luck,' was all he said, and then he was gone.

I was left alone with the rebel leader who had ordered the death of my friends. If ever I wanted vengeance, now was the time to take it.

Instead I shoved the stunned man in the chest and shouted: 'Fall back, you idiot!'

My aggression worked, but it was almost the end of me. Bato swung a punch that would have sent me over the wall had it connected, and then he was himself again.

Or so I thought.

'Abandon the walls!' he shouted. 'Abandon the walls!' Bato took his own advice then, and fled.

I stood astonished and alone on the town's defences. The guards were gone from sight. So too Ziva, and now Bato.

I turned back to look out at the gush of screaming men who charged towards me with nothing but plunder and rape and death in their eyes.

Raetinum was lost.

And so I ran for my family.

–

My feet pounded against the stone as I raced to the house that had been a home. Bells were ringing. People were shouting, fleeing. Panic was spreading, and fast.

I tried the door to our home. Locked.

'Miran!' I hammered at the wood. 'Miran!'

No answer.

'Sir,' I heard from behind me.

I turned, and saw two of Agron's household troops emerge from the house where he had stationed them. 'Lord Agron sent for them, sir. We were left here to tell you.'

I had no reason to disbelieve them, but I would not give room for doubt in my mind. I took a few steps back, then crashed against the door. It held.

'Sir, Lord Agron sent for them,' the soldier tried again.

I ignored him, pushed my sword down the side of the lock, prised it, and booted the wood.

The door opened and I crashed inside. 'Miran! Borna!' I checked every room. They were not there. I was about to leave when I saw the opened box of Cynbel's scrolls on the table.

'Sir!' the soldier shouted from outside. 'They're coming!'

Seconds matter in battle. I would risk my own life for Cynbel's gift, but not the two lives of the soldiers who waited with loyalty outside the door, and with silent apology I condemned my friend's treasured possessions, and ran back out into the sunlight.

The Romans were coming, spilling into the end of the street, forcing their way inside of homes in search of loot. They had not come as a disciplined fighting force but as groups of friends and bands of brothers. If the army was trying to bring their dogs to heel I saw no sign of it. Rather, I saw the legionaries fall onto the backs of civilians who had tried to hide. They were thrown from windows. Dashed against the stone. To the sound of cheers I saw a wailing baby tossed into the air. I did not wait to see it land.

'Come on!' I told the two men. 'Fall back!'

But they would not. They had seen the baby fall. Heard the Romans cheer. They shared a look between them, old comrades who knew each other's thoughts without a word.

And then they charged towards the Romans, and death.

I had no hesitation in leaving them to that end. My debt was to Miran and her child, and so I fled before Rome's legions.

–

I ran hard towards Raetinum's heart, then scrambled over the barricade that was the height of a man's chest. It spanned the width of the street, and bristled with steel and javelin.

'They're coming,' I told Ziva.

'How many?'

'All of them.'

The rebel spat but said nothing. His men were holding this barricade close to the centre of the town, and others like it. They had been chosen for the task because they were hard, they were steadfast, and they yearned for Roman blood.

They would soon get it.

'Here they come!' men shouted and, sure enough, the Romans appeared in their groups, and in their frenzy. Many took one look at the barricade and turned to looting houses instead, but a short and angry-looking centurion began to shove others into ranks.

'Form up, you shitbags, form up!' he shouted. 'You want loot? You won't find it here! Form up! The money's where it always is, lads, with the leaders! Do you want it or not?'

The centurion's fists and words worked well, and soon the Romans had formed ranks of shield and sword. It did not matter that these men were a mixture from different units – legionaries are trained to be replaceable parts, cogs in a killing machine.

And here they came.

'At the slow march, advance!'

Step after step, foot after foot. My gut tightened. My mouth dried. It felt like my tongue had been nailed to the roof of my mouth.

'Ziva,' I managed to say. 'Javelins.'

The Pannonian nodded. If he knew fear, then he hid it well. I doubted there was another place in the world he would rather be than here, with an enemy in front of him. 'Loose javelins!' he roared, and his men stepped back to aim, and arc, and throw.

'Shields up!' the Romans shouted, and the rain of death pattered harmlessly against their defences, as I had expected it would. Then, also as I had hoped, the Romans felt the need to retaliate with a volley of their own.

'Down!' Ziva ordered his men, and the Roman shafts thumped harmlessly into the barricade, or sailed over the heads of his men. We had robbed the Romans of a weapon and now, with only drawn swords, they charged.

'Up!' Ziva was shouting. 'Up!'

I stood beside him. There was no room for words. No room for thought. Roman shields were at the barricade, and I drove my sword into the first exposed skin that I saw. 'Kill! Kill!'

Something hit me hard across my helmet and I staggered back before regaining control of my legs. I looked up and saw the Romans were kneeling with their shields over their heads so that others could charge across the top of them, and onto the barricade. Through a break in their ranks I could see down the street, and witnessed more Romans rushing to join the imminent breakthrough.

It was time.

I turned to seek out the eyes of two men in an alcove. They had been waiting for my signal, and now I gave it.

'Burn the bastards!'

The men lit their torches, then ran to a gutter on each side of the street. They touched their flame to the oil and pitch that filled them, and fire raced along the gutters and towards the town's walls.

'It's working!' Ziva shouted. 'It's working!'

I held my breath. Following the last battle I knew that we could not defend the town indefinitely, but the destruction of the Roman siege engines had given me an idea of how we could still win the battle. It had been hard work to convince Bato that we should use Raetinum's walls as a cauldron to boil an army, but with Ziva and Agron's help he had been convinced, and so we had poured pitch and oil into the gutters, and now flame raced outwards. Once it reached the homes we had filled with fuel, a fire would take hold from which Raetinum would never recover. We would cook Germanicus's army alive.

But then I saw Ziva's smile fall away.

'Corvus!' I followed his pointing sword, and saw what I had missed.

No...

A catapult stone had brought a building down across the gutter, and the flame had been stopped before it could reach the houses where we had set our fuel and trap. In my haste I had missed it. I had failed.

And now we would die.

'Archer!' I shouted frantically. 'I need an archer!' I twisted and turned, searching for one.

'Sir!' a man reported, bow in his hand.

'I need you to—'

Blood hit my face, and my words were cut off as a javelin passed my shoulder by inches and drove into the archer's chest. He was dead before he hit the floor, and I reached out to pick up his fallen bow.

'You'll never do it!' Ziva shouted at me, and I already knew that he was right. I was no bowman, and to hit the pitch on the other side of the building required a lifetime of skill and training.

Ziva knew as much. He shouted something at his men in their tribal tongue, then turned back to face me.

'It's over,' he said.

And then he ran.

–

I watched with disgust as Ziva fled the battlefield. I thought about chasing him down and putting a blade between his shoulders, but that would do nothing to hold back the Romans who were gaining the upper hand at the barricade.

'Coward!' I roared, and then I turned to the fight, and resigned myself to selling my life dearly with the men that Ziva had abandoned. If they were panicked by his betrayal then they showed no sign of it. Rather, they fought with all the rage and fury of an iron tempest.

I drove my sword at one Roman. Beat another back with my shield. More came in their place. They smelled loot. They smelled victory.

They would not be held back.

I cut, parried, thrust. There was a second of space, and I stepped back to assess our position.

It was an awful one. A second was all it took to see that we were losing: my gamble to let the Romans into the town to trap them had failed. The flames in the gutter had burned out. The Romans would not be caught. Instead they would win, they would kill, and I would lose my family.

No. *No.*

'Clear a way!' I heard a man shouting. 'Clear a way!'

The drum of hoofbeats came from behind me. I turned, and the breath caught in my throat.

'For Pannonia!' Ziva shouted as he charged towards the barricade. 'For King Pinnes!'

Our eyes met only for a second, but it was enough.

He knew.

I knew.

What Ziva had done in the past he had done for Pannonia, and now he would show everyone that truth.

There was no sword in his hand. Instead Ziva gripped a blazing torch, and it left a fiery trail in the air as his horse cleared the barricade in a leap, and clattered into the Roman troops. I heard it whinny in pain as blades slashed towards its flesh, and Ziva cried out as he took his own wounds.

But he would not be stopped.

'For Pannonia! For King Pinnes!'

His men were roaring. Cheering. With a surge they gave up their defences, and instead threw themselves across the barricade at their Roman foe. It was a death sentence that they embraced. An end for heroes.

'*For Pannonia!*'

Ziva came free of the Roman ranks and spurred ahead.

He bled but he would not stop.

I shuddered as a javelin thumped into the man who had been my mortal enemy. Ziva gripped the shaft with his free hand, tore it from his flesh, and raged in agony as he faltered in the saddle.

He was only yards away from the collapsed building, but it may as well have been an ocean.

His horse stumbled.

Ziva fell.

'No...' My eyes were wet with dreadful tears. My throat was parched. My heart was a drum.

All around me men were fighting, killing, dying.

But my eyes were fixed on the death of their leader.

Their hero.

Our hero.

'For Pannonia!' A final cry. A pledge to his people.

And then I saw Ziva touch the torch to himself. I saw the flames take the man, and engulf him. I saw a human torch drag itself over the rubble, and fall into the pitch in the gutter beyond.

'*Ziva...*'

Flames raced outwards.

Buildings were engulfed in fire.

The Pannonian had lit the trap. There is only one thing that spreads more quickly than panic, and that is fire, and the flames rushed from house to house, a fiery rope around the neck of the Roman army. They came tumbling out of windows, aflame and screaming. Others raced down the street, trampling those that had lost their footing. It was chaos. Flames, and screams, and chaos.

'Go!' Ziva's Pannonians were telling me. 'This is our fight!'

I was stunned to stillness by the death of the rebellion's greatest hero.

'For Ziva!' his men were roaring. 'For Ziva!'

They gave their all.

They gave their lives.

I cried at the sight of their courage, and then I ran to join my family in the tunnels.

Above us Raetinum was dying, and an army was drowning in fire.

Part Three

Chapter 20

Ziva had saved the rebellion.

'My men will hold the barricades,' he had told Bato when I had presented my plan to trap the hungry legions.

Bato had not denied Ziva's wish. Not only would the fighting at the barricades be desperate before the flames spread, but the men would be expected to keep fighting the Romans until the very end.

'There must be no let-up,' Bato had said. 'I don't care if the Romans die in the flames or on your blades, but they must die, Ziva. Can you do that?'

The pride that had been absent in the failed usurper returned. He had held himself tall and righteous as he answered.

'All I want to do is kill Romans.'

And kill them he had. Ziva and his Pannonians had died with great valour, sealing the death of more than ten thousand Romans within the city. The walls that they had taken formed the lip of a cauldron. The pitch-filled houses had blazed and cooked the trapped Romans within.

Panic and flame had swept the streets. It was a stampede. A tempest. Every man for himself, and at the back of this fleeing mass the remaining Pannonian rebels had charged, and hacked, and chopped, and stabbed.

It was valiant butchery, and bought the lives of those who waited below, crammed into Raetinum's tunnels.

I had joined them there, black with soot and red with blood, my lungs straining as thick smoke swirled in the streets.

'Snake!' I sent the watchword. 'Snake!' It was the signal to be given when the town was alight, and the Romans were trapped. Leaving the tunnels early would have given them a chance to fall on our backs. We had to wait until the fire was on top of everyone – ourselves included. Only then we could hope to leave the mountain unmolested.

'*Snake!*' The word had been chosen by Ziva, and with a smile. Evidently, he'd been no stranger to what I had called him. I had meant it as nothing but an insult, but Agron had been right: a snake was the symbol of the protection of his people.

I worried that Agron and I would need protection now. Not only from the Romans, who still had a huge presence in Pannonia and Dalmatia, but from Bato.

How would he react if he ever learned that Agron, Ziva and I had hatched a plan to bring down a gap in the wall, and allow the Romans inside? Bato had agreed to the fires *if* the enemy carried the walls, but not before, but both Ziva and Agron had agreed with me that should we be engaged on the battlements before a break-in, we would either trap most of our own army in flames, or have to abandon the idea of burning the Romans. We needed them to get in cleanly, and quickly, and so Agron had seen that a section of wall had been undermined from *our* side. Thankfully, the mines and tunnels beneath the town gave us plenty of opportunity for such work, and a place to deposit the spoil so that Bato and the others would be unaware.

What had happened with the Roman cavalryman who threw the stone, I did not know. The work of the gods?

Fortune? Blind luck? Such things happened in life, and on the battlefield, and on this day we had been the benefactors of belief, as the Romans who witnessed the act saw the will of their gods, and charged to enact it. It was as good and as clean a trap as we could have hoped for, but still it had cost the lives of Ziva and his men, and though invisible, the sword of Bato's executioner once again pressed against my neck.

Should he ever discover what we had done…

It did not bear thinking about. Instead, with my family by my side, we pushed deep into the mountain, and slipped away from Germanicus's army.

—

'What are you thinking about?' Miran asked me.

We walked through wooded hillsides. Borna, seemingly untroubled by war, as children often are, was between us. The track was thick with Dalmatian soldiers and their families shuffling south. As the fire raged we had poured out of the mountain's tunnels. Through the evening and night we had pushed south-east, and continued through the dawn. There was to be no stopping. No rest. We needed a clean break from the Romans. Bato had ordered that his people leave with nothing that could not either kill the enemy, or feed those doing the killing, but I saw that the meaning of his words had been taken liberally. At first I had seen civilians and soldiers carrying all manner of possessions, and more of these burdens lay discarded along the track with every mile that we pushed south.

'I'm thinking about Ziva,' I said, leaving out that I had also been thinking about Bato's rage, and my execution, should he ever find out what I had done to his walls.

Miran nodded, and I wondered if I saw something of pride. Ziva's men had killed Thumper, but there was no doubt they had saved her life, and Borna's. 'He and his Pannonians wanted to show the Dalmatians how to fight.'

'They did that,' I nodded. No doubt the blood of some of those men was still on me now. I stank of the fire that they had fuelled with their sacrifice.

'Don't grieve for them, Corvus,' my wife told me firmly. Now there was no doubt – I could hear the pride in her voice. She was grateful to them. We all were. 'They died on their own terms. Not many people get to choose how they leave this world.'

We said little more. A hard night's march has a way of stealing conversation. I ruffled Borna's hair, kissed my wife on her cheek, and put one foot in front of the other.

—

My mind drifted for most of that slog. The summer heat was fierce, but my mind was more ferocious still, and it would not allow me to slip away to pleasant thoughts of one day visiting Cynbel on his island. I could not shake the image of Ziva as he had set himself on fire. I could not lose the sight of his men climbing the barricades, and charging the Romans. They had claimed as much glory as any force in any war.

And now they were dead, but we lived on.

What would come next in this rebellion? More sieges? More battles? When would the emperor and his empire look at the blood spilled and say, 'Enough!'?

Would it be so bad for them to make peace with Rome? I wanted to ask my wife. *Would it be so bad for them to say, 'You bested us, we will leave you be'?*

I didn't ask the questions, of course. Not only because we were as tired as flogged horses, but because I knew the answer.

The Empire was founded on conquest, pride, and held together by the knowledge that to take up arms against it meant death. If Rome allowed one rebellion to be victorious, word would spread, and other peoples would claim their freedoms. The Empire would fall, and so there could be no other option for them but victory. Either we kept killing the men that Rome sent against us, or we surrendered to slavery. Those were the only two options available to us.

Neither was a path that I would choose, but I knew I would die a hundred times over before I ever let Miran and Borna become slaves. Still, it was with a grim heart that I realised that the misery would drag on. The war would drag on. We had wounded the Roman beast, but like a bloodied bear it would no doubt rise again.

For a second I smiled. The image of that fictitious animal had brought back the memory of my fallen friend, Thumper. He had been fond of telling a story about how he had once punched a bear. The tale got taller every time he told it, and in truth it had often annoyed me to hear it, but I would have given almost anything to have that man beside me again. He would not be broken by our hard path. He would not be daunted by what was to come. I needed to look to Thumper's example, and find my own courage.

I would do it for him. I would do it for Varo, Priscus and Octavius. I would do it for Beatha, I would do it for Cynbel, and I would do it for my father. I would do it for Miran, and Borna.

And, gods help me, I would do it for Ziva.

I had known many hard marches – some had almost killed me – but the presence of Miran and Borna gave me strength, and I felt as though I were a witness to the army's flight deeper into Dalmatia, rather than a victim of those steep, winding tracks.

'How are your feet?' I asked Borna.

'Sore.'

'Do you want me to carry you?'

'He doesn't need carrying,' Miran answered for him. 'Do you, son?'

'No.' Borna shook his head, and the child meant it.

'You're a tough little soldier,' I said with a smile, and I saw pride and pain on his mother's face.

One foot in front of the other. Treasured items lay discarded along the trodden dirt: small chests; carved toys.

Bodies soon joined them. People died from exhaustion, or simply gave up. They fell like tears wept by the mountain. Soldiers tried to avoid them, until they too were beyond fatigue, and then the bodies of their countrymen became just another step. Men like Agron tried to act with decency, and have the dead dragged to the trackside, but I saw several trampled near-flat into the hot dirt by thousands of feet.

Children stood lonely with wide eyes after their parents fell. Plenty of hard hearts would pass them by, but at some point the child's misery would snatch at a man, and a soldier would risk his life for a stranger.

The tramp of feet. The gasp of breath. The whimper of the miserable. The march was not something one would wish to take any part of, had it not been for the knowledge that the Roman hounds were still at our back.

They had not given up. Cresting one ridge, I joined a group of soldiers stood watching a cavalry skirmish play out in a distant meadow. When the fight was over, the rebels around me sat down to rest.

'Don't rest now,' I told them, 'not unless you want to see their cavalry up close.'

Our own horsemen were few. Units that had been harassing the Roman supply lines had come to join Bato once they saw the town ablaze. No doubt they had been overjoyed to find the rebel leader alive, and after he had sent word to his different garrisons, he had taken horses for himself and his nobles, and formed a rearguard to fight the Romans that dogged us. Germanicus's army had been badly mauled in Raetinum, but they were Roman, and they were soldiers, and they would not give up while they had scent of their prey.

We pressed on. Misery. Panic.

Hope.

'Ranko?' I saw my old friend on the side of the track. He was trying to lift someone up. A soldier, his face bloodied and bandaged.

His brother, Zoran.

'Corvus...' Ranko was exhausted. I found some reserve of strength and helped them both to their feet. Then, Miran was beside me.

'Borna, out of the way. Wait by the track.' She told her son. 'I can help,' she told me.

'No,' I said. 'Save your strength.'

But my wife did not listen to me.

'Did you put this bandage on him?' she asked Ranko.

'I did.'

'In the dark?' It was said in jest, and despite the misery of the mountains – or perhaps because of them – we each of us smiled.

I heard shouting then. 'Corvus?' Agron was calling up and down the line. 'Corvus!'

'Over here!'

Agron came towards us. His sword arm was covered in bloody bandages. His left held the reins of the horse given to him by Bato. The back of the beast was thick with exhausted young children.

'What?' Agron felt my look.

'Nothing.' I would not tell him that I was proud of his selfless action. That I loved him because of it. Such emotion, I had been told, was not the way of men.

Agron looked from me to my comrades, then up and down the struggling line of refugees and fleeing soldiers. I saw no elation in him that we had burned Rome's soldiers alive. There was only the brutal resolve of the knowledge that the fight was far from done.

'I need your help.'

'With what?'

His answer was grim, and simple. 'Killing Romans.'

Chapter 21

I stood with the rebel leader and Agron in a clearing beside the track. Kicked up by thousands of feet, a cloud of dust choked the throats of his followers as they continued to stream by.

If Bato was exhausted then he showed no sign of it. Nor did he look uncomfortable that I was in his presence. I, a man who had seen him panic in the face of 'witchcraft'.

No. The man-mountain was *smiling*.

'We burned a legion's worth. At the very least, *a legion's worth*. Maybe two! Smile, Agron!'

Bato's scouts had been riding back and forth between our fleeing force and Raetinum, and now Bato clapped my friend on his uninjured arm, overjoyed at the casualties we had inflicted on Rome. He credited myself and Agron with a large part in that victory, but how would he react if knew that it was us who had collapsed the wall and enticed the enemy into Raetinum?

'Two legions wiped out!' Bato said, choosing to believe the most optimistic of the reports. Without seeing it with my own eyes I would not trust the numbers, but a legion's worth of dead at least seemed more than possible. The town had been stuffed with Romans before we set it alight. Few men can outrun panic and flame.

'Now for the bad news,' Bato went on. 'The bastard's cavalry units are untouched.'

'Germanicus?' Agron asked, in order to identify the bastard.

Bato nodded. 'He's only got a couple of cohorts' worth, but still, they're nipping at our heels and drawing blood.'

I thought of the small mercy that Germanicus's army had been made up by levies in Rome, then reinforced by Tiberius. A cavalryman and mount take a lot longer to train than a foot slogger. No doubt that was why the young general dispatched from home had a smaller contingent of horsemen.

'I thought you were bloody mad at first,' Bato said to me with some pride. 'Burning a town? Mad, but right. I owe both of you for convincing me. Ziva, too. He was a slippery one, but gods what an end. Him and all of his Pannonians. Glorious, weren't they?'

'They were,' I agreed, and it was the truth.

'I would have liked to have seen it,' Bato said of Ziva's death. 'Men will talk of that moment for generations. You were lucky to be there, Corvus.'

To this I said nothing. I could still smell the stink of burning flesh.

Bato eyed the column of refugees that continued to roll by in an unbreaking chain.

'They're giving it all they've got,' the rebel said of his followers, 'but we need to buy them some time. We need to teach this Roman cavalry some respect.'

'How?' Agron asked him.

Bato's eyes fixed on me. Where once I had seen nothing but anger, now there was comradely pride.

A predator's smile then crept across the warrior's face.

'Corvus isn't the only one with tricks, my friend.'

–

A group of women and elderly Dalmatians had fallen behind the main column of refugees. They were struggling along the valley floor. It was a farmed valley, abandoned for war, with ditches either side of the wide track. These people had pushed through exhaustion and beyond, but they had not been able to keep within the safety offered by Bato's soldiers.

They were easy prey, and so they would die.

Imperial cavalry burst into sight from the north. Most rode on the track. Many were in the fields. They were hot with anger after the burning of Raetinum, and desperate to kill, and rape, and plunder.

The struggling women and elderly saw their ends coming and fled. They abandoned each other in the face of death, and instead sought doomed refuge in the ditches.

The men who fought for Rome called to each other in a language that was not Latin. Thracians. They jested over who would take the first turn on their victims. Who would skin the elderly alive, while their comrades took their pleasure from the young ones.

The cavalry charged on. Heartbeats away from easy prey. Almost at the ditches.

Too late, they saw the trap.

'Up!' I yelled at Bato's warriors. 'Up!'

I was wearing Miran's clothes, and the seams bulged as I lifted my concealed spear from the bottom of the ditch, and prepared to receive the cavalry charge.

All about me, dozens of Bato's best did the same, and what had been a fleeing group of civilians transformed into a bristling hedge of wood and steel.

Too late the Thracians saw it. They could not stop.

'Ready!' I shouted. 'Brace!'

I gave myself over to fate.

The ground shook. The air filled with the cries of challenge.

And then they hit us.

—

The horses crashed against us. It was a terrible moment. A moment beyond fear and reason. Spears drove into the flesh of man and beast. Riders flew from their saddles. Others swung their blades into the faces of those that would kill them. Some of the horses passed clean through our trap. Others kicked and whinnied as their guts spilled into the ditch.

'Kill them!' I screamed. 'Kill them all!'

I drove my spear towards a horse's chest. The beast veered and I missed, but the shaft took its rider instead. He howled and took my weapon with him as he fell to the ground. My sword and dagger had been concealed beneath Miran's clothes, and the stitches ripped as I struggled to free them from the tight clothing.

I got the dagger into my hand just in time to stop the rider from rising again, plunging the blade downwards through his shoulder, and into his chest.

Blood spurted into the air as I pulled the weapon free. All around me, men were pulling riders from their horses, and falling to the blades of those who would not be taken down. I saw one skilful horseman pull his horse onto its hind legs, and the flailing hooves caved in the skull of a Dalmatian who had got too close. I saw a spear driven into the back of the rider. He fell.

'Kill them all!' I shouted. 'Kill them all!'

The Thracians outnumbered us, but those who followed their first wave quickly veered away as the second part of our trap was sprung. Bato and his cavalry erupted from hiding to our flank. They had laid down with their horses in a wide ditch, hidden from view, and now they mounted quickly and charged.

The exhausted Thracians had expected easy blood. Instead, it was their bodies leaking into the fields.

They broke. They routed. They fled.

They died.

'Run, you bastards!' Bato was laughing from the saddle. 'Run, you sons of dripping whores!'

The rebel leader dropped from his saddle, and joined in the work of killing the enemy wounded. 'Leave that one for me!' he called out to his soldiers.

The horseman's screams were terrible as Bato went to work with a small knife.

'Louder!' he told his victim. 'I want them to hear you wherever it is you're from! You should have stayed at home, boy! Louder!'

The screams got louder.

I watched Bato smiling as he tortured the Thracian. He loved every moment. This was the man whose walls I had brought down.

What would he do to my family...

'Corvus!' Bato called. He was taking out his cock, and for a moment I stood rooted to the spot.

'Don't worry, you don't look that good in a dress!' Bato laughed, and then he began to piss over the bodies of his enemies. 'Drink up, Thracians! Drink some Dalmatian wine!'

185

I wondered if I had sustained a head wound as I surveyed the scene in front of me. Dozens of Bato's killers, wearing women's clothing and decorated in gore, began to piss over a carpet of enemy dead.

'Drink up!' Bato was weeping with laughter. 'Corvus!' he shouted again as he put his cock away. 'Come on, don't be shy!' More laughter from his men.

'Gather their weapons and equipment,' Bato told them before turning back to me. 'Good fun that, wasn't it? Should give them something to think about.'

I nodded. At least fifty horses were down, and more rode away riderless. It was a bloody nose for the cavalry force that pursued us through the mountains.

'Should buy us some respect,' Bato said, kicking the face of a dead man.

It would do that, I reckoned. We didn't need to lose the Roman tail. We just needed them to be cautious, and that would buy us the shallow breathing room we needed to continue our escape into Dalmatia's hinterland.

The predator's grin was back on Bato's face. 'I've changed my mind,' he said.

'About what, lord?'

'You.' I expected he would talk about warriors and war then, but instead the rebel leader ran a bloody finger down my cheek.

'You look pretty as a woman, Corvus. Grow your hair, then we'll talk some more.'

His bark of laughter was full of the thrill of victory.

'I love this,' he told me. 'There is no better place to be, eh?'

I said nothing. Bato laughed again. 'You know, for someone so good at killing, you should enjoy it a little more, Corvus – or are you still hoping I'll shove that stick up your arse and turn you into an eagle?'

I was too tired to laugh, too bloodied to smile. That only made Bato's humour grow.

He placed a massive hand on my shoulder. 'Come on, you pervert. Let's get those clothes back to your wife.'

Chapter 22

Miran had said little when I'd handed her back the bloodied clothes. She didn't need to hear the stories.

'You're alive. That's all that matters.'

I kissed her on the forehead, and gave Borna a tired smile. The lad grinned back, but I could see red in his eyes, the product of fatigue, and the dust of the track.

'I'll carry you,' I said.

'I want to walk,' Borna told me, and secretly, I was glad – the fighting had left me drained – and so we walked on. One foot in front of the other.

By tricking the Roman cavalry into an ambush we had bought their respect, and forced their caution. They continued to trail us, but they were a sniffing hound now, and not a snapping wolf. I caught glimpses of them, now and then – bands of riders on distant hillsides – but it was no force to fear. Bato's scouts promised him that, so long as we kept pushing hard, we would reach our destination before an enemy army could face us.

I could *taste* the track that aided our escape. Thousands of feet and hooves had churned it into a cloud of dust. I was towards the rear of the column of refugees and soldiers, and before the sun set I saw that many more had dropped from exhaustion. They lay dead, or they lay dying. No one stopped to help them up. People saw only to their closest friends or family. In times like these, a person's tribe fell to a number that could be counted on their fingers.

But two dead men did catch my eye, because they were not lying on the roadside, but hung from a tree.

'Deserters,' Agron guessed, leading his horse and its cargo of orphans.

I heard the branches creak. Saw the rope strain. Pictured my own father, and how I had found him in death.

'They're idiots,' Agron tutted. 'If they wanted to run they should have done so after dark.'

I said nothing. How many would do just that when darkness fell? The mountains were steep, hard and full of peril, but they had been an army's sanctuary. They could be a person's, too. It's easy enough to vanish in such lands. I had done so myself, with my friend Vuk, to evade capture when King Pinnes had surrendered to the Romans. We had watched like gods as the manoeuvres of armies played out beneath us.

Vuk. Pinnes. So many gone, and no end to the rebellion in sight.

At least, no end that was desirable.

I didn't know where we were going, save that Agron had told me Bato had chosen a place that could be well defended. We were an army on the run, and then, sure enough, we would once again become an army under siege. The chance to stand and win against Rome in open battle had left this world with King Pinnes and his surrendered force. Now we could mount a defence on a town's walls, but anything else would be a slaughter. We could not stand against Rome's legions in the open, and there was no saying how long we could do it from a fortress. If we could hold out until deep winter then conditions for the Romans would be made harsh, miserable, even deadly. But winter seemed so far away...

I looked back at the dead men in the tree. Winter was far away, but darkness would fall soon. We could desert, tonight. I could take Miran, Borna. I was sure Ranko and Zoran would follow my lead and come with us. Agron would not, and the idea of leaving him felt like a dagger in my chest, but the thought of losing Miran and Borna was more terrible still. We could sneak away after dark. We could find someplace to hide. Let the hot waters of the rebellion flow by us, and then strike for the coast. Strike for Iadar. The boys' father would be happy to see us. He could find us somewhere to wait the war out. He could put us on a ship. He could—

'*Traitors*,' I heard someone say in an acid tongue. At first, the tone was so unfamiliar that I had no idea who had spoken.

'*Bastard traitors*,' Miran said again, then she spat in the direction of the swinging deserters. There was fire in her eyes. She was as tired as any of us, but something about the sight had given her a furious energy.

'They would have left us, Corvus,' she seethed. 'They would have left these children to save their own skins. They would have abandoned the rebellion to save their own pathetic lives. *Traitors*. They deserved worse than death!'

I was stunned to silence. I had seen fatigue turn the happiest of soldiers into cantankerous bastards, but what gripped Miran was not tiredness, but rage at those who would have abandoned her son, and those like him.

Any thought of taking flight from the army died instantly, and I resolved never to tell my wife what had been on my mind. There are fates worse than death, and having Miran believe me to be a lesser man was one of them.

'Bastards,' she spat one more time, and then we were past the bodies hanging in the still, dead air.

Soon after the skies turned red. We crossed a ridgeline as the sun was setting. There, as night came, I looked down at the pathetic snake of an army, slithering for cover in its death throes.

The end was near.

I wanted to run.

Instead I lifted Borna onto my aching shoulders, and kissed the dust on my wife's hair.

We were damned, but we were free.

—

To stop was to die. We had marched for more than a full day, but no one dared take more than a short break by the trackside. Eagles see weakness from a distance. They strike at the slow and the sick. Rome's legions were no different. If we gave in to the temptation of sleep, then we would wake as slaves, if we ever woke at all.

'Just put one foot in front of the other,' I said in the darkness.

There was nothing fun about tramping through the night. Nothing fun about the steep slopes that came from nowhere. Nothing fun about tripping, and eating dust, even though you already had a mouthful of it from the air. My nose had long since blocked. We breathed through our dry mouths. Said little. Said nothing. Not so much as a curse if you stepped on a body. Not even a whimper when your mind told you to give up, and join the dead. We had left our words with the sunset. In the darkness, there was only survival.

Such thoughts took me to pondering the Roman leaders. We had not just given them a bloody nose at Raetinum – we had cut their nose from their face. Germanicus would need to be reinforced before he could mount an offensive on our next sanctuary. Would Tiberius be more or less likely to favour siege – even talks – now that the Roman army had taken such large losses? The original reason for the raising of the Pannonian and Dalmatian forces had been war against the German king, Marabodus. He and his tribes still waited beyond the Danube. Would Tiberius want to return there as soon as possible, with as many men as possible? Would he concede to a peace with Bato if it allowed a war with Marabodus? The lifeblood of Rome was glory, and glory was not won in ambushes in the mountains. It was won on sweeping battlefields, in the mighty clash of armies against armies, where men fell and eagles soared.

Try as I might, however, it was hard to believe that the powerful Romans would wish to end this campaign on a note of failure. No doubt they would want a great victory to stamp out the flames of Raetinum once and for all.

And yet…

Germanicus was a young commander, beloved of the mob in Rome. Tiberius was heir to the Emperor Augustus. Would he want Germanicus to go home covered in glory, or would he want people to whisper, '*He lost*'?

Politics was a viper's nest, and aristocrats had long been fond of smearing – even murdering – their competition. I prayed that Tiberius was cut from the same cloth, that his own vainglory would trump the needs of his soldiers, who no doubt yearned for retribution against those who had killed their comrades and kinfolk.

The hope of it kept me marching through the night. Slope after slope. Agron was somewhere in the dark close beside me. Ranko and Zoran, too.

'Do you see that?' Ranko asked no one, and everyone. 'The sea!'

'You're hallucinating,' I told him. Extreme fatigue would do that to a man.

'I'm telling you, I can see the sea.'

I heard a slap in the dark.

'You're hallucinating,' his brother told him.

Ranko stopped talking about the sea.

We put one foot in front of the other.

–

Dawn threatened the skies. Soon, there was enough light to make out the silhouettes of loved ones.

'Lord Agron!' someone began shouting.

'Over here!' My friend's voice was parched, but strong as ever. He was a leader, and leaders do not let their discomfort show.

I heard a horse's hooves and breath, then quiet conversation. The dispatch rider rode away.

'Corvus!'

I joined Agron. 'Here,' I said when I was by his side. I knew what was coming. Another chance to get myself killed.

I was wrong.

'Seretium has fallen,' Agron said quietly. 'Tiberius's men have captured the town.'

I felt grief flood into my limbs. A grief for strangers.

Thumper's sons had been there.

'Did any escape?'

'The Romans carried it with the sword,' Agron told me. 'Our scouts do not believe that there are any who got out. I'm sorry, Corvus.'

He knew who was there, and why they meant so much to me. For saving Miran and Borna, Thumper was a hero in Agron's eyes as much as my own.

'They're with their father now,' I said, and there was some consolation in that.

'Are you all right?'

'Yes.' And I was. Miran was alive. Borna was alive. 'What happens now?' I asked him.

Agron knew what I meant. If Seretium had fallen, then Tiberius's army could be re-tasked. 'Tiberius will come,' he said finally.

'And what of Bato?' I asked. 'Does he plan on meeting Tiberius on the battlefield?'

'Bato is a warrior, but he is not an idiot. He knows he needs to be behind a town's walls when Tiberius and the remainder of Germanicus's forces arrive.'

Raetinum burned.

Seretium fallen.

We were running out of places to hide.

'Where next?' I asked.

Bato had not told us. His scouts were under pain of death to reveal nothing. Darkness and fatigue had robbed us of our landmarks, and curiosity. There had only been one foot in front of the other, but I knew that we could not march for ever. Not without rest. We would stop soon, or die, and sure enough, by dawn's light we were given our answer.

Tears cut tracks through the dust on Miran's face when she saw the town.

194

'I never wanted you to see it,' she said honestly. 'I told you that. If we came here, it meant that the war had come, too.'

Arduba.

Miran's home.

The last bastion of the rebellion.

'It's beautiful,' I told her, and that was no lie.

The light of day began to fill the valley. Surrounded on three sides by a wide river, perched atop of steep cliffs, Arduba sat high and proud in the green valley. There was only one direction from which it could be approached, and across that neck of land stood thick battlements. It was a formidable place, likely unconquerable in Dalmatian warfare. But this was no tribal feud. There was an empire coming for our lives, and though I sensed great relief in the refugees to finally lay eyes on their sanctuary, the warriors around me all saw the same thing.

There would be no escaping this place.

Miran saw it, too. 'There's nowhere left to run.'

Her home would be the site of the rebellion's last stand.

Chapter 23

I woke beside Miran in the home of her childhood. It was of modest size, but well kept, clean and proud. Space was at a premium on Arduba's clifftops, and though it was smaller than the villa in which I had grown up, I did not doubt that it was doubly expensive. Furniture remained, but all ornaments had fled south with the residents.

The town's small garrison had been ready to receive us, but its people were absent. Bato's scouts and quartermasters had brought word of our coming, and there was no shortage of empty buildings for the army to occupy now that Arduba's population had fled before the war. Bato's refugees and soldiers were glad of their absence, but I was not. What did it say that the town's own citizens had fled? Against an empire, they recognised Arduba for what it was.

The end of the rebellion's road.

The walls that we had entered through were as stout as any I had ever seen, but they would keep us in as well as they kept the Romans out. There were no tunnels here. No mines. Arduba sat high on its cliff perch like an eyrie, and the legions were bringing their eagles to roost.

With care I moved Miran's arm from my chest, and slipped from our bed. We were both fully clothed, having fallen to slumber the moment we lay down. Though my body still ached, my mind was alive, and so I gently left my wife's side, careful not to wake her.

I needn't have worried. Miran was in the bliss of deep slumber. My heart warmed to see something of a smile on her sleeping face.

I wanted her to enjoy those dreams for as long as she could – I imagined that there would be little of them to come.

I spared another moment to look at Borna, curled up on the bed, his mouth slack and drooling.

I loved this child.

I loved them both, and that was why I left the bedchamber, and stepped into the hallway. I knew that I would not meet any members of her family in the house. Miran's parents had died before the rebellion. The rest of the family had fled south. Two of Miran's cousins had remained behind with the garrison, but their reunion at the gate had been brief.

Walking into the kitchen I saw two figures asleep on the tiles. Miran had insisted that Ranko and Zoran join us here, and such an arrangement worked well for me. I trusted that the pair would watch my family when I was away. Of course, one of them would need to be awake for that.

'Sorry,' I apologised to Zoran as I shook him awake. 'I'm going to take a look around.'

'What time is it?' he asked, rubbing at red eyes.

I opened the door, and sunlight flooded in. 'About midday,' I said, checking for the high sun. 'I'll be back soon. Are you awake?'

'I'm awake,' he said, pushing himself to his feet. 'I could use the latrine.'

'You're in a kitchen,' I told him, tossing the man a jug. 'Be inventive.'

Zoran caught it and I closed the door. The air was hot but not as stiff as I'd expected. I guessed that the winding river beneath the cliffs had something to do with that, and I enjoyed the kiss of a breeze that carried through the tightly packed streets.

I felt eyes on me then. Saw the culprit. He was peering at me from atop a low wall opposite my door. His eyes were dangerous, and for a moment I was reminded of Ziva.

'Good afternoon,' I said to the cat.

The feline said nothing back. It continued to stare, and I laughed to myself as I felt the creature judging me. 'You should leave,' I told it. 'There's going to be a lot of hungry mouths here come winter.'

The cat said nothing.

'Fair enough.' I stepped across to pet the animal but the cat jumped back, and out of sight. For a moment I thought it had plunged to its doom, but looking over the wall I saw a rooftop beneath us. Arduba's streets were tiered, and tangled, and that was exactly why I wanted to walk them now, and become familiar with what would inevitably become a battlefield.

It was a pretty town. A clean one. The buildings were densely packed, but it did not reek of excess filth. The latrines were on the town's edge, the waste carried down and away over a cliff's edge. If one needed proof that shit rolled downhill, then they could find it here.

Despite the late hour of the day, the whole town felt asleep as I paced the streets. There was little wonder at that, as the flight from Raetinum had pushed many to their limits, and some beyond it. How many had died or given up on the track? Hundreds, at least.

I walked on, and saw knots of soldiers sleeping in the most unnatural-looking positions. For a horrible moment they reminded me of the dead on a battlefield, but then I heard their snores.

I had come to love these rebels. They had been my enemy once, but now they were my comrades.

I realised then that it was not one side or another that I thought of as kin, but soldiers themselves. Soldiers of all races, of all colours and of all tribes. They were the most brutal and brilliant of men. The most honest in their manner, the most dishonest in their deeds. They could be trusted to give their word, or take your life. Bring home one mother's son, and end the life of another's. They were complicated, and yet so simple. They were witty, hard, and ever-loving of those that they found deserving of it. They were mankind's greatest gift, and his most violent poison.

They were my brothers.

I left them to their sleep and walked the clifftops that surrounded the town. There was no wall here, nor was one needed. The cliffs were high and steep. Some distance beneath them a wide, fast river flowed. I didn't put any physical feat beyond determined men, but it would be impossible for the Romans to come in force, and armoured. Bato had placed sentries to watch for them. He would not be tricked as he had tricked the Romans.

Taking stock of my surroundings, I realised that Arduba clung like a teardrop to one side of the steep-sided valley, and the most narrow part of that tear was protected by walls that appeared thick and dependable. They reminded me of my old friend Varo.

I half-expected to find Bato on the walls, but there was no sign of the massive man. Even the leaders of the rebellion must sleep.

I looked out over the approach to the town. It was a sloping climb, but no great hill, and certainly no mountain. From my vantage I could see the outline of traps, and ditches, but nothing that would stop an army from reaching these walls once they had paid the blood price. Surely it would be Tiberius who led his army here for the final battle. How many men was the emperor's heir willing to lose? How long could we withstand his siege?

I looked down and across the green valley, expecting it to turn red at any moment with the shields of Rome.

There was a reason that I was awake, and that reason was a legion.

The Eighth Legion. Men that I had called comrade. Men that I had fought alongside. Men who I had been willing to die for...

The Eighth had been with Tiberius at Seretium. Would they come here now?

Would Marcus?

My gut turned to stone. I felt light-headed at the thought. The man was a bastard, a shit, a killer, but...

He was – *had been* – my brother.

Marcus had taken much from me. So had three of his fellow killers. They were cruel, but life since had been kind. I had a family now, a reason to live. Those with the most to lose are the least likely to risk it all to seek revenge. I didn't need honour, I needed Miran. I didn't need glory, I needed Borna.

I would not seek vengeance, not while they lived, but nor would I shy from protecting them. Nor would I shy from ending the lives of others to preserve the ones of the people that I loved.

A tear ran over my cheek. Then another. Then another.

I was in a state of terror.

I was grieving.

Because if the Eighth came here, I would be forced to kill my brothers.

Chapter 24

I woke up screaming. It took a brief second to realise that I was in my bed, with Miran by my side, and then the headache came.

White sheets of pain struck me like lightning. My skull felt as though it was in a giant's palm, squeezed and cracking. The agony was so great that I only wanted to die so that it would end.

I felt Miran's hand on my forehead. Heard her soothing words. The pain beat a retreat, but left me wretched in its wake.

My nightmares had returned. I'd never seen Miran more concerned.

'Corvus… what's wrong?'

I pushed myself up on my elbows. The pain had gone, but shame had come in its place. 'Nothing,' I said with misdirected anger. 'I'm fine.'

Miran tutted at that, and pushed me firmly back down as I tried to rise. 'Play the hero to yourself all you want, Corvus, but you have an obligation to me. You have an obligation to Borna. *Tell me.* Speak. If not for your own good, then for ours.'

The fire in her eyes was back. I wondered if she would hit me if I said nothing.

There was no need to find out.

'I'll tell you,' I promised, 'but not here.'

We sat on a rock on a clifftop and looked out over the valley beneath us. The river was a twisting ribbon of silver amid the green, the blue sky empty of everything but soaring eagles.

I held Miran's hand. Her eyes were red. So were mine. We had been crying. For Beatha. For my father.

I had told her everything. Beatha's rape. Her murder. The death of my father.

I wanted to tell Miran that it would be different this time. I wanted to tell her that everything would be all right.

But how could I?

We would soon be surrounded, and then we would fight.

'I would die for you,' I said. I hoped that the words would bring her comfort. Instead they brought a tut. 'What?' My pride was hurt.

'I don't want you to die for me, Corvus,' my wife explained, as though to a child. 'I want you to *live*.'

There was an edge to her voice. A frustration. 'Men are always saying they will die for this, and die for that, and what does that leave? *Who* does it leave? The man gets a hero's death, and their family is left to pick up the pieces.'

I couldn't believe what I was hearing. 'You're telling me that it's selfish to die in battle?'

'Don't put words in my mouth, Corvus. I'm saying that when a soldier's battle ends, his family's begins.'

The words struck a blow. I felt chastened, and did not know what to say. I heard truth in what Miran was saying. As hard as it could be to overcome fear and charge into battle, the world did not end when a soldier died. It would go on, and his family would have to go through it without him. Life was not sparing of hardship.

'Then I will live,' I promised her. 'Whatever it takes.'

'That's better,' she smiled.

We drifted into melancholic silence. 'How does it feel,' I asked after a long moment, 'to be back?'

I had deliberately avoided saying 'home', but Miran flinched nonetheless.

'Tell me a story,' I tried with a smile, 'about when you were a child.'

'Why?'

'Because I want to know more about my wife,' I said, laughing at her expression, and the roll of her beautiful eyes.

'You don't know enough? What difference does it make if you know about my life as a child? Those days are gone.'

I tried a different tack. 'Does Borna take after you?'

Mention of her boy brought warmth to her face. 'I was not quite so quiet,' she admitted.

'You mean you were trouble.'

Miran pushed my shoulder. 'You're one to talk.' A smile. 'No, I was not trouble, my love, I was a little girl in a good family. I helped around the house. I was educated. Life was dull, and happy. I liked it.'

'Did you go on adventures?'

'Not like this.' She squeezed my hand. 'What would you like me to say, Corvus? I've had a good life.'

She smiled as she said it, but the word delivered me a blow nonetheless. 'You *have* a good life, my love. And we have many more adventures ahead of us.'

Miran kissed my cheek. 'I hope not, my darling. I'd rather like life to be boring, again.'

I looked into the eyes of the woman that I loved, and brushed my fingers through her hair, still filthy and tangled from our flight from Raetinum.

'What?' She was smiling.

'Back in Bato's camp, before we were married, Agron told me that I was a lucky one.'

My wife laughed, and playfully knocked my hand from her hair. 'And you didn't believe him?'

'I could see the truth of what he was saying,' I said after a moment, 'but I didn't believe it. I didn't feel like I deserved to be lucky, or happy.'

'And how do you feel now?'

'Very lucky.' I smiled, and kissed her. Life had taken so much from me, but it had given me much in return. I would never forget Beatha, my father, my friends, nor stop loving them, but neither would I stop living. I owed them that.

I would live for them all.

'Finding you has been my greatest gift,' I told my wife, and I had never spoken truer words. 'I love you.'

'I know you do.' Her frustration was gone. There was only love. 'Kiss me.'

I pulled her close.

The war could wait.

Chapter 25

Two days passed. There was still no sign of our Roman enemy.

I walked the streets with an aspiring soldier, Borna. He stuck his chest out and walked with pride, narrowing his eyes whenever he appraised the other warriors in the town.

'Why are you looking at them like that?' I laughed.

'Because that's how you do it.'

I didn't know what to say to that. 'Come on,' I ruffled the lad's hair, 'let's get some bread.'

We broke it back at the house with Agron and the brothers. Miran sat by my side, and Borna watched on from the corner of the room.

'No news?' Agron asked me.

I shook my head. 'No sign of their army.' There was no sheltering my loved ones from war, and they were entitled to know the warriors' thoughts as much as anyone.

'They'll be gathering all of their forces,' Agron guessed. 'Tiberius will have come down from Seretium, and they'll want to awe us when they reach the valley. Give us a display of power.'

'How far are we from the coast?' I asked Agron.

'A few days' ride,' my friend replied, giving me the answer for the fifth time. In the days since our arrival at Arduba, we had done little else but speculate about how and when the Romans would come. At any moment I expected to hear the call.

'Maybe they won't find us,' Ranko said hopefully. There were clean bandages on his head, and my old friend was in good spirits.

'They'll find us,' Agron promised. 'This isn't the biggest town, but it's an important one. Nature has built us great defences here, but it hasn't made us invisible.'

'More wine?' Zoran asked him.

'Why not? Can't take it with us, can we?' Agron said, and I saw my friend immediately regret the words. 'A soldier's joke,' he apologised to Miran.

She smiled as she reached over and took his newly filled cup. 'You're quite right, Agron. Cheers.' Miran drank, then wiped her wet lips. I fought back the surging urge to kiss them, and listened as my wife went on in a calm and even tone.

'Germanicus didn't wait at Raetinum,' she said. 'And Tiberius didn't wait for surrender at Seretium.' Word had spread through the garrison. All knew that the town on the Sava had fallen. 'The Romans have shown us their tactics. There's no reason to believe that they will be content to starve us out here.'

Agron nodded in agreement as Miran went on.

'We're the last town standing in the rebellion. The last one of size, at least. The Romans will want to crush us, and then get back to their *glorious wars*.'

'They want to fight battles that expand Rome's borders,' Agron agreed. 'Not put down rebellions within them.'

'And yet here they are,' Ranko said. 'How long now since Bato led us against them?'

'Two years,' his brother answered, almost wistfully. 'I can still remember it like it was yesterday.'

'You were with Bato when he declared the rebellion?' I asked.

Zoran shook his head. 'I was ploughing a girl in the village,' he said proudly. 'I'll never forget her.'

'She looked like Bato, though,' Ranko said.

The adults laughed. Borna wasn't sure why ploughing someone that looked like Bato was so funny, but he joined in anyway.

'I think we're at the part where you need to go to an inn,' Miran told us. 'I'll make us some food for later.'

I didn't move. I gazed at my wife.

'Why are you looking at me like that, Corvus?' she laughed. 'Are you a soldier or a puppy? Go and have some fun with the boys.'

She leaned across and kissed me to cement my orders. 'Go.'

Agron and the brothers thanked Miran for having them in her house, and then walked out into the sunlight. When the door closed behind me, all were smiling.

'What?'

'Does she have a bigger cock than you?' Zoran grinned.

'Does she spank you when you've been bad?' his brother wanted to know.

I half-laughed, half-tutted.

'Don't look at me,' Agron put his hands up. 'I'm not getting involved in this discussion.'

'At last,' I said. 'Someone with some manners.'

'Manners? No, no, I'm just terrified of your wife.'

The brothers laughed at that, but there was an edge of seriousness to Agron's tone, and he explained why as we walked towards the centre of Arduba.

'You'd do well to have a little fear of the mothers in this town, lads. Think about it. They saw Raetinum burn. They've been close enough to battle to *smell it*, and then they had the toughness to survive a forced march here through the mountains. There's no one behind these walls that doesn't have grit, and I doubt there are many who don't see this place for what it is.'

Agron didn't need to spell out what that was – the rebellion's final stand.

'You ever seen a bear protect its cubs?' he went on. 'That's what we have now, with the women in this town. They know there's nowhere left to run. Arduba's walls, and the men on them, are the last chance to save their children, and gods help the man who falls short of their expectations.'

The sun was high and flooded the small town square. It was packed with soldiers who'd had the same idea as us, and the few inns were heaving and flowing as men came outside with their wine. Shouts flew back and forth in a variety of languages, and though I did not speak them, I could tell that each was spoken in the same tone – that of comradeship.

'There's nowhere to sit,' Zoran said. 'Sir,' he said to Agron, 'can you tell someone to move?'

'I could,' the nobleman replied. 'But I won't.'

I smiled a little at that. Agron understood leadership, and that just because you could do something, didn't mean that you should.

'I was told that Tiberius sits at a table and takes food with his men,' I said, thinking back to the fondness that my brothers had had for our leader in the legions.

'Probably stealing their dinner,' Ranko grinned. 'Doing what commanders do best. Present company excepted, sir.' He nodded at Agron.

'You can both drop the "sirs",' he told the brothers.

'Yes sir!' they chorused.

'Oi! Ranko!' someone was shouting. 'Zoran!'

I looked over my shoulder and saw a knot of soldiers at a table. From their half-closed eyes, I guessed that they'd been there for a while.

'Come sit with us!' the soldier shouted. He was rowdier than his mates. Either a latecomer to the wine, or a man with a stronger constitution.

'We were in the same garrison together,' Zoran explained with a smile, and then introductions were made, and we crammed onto benches.

'Wine!' several voices shouted, and the overworked innkeepers rushed back and forth to fill cups that rapidly emptied.

I kept silent. Not out of choice, but because it was impossible to get a word in edgeways while Ranko, Zoran and their friend Goran were spilling gossip at high speed.

'Did you hear about him?'

'Did you hear about *her*?'

Dozens of mutual acquaintances were discussed, laughed about, grieved for, or subjected to brutal criticism. When I turned to speak to Agron, I saw the older man had fallen asleep, a serene smile on his face as he drooled onto his chin.

'I've fought against you,' I heard then.

It was Goran speaking. 'Excuse me?' I asked.

'I fought against you. Outside Siscia, when we marched on Italia.'

I searched his face for hostility. Doubtless he had lost friends that day.

'I saw you hold the eagle,' the man said. 'Well, I saw someone hold it. I don't know if it was you or not, but I definitely saw an eagle.'

'What was it like?' one of his friends asked. 'Fighting against us?'

'Terrifying,' I answered honestly. 'And hard.'

They liked that.

'You had us in the day,' I admitted. 'If your commanders had set better watches, there would have been no beating you.'

'Told you it was their fault!' one of the rebels tutted. 'More wine?' he asked me.

'Why not?' I said, copying Agron's words. 'Can't take it with us, can we?'

They liked that, and drunkenly filled my cup until it ran over my hand.

'How many men have you killed?' one of them asked me.

The question took me by surprise. 'I'm not sure,' I said honestly.

Goran turned to his friend. 'He's not gonna tell that to people he used to fight against, is he?' He looked at me. 'It's all right though, honest. Water under the bridge, my friend. So how many? Fifty? Hundred?'

'Three hundred,' Zoran said.

Goran narrowed his eyes. 'How would you know?'

'I'm writing his biography.'

'Ha! You couldn't write your own name, you dickhead. I've had turds with more artistic talent.'

'That's no way to speak of your children.'

And so it went. The insults. The laughter. More wine flowed, and it wasn't long until one of the Dalmatians got naked. Then another, then another. When one of those men pissed in his comrade's cup, and the man drank it down in one, I knew it was time for me to gather up the sleeping Agron, and leave.

'Where are you going?' Zoran slurred.

'Home.'

'We'll come with you,' he said, though I knew the words were simply out of duty.

'Stay,' I told him. 'Have fun.'

Agron was alert once I woke him. He took one look at the naked rebels and didn't need to hear my explanation about why we were leaving.

We left the rowdy assembly and said our goodbyes on one of the streets. Agron was accommodated close to the inn, and Bato's new headquarters.

'I'll see you tomorrow,' I told him, and then, as I walked to my home, and to my wife, my mind drifted back to the soldiers in the square, and other comrades that I had known. Irregulars like Thumper. Pannonians like Vuk. Legionaries like Priscus, Varo, Octavius and Brutus. Old warriors like Cynbel, who had fought on the island of white cliffs. I had been honoured to know such men, and I could only hope that I was proving worthy of their friendship.

I found the door to my new home. Miran was in the kitchen.

I put my hands on her waist, and kissed her neck.

'I love you.'

She giggled. 'You're drunk.'

'I'm drunk on your love.'

She laughed at that and pushed me away. 'From the smell on your breath I'd say you're drunk on wine.'

'That too.' I shrugged, and before I could utter another word my wife had gripped me by the hair, and bitten my ear.

'Shut up and fuck me,' she told me.

I listened.

—

Later that night I lay in bed with my wife. The sex had done a lot to sober me up, and I was basking in Miran's naked presence. There was sweat on our skin, and our hot flesh pressed against each other's.

'Did you have fun with the boys?' she asked, her head on my chest.

'I did,' I answered honestly, leaving out that there was a price to be paid for that enjoyment – the memory of my fallen friends was now vivid in my mind.

I missed them so much.

Miran began to run a finger up and down the inside of my forearm, and onto my sword hand.

'We should be training,' I said then, surprising myself. 'The army is drinking, when we should be training.'

'Men need their fun. They're scared, my love. They need distraction.'

'Drill can be a distraction,' I told her, though in truth I knew that she was right. Men wanted to drink, and tell stories about the good old days. To drill was to acknowledge that the Romans were coming.

'There'll be time for war,' Miran said. 'Let them enjoy their brothers' company while they can.'

'You're right.' I kissed the top of her head.

Miran turned her face up to mine. I knew the look in her eye before she began to crawl on top of me, then stopped with a smile when someone banged at the door.

'Wrong room, boys!' I shouted, glad that Ranko and Zoran had found their way back through the narrow, winding streets.

'I'm here from Lord Bato,' a stranger's voice replied instead. 'You're needed on the walls, immediately.'

Chapter 26

Beneath the stars I made my way quickly to the walls. Arduba was something of a winding maze, with streets tiered at different heights, but I had spent the time wandering them either alone or with Borna so that they became familiar. When battle came, we could not afford to get lost.

Bato was on the walls. There was no mistaking the massive bulk of his silhouette, nor the glow on the horizon.

'Camp fires,' I said to him.

'A big army,' Bato replied. 'They're not in the valley yet. I expect they'll want us to watch their arrival in the light of day.'

For a moment I said nothing. I had seen Bato flushed from victory, and panicked by witchcraft. His voice was calm and even now, but I could not help the worm of worry in my guts:

Did he know that I had persuaded Agron to undermine a section of wall?

'You sent for me?' I said at last.

Bato's eyes remained on the distant fires.

'Your plan got my people out of Raetinum,' he said after a moment. 'You fought bravely, Corvus the Dalmatian, and for that I want to give you the chance to leave with your wife and child while you still can.'

His words shocked me. I said nothing.

'The Romans will be here in the morning,' Bato went on. 'We will win our freedom, or we will die trying.'

'And I will try with you, lord.'

Bato grunted. 'You would decide your family's fate that quickly?'

I thought on it for a long moment, then gave him truth that he was owed. 'I would leave, lord. I would take my family and never look back, but my wife will not abandon her people.'

'She is your wife, Corvus,' Bato said with some amusement. 'She will do as you tell her.'

I smiled in the darkness. 'If she were that easy to control, lord, then you would have taken my head from my shoulders a long time ago.'

Bato laughed at that. 'True. She's a good woman, Corvus. This country is full of them. No wonder the Romans want it for themselves, the bastards.'

'How big is their army?'

'I haven't had any scouts return in a day,' Bato said evenly. 'They're either dead or have deserted. I expect the hills are full of Roman scouts now. No doubt their engineers will have snuck ahead of the army to plot their siege.'

For a second I thought of Ziva. If he were here, he would be desperate to leave the town and hunt for such men.

'Do you regret it?' Bato asked me then.

The question caught me off guard. 'Marriage, lord?'

'Desertion, you idiot. Turning traitor.'

I didn't have to think about my answer. 'No.' And that was nothing but the truth.

'That's good. A man should not die with regrets...'

He turned to me then. By the moon and stars I saw the smile on his hard face.

Bato put out his massive hand.

I hesitated in taking it. 'If this is about me wearing women's clothes again...'

Bato boomed out a laugh that sounded like a clap of thunder. 'And now you make jokes? That woman and child have been good to you, Corvus.' He thumped me on the shoulder. 'From standard-bearer to comedian!' Bato leaned forwards and sniffed at me then. 'Ah, that's why! I can smell the sex on you!'

I stepped back.

'Where are you going?' he laughed. 'Just one more sniff!' Bato cackled at his own joke, and then the man-mountain spoke in a warm tone. A tone that made me believe that I had earned this rebel's friendship.

'Go home to your wife, Corvus,' he said to me. 'I have the watch.'

'Good night, lord,' I said. I took two steps from him, then hesitated. 'Lord Bato?'

'Yes?'

'Thank you,' I said to the man I had once wanted to kill, and I did not need to tell him why.

Bato understood. He had given me a chance – grudgingly at first – to fight on the right side of history.

'I would have liked your eagle, Corvus, but your sword will do. Good night.'

'Good night, lord.'

'Oh, and Corvus?'

'Lord?'

'Did you really think I believed in Roman witchcraft?'

The words stunned me.

'I know what you and Agron did to my wall,' he said, and all peace fled from my limbs.

'You can unclench your arsehole, Corvus. You're not in danger. *I* gave Agron the orders to do it. I just couldn't say so in front of the other nobles.' Bato laughed. 'Men do not willingly give up walls.'

I was stunned.

'Why are you telling me this, lord?'

'Because I don't want you dying thinking you got one over on me.' The rebel general grunted. 'How many times do I need to tell you about not showing your true faces?'

'Then why are you doing it now, lord?'

'You know why,' he said, and I did.

Because tomorrow the Romans would come, and we would win our freedom, or we would die.

Chapter 27

Sometime after dawn I awoke to panic in the streets.

My arm shot out of bed and gripped my sword – were the Romans already in the town?

Fearing for such an eventuality I had gone to bed in my chainmail, and now I wasted no time in throwing the window open, and peering down at the street below – people were flocking to the wall.

'What's going on?' I shouted to a soldier.

The man looked up, his words painted in nervous excitement. 'The Romans are coming into the valley, sir!'

'I'm going down there,' I told Miran, half expecting her to follow. Instead my wife barely moved.

She felt my look. 'What? I'll not let Tiberius chase me from my bed.'

'I love you,' I said, and kissed her savagely. I didn't worry that this would be our final farewell, certain that the Romans would at least try and intimidate us into surrender first. The more men they lost here, the fewer they had for their next inevitable campaign.

Then I was in the street. I thought about running with the rest of them, but I was known, as was my reputation, and so I walked at a leisurely pace. I heard soldiers say 'that's Corvus', and soon they were walking too.

The wall was choked with people, but they made way for me, many with pleasant greetings, and something of pride swelled in my chest. I had flaws, and I had a past full of mistakes, but I had earned my place in this rebellion.

I saw Bato's massive bulk and moved to him. The rebel leader did not break his gaze to meet mine, and so I followed his eyes into the valley, and to a scene of brilliant majesty.

Legion after legion covered the landscape, a blanket of martial might. Never during my days in the army, nor while watching the surrender of King Pinnes, had I seen such a gathering of force.

'There must be five legions...'

I tried to count the eagles. They had been gathered together, a knot of shining brilliance. Perhaps they had been put there to overpower us with awe, perhaps to entice Bato into launching an attack to claim the sacred totems. Either way, we were knocked into stunned silence. There were fewer than thirty legions in the world, and five of them were here.

Here for us.

'Quite a sight, isn't it?' Agron said. 'What was in that wine, Corvus? My head feels like a drum.'

My friend was smiling and calm. Was he truly so unworried about what lay before us?

Of course not. Agron was simply doing what good leaders do, and not letting his fear become infectious.

I followed his lead. 'It's your age,' I told him. 'My head feels fine.'

He smiled. We lapsed into silence. There was an odd sense of detachment in the air, as though the rebel army was looking at a wonder of the world, and not at the instrument of their own destruction.

And then it happened.

'What's going on?' Agron asked, but I said nothing.

A solitary figure was breaking free of his comrades' arms and walking forwards with intent from the Roman ranks. He carried no shield, and the crested helmet that marked his centurion's rank was tucked beneath his arm.

Before I even saw his face, my heart turned to ash.

'Corvus!' the soldier shouted, and the challenge echoed across the valley like an eagle's cry. 'I am here, Corvus, and you have nowhere left to run!'

My hand gripped my sword. Grief gripped my heart.

At last I was reunited with my brother.

My betrayer.

Marcus had come.

Chapter 28

I had seen Marcus many times since deserting the legion. He had come to me in visions. We had talked on mountains, and in the fields of bone. But since knowing the love of Miran, and the life of a family, those nightmares had largely left me.

Please, let this be another nightmare.

'Corvus!' he called. 'Show yourself!'

It was the crammed wall that convinced me that this was no vision. The greatest friend of my youth always came alone to my nightmares. The one I had trusted above all others now had five legions at his back, and my own flanks were thick with rebel soldiers. This was no meeting in my mind. This was reality.

'Corvus!'

I *wanted* to reply. I *knew* I should reply, but my lips were nailed shut. It was only by force of will that I kept my feet. It was only with the greatest effort that I did not throw up onto the wall.

My oldest friend.

My greatest betrayer.

Here.

There had been a time when I loved him more than anyone else. It was us against the world, and Marcus made plans for us to conquer it together. I went along with them – I loved the friend who became my brother – but when I was old enough to recognise the beauty of Beatha, and the magnificence of her soul, her life became the focus of my own. I had less time for Marcus, no room for his dreams. He had smiled when he had left to join the legions, but that smile had been a feint. A distraction. With my beloved I planned to take ship to Rome, and when Marcus was on leave I confided in him the details of our plans.

And then…

Every muscle in my body wanted to shake as I looked at the man who had raped and murdered Beatha, and killed my father. A voice raged in my head to drop over the wall, and gut him. Another whispered mercifully…

'*He's your brother. He's sick. You must help him.*'

'Corvus!' His sword was in his hand now, and he called my name with prideful rage. He believed me weak. He believed me a heretic. I had turned my back on *his* first love. His only love.

Rome.

'Come out and fight me!'

I could not.

I would not.

I did not want Marcus's blood on my hands, even after all he had done. I was sick of war. Tired of death. I lived with a skull full of ghosts. Must I be forced to carry the weight of Marcus, too?

Yes! the soldier in me was saying. *Yes, Corvus, you must kill Marcus! Honour demands it! Decency demands it! To do anything but kill him is to be a coward! Draw your blade, you bastard! Draw your blade, and fight him!*

My hand trembled, but I felt it grasp the pommel of my sword.

If I drew it before this crowd, there would be no turning back. There would be a duel before the two armies, like I had wanted when I first ran to the rebels – but even if I killed Marcus I could never return to Miran, not truly, for what man can claim to be whole when he has ended the life of his brother?

'Corvus!'

It was my erstwhile comrades of the Eighth that saved me. Several of them came forwards, and persuaded Marcus against his will to rejoin the legion. He struggled against their guiding hands, throwing one final word against the battlements.

'*Traitor!*'

I said nothing. I simply watched my brother – my betrayer – until he was lost to the red ranks of Rome.

'Are you all right?' A quiet voice on my shoulder. Agron.

'I'm all right.' Lies.

'Who was that?'

'No one.'

'Would you like some wine?'

'I would like some wine.'

I took the skin that he offered me and made a great effort to drink with nonchalance, spitting some over the wall to show my disdain for the enemy, as a soldier should do. Whether I fooled anyone, I did not know. The truth was that I was shaken to my core. I did not dare even walk.

'I'll go with you,' Agron said. 'Back to Miran.'

I almost snorted at that – the idea of running to my wife sent a shiver of disgust through my body, but the truth was that there was nowhere I would rather be than in the presence of my love.

Still…

'I'll stay here,' I told Agron. 'I'll man the walls.'

Panic was contagious. Weakness was contagious. I would show neither, for the good of Arduba. For the good of Miran, Borna, Agron and the army.

'All is well,' I promised my friend. 'Relax, Agron. Go and get some water for that headache of yours. Eat. Go. I'm all right, I promise.'

There was sadness in my friend's eyes. He knew that I was a bag of lies, and yet…

And yet he was a man, and so was I. We were soldiers, and soldiers do not talk about what ails them. They fight, and they drink, and so I took a shallow pull from his wineskin, and prepared myself for the battle that would come. 'I'm fine, Agron,' I told him.

But in my heart I hated myself. I hated myself because I wanted to be merciful. I hated myself because I wanted to spare life, not take it.

'I'm *fine.*'

Grudgingly, Agron left my side, and as the legions began to dig the defences of their camps, the crowded walls began to thin.

Eventually I stood alone.

And I was not fine.

–

That day, after Marcus had come forward from the army, I stood a lonely vigil. I was attacked, again and again, but not by any army. It was memories that laid siege to me. Memories of a better time. Recollections of death. Echoes of pain.

Remembrance of the love I had for Beatha was quickly poisoned as I recalled her death. It was hard to picture her as she had been in life, when I knew how violently she had left it. So, too, my father. Though I had never felt truly close to the man, I had never expected that I would hate him, and yet I had mistakenly attacked him, when I had believed he was Beatha's murderer. That Marcus then murdered my father before I had a chance to make amends haunted me. He deserved better than leaving this world believing he was hated by his only child.

Where my happy memories of Beatha were laid to waste by the manner of her death, so my hatred of Marcus was tempered by the fondness of our childhood. We had been an army of two, and we were unstoppable. I wanted to picture him as the cold killer he had become, but it was impossible for me not to see the smiling young child he had been. The boy who was quick of wit, and even quicker to defend me. Marcus had taken beatings for me. We had lost fights, but never our courage. How had he become the monster that I now knew him to be? How?

Darkness claimed the walls before I left them. I had drained the wineskin given to me by Agron, but I was as sober as the stone of the battlements.

My body ached as I walked back to the house. I felt as though I'd fought a battle, though I had done nothing but stand, and think. I tried to hide my fatigue from my wife.

I failed.

'What happened?' Miran asked me when I came through the door.

'Nothing.'

'Corvus, speak to me.'

And so I did. I only had to say one word, but that word said everything.

'Marcus…'

She put her arms around me then, as though I were a child. I suppose in many ways that I was. It did not feel like it was Corvus the Dalmatian who would have to fight Marcus. That burden seemed to fall on Corvus the Youth. I could not separate our boyhoods from the man who had wrought such pain on my adult life.

'I don't want to kill him,' I confessed to Miran.

My eyes were wet. Hers were not. 'Why?' she could not understand. Marcus had killed my love. My father.

'Because I still love him,' I told her, and tears ran out over my cheeks. 'He's sick. He didn't want to do it, he can't have. *He's sick.*'

'He's not sick.' Miran squeezed my hand. 'He's a killer, Corvus, and he chooses to be one. You should shed no tears for him. He chose his path, and he has walked too far to come back.'

'I can help him,' I tried, 'it doesn't need to be this way.'

But it did, and we both knew it.

'Answer me honestly.' My wife looked into my eyes. 'If Borna and I were captured, would Marcus spare us?'

I could not speak. We both knew the answer.

'He would rape me.' My wife's words fell like stones. 'Perhaps he would rape Borna, too. He would torture us both, wouldn't he? He would kill us, but he would do it slowly.'

I wanted to be sick. Nothing that she said was a lie.

Miran saw that I understood, but she wanted me to kill my misplaced mercy. 'Say it, Corvus. Say it out loud.'

I couldn't.

'For me, and for Borna, say it out loud.'

I choked. The words felt like wet ash in my mouth. 'He would rape you.' I purged the thought. 'He would torture you both. He would kill you.'

Miran squeezed my hands. Her eyes were defiant. 'And will you let that happen?'

'I will not,' I promised.

'Then what will you do?'

'I will kill Marcus.'

'You will kill him.' Miran's eyes held mine. 'Not because you want to, and not for revenge, but to protect our lives. That does not make you an evil man, Corvus. It makes you a just one.'

Then why did I feel sick?

I asked her.

'Because you have grown,' she told me. 'Because you are no longer just a killer. You are a protector, a warrior, and I love you.'

She kissed me. Then, together, we grieved for those that we had lost, and the ones that had yet to fall.

To protect my loved ones, I would kill them all.

—

A week went by with no sign of Marcus, or a Roman assault. Still, knowing that both were close was a torture, and I avoided sleep and the dreams that waited there in ambush. Instead, I spent a lot of my time on the walls, watching the Roman camps, and committing myself to killing those whom I had once called brothers, comrades. The very eagle that I had carried was here, and though at the time I had felt little affinity for the totem that I had named Gallus – famed chicken of the Eighth – I had now come to realise the power and importance of such a device. The eagle wasn't just a symbol of current conquest, but of the sacrifices of the past. Brutus was an invalid, and Priscus, Octavius and Varo were dead, but so long as the eagle was carried, their service would live on. *That* was the power of the standard.

There was a time when I would have snorted at such sentiment. I had believed in what was in front of me, and little else. It was only now, after the death of comrades, and years to mourn them, that I had come to understand the power of standards. The men of the legions facing us fought not only for their own lives, but for the reputation of their legion. Their lineage was one of conquerors. One of heroes. Most men fear death, but all men fear shame. Fighting under the eyes of an eagle inspired a man to give his own life more readily, and encouraged him to greater acts of valour, because it was not only the acceptance of his comrades that he would receive – it was the pride of his ancestors in the legion. The men who had fought for Octavian. The old breed who had conquered under Caesar. All would know. All would feel pride. Generals could inspire with words, even coin, but the mere presence of an eagle *was* inspiration. *Was* reward. Without the eagles, there was no Rome.

Bato had gathered us in his headquarters to discuss stores, and duties, and plans. It was smaller than the building he'd possessed in Raetinum, but that didn't matter – after that battle, there were fewer men to fit in.

One of the nobles finished boring his fellow warriors with talk of grain supplies.

'Anyone else?' Bato asked his assembly.

I spoke first. 'We should launch a raid, lord.'

'A raid?' Bato laughed in surprise. 'Didn't I say that after a bit of marriage you'd be begging me to kill you!'

Others laughed at the joke. I did not. 'We should go after their eagles, lord.'

'No,' Bato said without hesitation.

No one else spoke. 'Lord, if we—'

'No.' Bato cut me off. 'What have the Romans been doing this past week, Corvus?'

'Nothing, lord,' I said at last.

'And what do you think they'll do if we go and raid their precious eagles?'

I said nothing. I didn't have to. They would attack.

'I know what you're thinking,' Bato told me. 'To take the eagles would be a great blow to their pride, and a boon to us, and were this any other situation I would agree with you, but this is no ordinary battlefield, Corvus. Our aim here is to hold.'

Bato looked around the room. 'My spies tell me that Rome's enemies are stirring,' he announced. 'We need only hold out until they attack the Empire, and Tiberius will be forced to make a favourable peace with us. We can still win this war!'

There was no cheer, but the sound of agreement ran through the room.

Bato turned back to me. 'When a bear is asleep, you do not shove a hot poker up its arse. If Tiberius is content to sit outside the walls, then we will not disturb him, understood?'

'Understood, lord.'

Bato dismissed his commanders. 'Not you, Corvus,' he said as I walked towards the door. 'You too, Agron.'

Some of the other rebels looked our way. I heard one utter something about pets, but I let the gossip go. For my family, I would not rise to bait and insults. My only purpose now was to see them alive through this siege. *That* was why I had proposed the raid. I wanted to strike first.

'They'll come, lord,' I told the rebel leader. 'Hot poker or not.'

'Maybe.' Bato shrugged. 'But it's been a week, and no assault. What does that tell you?'

I said nothing. Neither did Agron, and so Bato spoke for us.

'It says that Tiberius has given up on any other campaign this year. If he wanted to end this quickly, and still have time before winter to campaign on the Danube, then he would not have wasted a week sitting outside our walls. No, he has resigned himself to another winter in this region, and with that being so, he may be content to try and starve us out.'

Agron spoke up. 'What you said about the spies, and enemies preparing to strike Rome, is that true?'

'There are enemies of Rome preparing to strike,' Bato confirmed, but he would not say who, or where. 'It will shock the world,' he promised us, 'as we have done here. We need only hold out, and to that end, we will not provoke the Romans. If we attack them, pride will demand that they launch an assault.'

'Tiberius has five legions here,' I said. 'He doesn't need that many if all he plans on doing is starving us out, lord. This is a hard place to resupply, is it not?'

'I have men harassing their supply lines,' Bato confirmed, 'units that were not with us at Raetinum.'

'Then if Tiberius is making the effort to supply five legions, lord, it's because he plans on using them.'

'It could be part of a ruse,' Agron said. 'Five legions are a lot harder to look at than two.'

That was true.

'We just need to outlast them,' Bato said, echoing the words that King Pinnes had once spoken. Bato had been wary of such sentiment then, and now it seemed that I was the one to carry that torch.

'We can't outlast Rome,' I said sullenly, immediately regretting my tone. Fatalism helped no one. 'I'm sorry, lord, I've not been sleeping well.'

'Your friend that came to say hello?' Bato guessed. 'Who was he? A lover?'

'He's no one,' I said. 'No one that matters.'

Bato looked pleased. 'Not letting me see your true faces, eh? You're learning, at last.'

It struck me then why Bato had held me behind: he and Agron were grooming me for command.

The rebel leader saw my recognition of that, and shared a smile with Agron. 'He's the most resourceful idiot I've met,' he said to my older friend. 'And you don't lack courage,' Bato said to me. 'Now learn patience, Corvus. If you have debts to settle, life will present you with the opportunity to do so, no doubt, but for now enjoy the gift of time, and spend it wisely.'

I looked up at this mountain of a man, and wondered at the winding roads of life. My enemy had become my mentor. My brother had become my foe.

Agron placed a hand on my shoulder, and squeezed. I knew that look. My friend had an idea.

'Let's get shitfaced.'

—

After a night of drinking in the company of great men, I spent my time wisely, as Bato had suggested, and I was either on the walls to appraise the Roman positions, or a shadow to my wife.

'You hang around like a bad smell,' she told me fondly, glad to see that something of my spirit was restored. Though the ghost of Marcus lay beyond the walls, my love was within my reach, and my mind triumphed in its battles to be grateful for what I held, rather than to lament what I had once possessed.

I talked with my wife. I made love to my wife. I played games with Borna. I taught him what lessons I could remember from Cynbel.

I was winning my own war, but others were falling to despair. I heard about fights amongst the soldiers. Most with fists, some with blades. It seemed that the army was intent on being drunk, and so Bato ordered curfews, and made rules to curb men's inclination to excess. This worked to curb violence, at least against one another.

'A woman jumped from the cliffs,' Miran told me. The gossip had shocked her. My wife's eyes were wide. 'How could someone do that?'

'They lost hope,' I said, but we would not. So long as I had Miran, so long as I had Borna, not even five legions could kill the promise of our future.

'We'll be all right,' I said, and the gods smiled on me.

Later that day, a Roman herald came to the walls.

Tiberius was ready to talk.

Chapter 29

I watched from the walls with Bato as Agron walked his horse forwards, and through the half-open gate. The beast that he sat astride was a fat one, the best in the garrison; most of the others had already been slaughtered, their meat salted for winter – Bato knew that we would either win here or die, and there would be no room for cavalry in that battle. It would be infantry against infantry. Shield on shield. Sword on sword.

I was nervous, worried about Agron's safety. There was always a danger in parlay. I heard a whisper of worry in Bato's words too, and with good reason.

'The Romans sent an officer to speak with us in the first few days of the rebellion...' he said to me.

I had served in the legion at that time, and I could recall hearing the news of that brave man's death.

'Ziva?' I asked.

'Ziva,' Bato grunted. 'There was nothing he loved more than a Roman's screams.'

I looked at their army. A guard force was ever-present as a deterrent before their camps, but there was no fanfare or show of force for the horseman who moved slowly towards them.

'He's a clever bastard,' Bato said of Agron, and it took me a second to realise why – my friend was carefully walking his horse around traps that did not exist on the slope, and going perilously close to ones that did.

I smiled at my friend's deception. 'Their engineers will be watching.'

'Clever bastard,' Bato said again.

Agron had been chosen to be Bato's envoy for that reason, and others. Though my friend was fierce in battle, he had a level head and could be trusted to control his temper. Agron had been born a nobleman, and he lived a noble life. His bearing, his decorum, and his intelligence were all virtues that a Roman could appreciate. If they killed Agron, then they would do so grudgingly. Still, that would be no consolation for those of us that loved him.

'How long have you known him?' I asked, suddenly desperate to know more of the man who had saved my life.

'Since I was a boy,' Bato replied. 'You know Dalmatia, Corvus. It is not the most populous of places.'

'You were friends, as children?' It was hard to picture the huge man as anything other than an armoured god of war.

Bato shook his head. 'Not friends.' He chuckled. 'From my earliest memories I knew that I'd one day lead the tribes. I didn't want friends, Corvus. I wanted allies and followers.'

'And that was Agron?'

Bato pointed to a nose many times broken. 'Ask this.'

I was astounded, and fell into silence.

Bato smirked. 'You're wondering why I have the tribes, and not him?'

Yes. But I said nothing.

'Agron doesn't want to lead. Not an army, at least.'

'Why?'

'Because then he wouldn't be allowed to have friends.'

For a moment we said nothing.

'Why did he hit you?'

'Why does anyone hit anyone?' Bato laughed. 'A woman, of course.'

I was amazed that the violence had ended with punches, and said so.

Bato shrugged. 'We were children.'

'If only war were like that, and we could stop at broken noses.'

Bato tutted. 'And where is the joy in that? Look at that army of theirs, Corvus. *Five legions*. When we defeat them we will have won one of the most famous victories in all of history. We will be remembered. We will be as immortal as gods. Is there no part of you that has dreamed of such a fate?'

'No,' I answered honestly. 'I've never wanted immortality.'

He laughed at that. 'Horse shit. I've never seen a man cling to life as determinedly as you. And what of your friends?'

He had me there. 'I would like them to be remembered,' I admitted, 'for ever.'

'Well there you go. If you want their memory to live on, Corvus,' he pointed to the Roman camps, 'then help me beat that.'

'I will, lord.'

I fell silent then. A detachment of Roman horsemen was coming slowly from their camp.

'Do you think they'll kill him?' I asked, the words escaping me of their own volition.

I expected Bato to tut, or shrug. 'Yes,' he said instead. 'Yes, I do.'

His words were a blow to my stomach. Seeing Agron leave the camp, I had felt like my insides had been filled with cement. Now, my gut rumbled with fear. 'Then why have you let him go?'

There was an impertinence to my words, and for a moment Bato looked as though he was about to add another broken nose to his record. 'Because we're all dead without some magic, Corvus, and Agron is as close to a magician as I have.'

I saw it in his eyes, then. For all his bluster, for all his dreams, Bato knew that we could not hold out against five legions of Rome.

Who could?

I turned and looked out at our surroundings. The wall across the neck of land. The steep-sided drops of the cliffs. Bato had been deliberate in bringing the army here. He had given his soldiers no chance of retreat. They would find death, or glory.

'Did you send word ahead that the townspeople should flee?'

Bato nodded. 'Fewer mouths to feed.'

He knew the rebel army was likely coming here to die.

Bato sensed what was on my mind, and laid a thick hand on my shoulder. 'Relax, Corvus. If we win this battle your name will be known forever more. And if we lose?' He smiled. 'Well, then our days of worry will be over, won't they?'

Agron was almost at the horsemen, and for a moment I remembered another hero of the rebellion, and how he had ridden through steel, and fallen in fire.

Ziva was one man I could never have imagined becoming a comrade. Bato and Agron were others, and now that noble man was at the enemy's camp. His life was in the hands of Rome, and her taste for vengeance.

'He'll be all right,' I said out loud.

Moments later, Agron disappeared from sight.

–

There was no way to keep sight of Agron as he was lost to the Roman camp. I stood in silence with Bato on the walls, both of us motionless except to wipe sweat from our eyes. It was a hot day, and only growing hotter as the sun climbed higher.

'Let's go and have a drink in the shade,' Bato suggested as the sun reached its zenith.

I didn't want to leave the wall while Agron was with the Romans.

'It's been hours, Corvus. He's either dead or he's getting fat and drunk with their generals. Either way, I want a drink.'

Bato walked away, and after a moment of hesitation I followed – he was right. Agron would either be dead or taking food and wine with Tiberius.

The houses closest to the wall were occupied by that day's guard force. Men stood in deference to their leader, and had the sense to leave when Bato took a seat. Nothing about the man's manner said that he was in the mood for conversation.

'Have my servant bring wine,' he called after them, putting his feet up onto the table.

I expected that we would fall into silence then. Instead Bato picked at a dirty fingernail, and wondered aloud, 'Do you think it's as grand as they say it is?'

'What, lord?'

'What do you think? *Rome.*'

'There's not much that lives up to stories.' I shrugged. 'I doubt that Rome is any different.'

'Huh, you think so? You're like a bloody puppy with that wife of yours. Has she not lived up to the story?'

'War, then,' I amended my statement. 'The achievements of man.'

Bato heard the bitterness in my voice, and looked up from his nails. 'You hate Rome that much, eh?'

'Don't you?'

Bato went back to his nails, and for a moment I was reminded of the time I had fought against him. Our Centurion, Justus, had picked his nails to feign nonchalance before Bato's army attacked us. Was the rebel leader now doing the same?

'I don't hate Rome.' Bato surprised me. 'They build roads, they bring trade, and they have brought stability to borders. If they could have stopped at that, I would have been their willing ally.'

'But they ask too much,' I guessed.

'They ask too much,' Bato agreed. 'Rome wants subjects, not allies. Slaves, not soldiers. Look at the Thracians and Germans we have in our ranks. Men who deserted Rome. Rome would take their blood, and gladly, and they get it with just the dangled carrot of citizenship, after *twenty-five* years' service!'

A look of pride crossed Bato's face. 'Not me. When those men joined my army, they were treated the same as any Dalmatian. Look at yourself. Look at Ziva. Birth is important. Tribe too. But I would never ask a man to fight for me unless he was a part of mine.'

'You asked me,' I said, regretting the words immediately. Bato was being cordial enough, but I had seen how quickly he could lose his temper.

He laughed instead. 'How many lessons have I taught you, and yet you still think I'm a fool?' Bato's chuckle grew deeper. 'You think I didn't know that Agron was bluffing about protecting you?'

The words struck me. I coloured.

'I told you, Corvus, I've known Agron since I was a child! He would not have risked the lives of his tribe for a stranger, no matter how persuasive your wife. I saw a chance to give him a small victory, and bring you into my army, and I took it.'

I didn't know what to say.

Bato laughed some more. He was pleased with himself. 'Oh, poor Corvus. Don't look at me like that. I did you a favour. I saw how well you served Pinnes, but I knew you would never come to my side willingly. Unwittingly, Agron did all of the work for me.' The rebel laughed again. 'Oh, the look on your face is worth all the treasure in Rome.' He slapped the table in pleasure. 'And now you are a willing comrade, are you not?'

That was the truth.

'You've been a great fighter,' Bato said then. 'A killer. A warrior.' The rebel leader leaned across the table, and held my eyes. 'You should be a lot more than that, Corvus. You should be a leader of men. Open yourself up to it. I tell you these things so that when that day comes, you will have had insight into the mind of such a man.'

'You lead well,' I said honestly. Bato was not a man of tactical brilliance, but the fact that he had held together an army in the face of Roman might spoke volumes about his character. 'People would die for you.'

'People *have* died for me, tens of thousands of them, Corvus, and the burden of their loss is a part of leadership you can only learn from experience. I can't tell you how to remember their names, and forget their screams, except that I take solace in knowing that every man followed me willingly.'

I thought back to the deserters hanged by the road, but said nothing.

'What will you do when the war is over?' I said instead.

'Prepare for the next one.' Bato laughed.

'You think there will be more?'

'Of course. It's what men do best.'

'It doesn't have to be.'

'Of course it does. What else would we do?'

'Farm,' I suggested. 'Raise children.'

'You? Farm? You're as much of a born warrior as I've ever seen. You think you want peace, Corvus, but it would crush you more than any war.'

'Then why do we fight, if not for peace?'

'So that we can dictate the terms of the next war.' Bato laughed, and thumped the table. 'And to honour our ancestors, and set good examples for our children.'

'Where are your children, lord?' I asked with a little bitterness. Agron had spoken of them, but I had never set eyes on Bato's family, and I did not believe they were trapped in the Roman vice.

'They're somewhere safe,' Bato admitted. 'Far from here, and with a friend. One day my son will march by my side, but he was too young for this war.'

'You seem disappointed.'

'Of course I am. How many children can say that their father forced the Romans into negotiations?'

'Not many,' I admitted.

'Not many indeed.' Bato slapped the table again. 'Seeing the pride on his face will be worth every dark day.'

Dark days paid for in the blood of other people's children... 'You miss him,' I said as a way of remaining cordial.

'Of course I do. What father would not miss his son? And what father would not give his greatest effort to provide for him?' Bato asked rhetorically. 'Now what about you? What will you do after this, Corvus, and do not say farm, or I will send your head to Tiberius.'

'All right. I would like to see Britannia.'

'Britannia? Leave the Empire, eh?'

'If such a thing is possible.'

'It's possible, Corvus.' Bato's eyes were deadly serious. 'And we will prove that here.'

There was a knock on the door.

'Finally, the wine.'

But it was no servant who entered, and my heart leapt into my throat to see him.

'*Agron!*'

—

The wine followed soon after my friend. I embraced him for a long time before I let go.

'Put your erections away,' Bato snorted. 'I imagine we have a lot to talk about.'

I couldn't tear my eyes from Agron as we sat around the table, and Bato poured the wine. My friend was untouched and unharmed by the Romans. Indeed, he seemed to be happier than I had seen him in a long time, and little wonder – he had taken a deadly gamble, and survived.

'It was something,' he said, 'to sit and talk with the heir of the Empire.'

Bato looked up from the wine he was pouring. 'Oh, I'm sorry. No longer good enough for you am I, you bastard?'

'You'll do fine, lord.' Agron smiled.

'I bet Tiberius didn't pour your wine.'

'He did not, my friend.'

'Well, drink, you shit. It's good to see you alive. Our expert on desertion here reckoned you'd gone over to the other side, didn't you Corvus?'

'I said no such thing!'

Both Agron and Bato laughed at my embarrassed defence. 'So tell me about Tiberius,' Bato said.

'He's a dour man.' Agron shrugged. 'He looked fit, and able, but there was no humour about him.'

'Sounds a bit like you Corvus,' Bato snorted. 'How did he speak to you?'

'With manners,' Agron said. 'He was not as aloof as I expected him to be.'

'Did he feed you well?'

'Very well.'

Agron proceeded to list the dishes that he had taken with the Roman general. I paid little attention to the menu, wondering instead why Bato did not want to immediately hear the terms that Tiberius had surely proposed.

It was only when I saw the laughter and jokes pass between him and Agron that I realised why that was — the words that Agron spoke could be the nails that built a bridge to our future, or the ones that put us up on a Roman cross. Bato was delaying that moment, enjoying a smile while he could.

At last he breathed out. 'Come on then, Agron, let's hear them.'

Agron gave a single nod and a brave smile. 'The terms are these. Firstly that you, lord, must leave Dalmatia, never to return.'

Bato shook his head. 'Unacceptable,' he said, but Agron continued regardless.

'You must also break up the army, providing five thousand troops to serve immediately as auxiliaries in the Roman army, with regular levies after that.'

'Unacceptable,' Bato said again.

Agron could not hide the pain in his voice as he delivered the next of Tiberius's terms. 'Finally, all deserters from the Roman army will be handed over to face Roman justice.'

My throat closed.

I felt Bato's eyes. 'Well that one's not so bad,' he said, but not even he was convinced by his joke.

'The terms could be worse,' Agron tried.

Bato snorted at that. 'I'll not leave my home,' he said. 'And you would hand over the people who have bled beside us?'

'Of course not, but we can negotiate.'

'I dare say we can,' Bato said bitterly, 'but not on all points. Does he really expect that I will leave my home?'

'Tiberius said that you will be given an estate in Italia.'

'If I wanted an estate in Italia I would have taken one for myself,' Bato snarled, though the truth was that my old legion had put an end to that dream.

I should have been terrified by Tiberius's last term, though the truth was that I was certain Bato would not give up the Thracians and Germans in his ranks, and now he confirmed as much.

'I cannot accept these terms,' he said, and then the rebel sighed heavily, as though he had taken a spear in his chest. In a way he had suffered a mortal wound, and it was Agron's words that had delivered it.

For a long time he said nothing. The silence was heavy, and weighed on us all. At times Bato looked like he would explode, at others like he would drop his head into his hands.

Finally he stood.

'Go back to Tiberius,' he said. 'Tell him that I will leave Dalmatia.'

The words shocked us both.

'Lord…' Agron began, but Bato waved him to silence.

'I will leave Dalmatia, and I will break up my army, but I will only do so with the guarantee that the lives of *every* man in my army is spared, regardless of where they came from.'

Agron said nothing. I said nothing.

'Remind Tiberius that this entire army was in the service of Rome,' Bato added. 'We are *all* deserters.'

'Is that wise, lord?' Agron asked.

'It is fair,' Bato said with finality. 'And what goes for one of my men must go for all.'

I knew his words were not spoken simply for my own skin. There were hundreds of others who had thrown in their lot with the rebellion, and many from the very outset of the war.

Still, I took great pride in his statement.

I belonged.

'I will not abandon my men,' Bato declared, and his words were grim, and final. 'Go back to Tiberius, and tell him that.'

I sat in heavy silence with the rebel leader until Agron returned.

He was not smiling when he came through the door.

'Tiberius rejects your proposal, lord, and bids you make ready for battle.'

Chapter 30

The day was long by the time that Agron returned with Tiberius's rejection of Bato's terms, and a warning that we should prepare for battle. I did not expect that the Romans would come that evening. Fighting at night is a difficult proposition. Better for the legions to come in the morning, and against an enemy that would have known little sleep.

'We should double the guard,' Agron suggested to Bato, but Bato shook his head.

'If we do that our men will know that things went badly. I'll have a rumour spread that talks are to continue tomorrow.'

Bato didn't say it, but I reckoned I knew what was on his mind. His rebel force was an alliance of tribes. With Tiberius's words in their ears, would they hold together, or would some look to their own salvation?

I said nothing, and watched the big man grind his jaw as he thought on his position.

'I'll put my household troops on the walls,' Bato said at last. 'They're the best we've got, and it's about time they took a turn at guard duty. People will see it as that, nothing more.'

Agron nodded. 'Very well, lord.'

'Put a hundred of your best in these houses, Agron, close to the wall. They can sleep, but they must be ready.'

The rebel leader looked to me then. 'When do you think they'll attack?'

'Sometime in the morning. Their numbers are a weapon in themselves,' I told him. 'They'll want the men on the walls to see how many they're facing. They'll come after the sun has risen, lord.'

'Not tonight?'

'They'll send engineers up the approach to look for traps, lord, but they've probably been doing that every night, anyway.'

'Sneaky bastards,' Bato grunted, then leered. 'I expect you'll want to hump your wife, eh?'

'I would like to see my wife, lord, yes,' I answered more politely.

'Then go. Be back on the walls before dawn, and don't leave them until we've killed the bastards.'

I looked to Agron, and he gave me a fatherly nod. I was no longer needed, and so I said my good nights to both men, and walked through the door.

Bato had given me a great gift, and I would not waste a moment of it.

–

That night I ate one of the most pleasurable meals of my life. The meat was heavily salted, the bread stale, but the company was magnificent: Miran and Borna, my family; Ranko and Zoran, great friends of my youth.

'How's your head?' I asked Ranko.

'The wounds cleaned up nicely,' Zoran answered on behalf of his brother, as brothers do.

'No thanks to you, you cock. I wasn't sure if you were trying to bandage me or strangle me.'

'It was a bit of both,' Zoran admitted. 'I wanted to stop you whining. *Oh, the nasty Roman hurt me!*' he teased.

'He tried to cut my head off!'

'Do you see what I mean?' Zoran asked the rest of the table. 'Such a whining baby.'

Ranko dug a knuckle into his brother's ribs, and we laughed as Zoran let out a yelp. The brothers were exactly as I remembered them from Iadar, full of life, and full of horseplay.

'You got any sisters, Miran?' Ranko asked.

'I'm afraid not.'

'Cousins?'

'All ugly.'

'Perfect. I won't have to worry about them running away with a rich man.'

Miran smiled. 'Did you marry?' she asked them. 'Before you were conscripted?'

Zoran shook his head. 'We were keeping our options open.'

'Father wasn't happy, of course,' Ranko said to me, 'but he'd heard rumours through the port that there were going to be levies. We quite liked the sound of it, to be honest, and neither of us wanted to get married before we went away. What if we got rich on campaign? We wouldn't want to come back to Iadar, would we?'

'No, we would not,' Zoran backed up his brother. 'Fat and rich somewhere across the Danube was the plan, but then Bato told us we were fighting *against* the Romans, not for them, and here we are.'

'Not rich,' Ranko smiled. 'But the company's not bad.'

'It's not,' I agreed.

'I heard Lord Agron's men are the reserve at the wall tonight,' Zoran said to me. 'Should we be with them?'

I shook my head. 'You're to watch this house, and nowhere else.'

'And what if we want to fight on the walls when the Romans come?' Ranko asked me.

'Do you?'

'Fuck no, I'm not an idiot.' He laughed, and his brother joined in. 'Not that Rome gave us the choice, or Bato after them… We both thought war would be an adventure.' The tone of his voice spoke to how wrong he'd been. 'No, we are very grateful to be the guards of this home, Corvus, and consider ourselves blessed to be in the company of those who live here.'

I didn't know what to say. 'I…'

Another burst of laughter burst from the brothers' lips. 'We're talking about Miran and Borna, you dickhead!'

Now, even my wife and stepchild – *my child* – were laughing at my expense.

Good. Let them. The sound was music to my ears, and I enjoyed every second. I had not told them that the Romans would attack tomorrow, nor would I. Let them sleep. Let them dream. Let them hope.

When the food was finished I took hold of my wife's hand, and kissed it.

'Let's go for a walk,' she said.

—

The sun was setting as we left our home. Ranko and Zoran insisted on clearing away the dinner, and I was grateful to the two men for their tact. Now, alone with my family, I walked through the streets of Arduba, and to the cliffs.

'I always used to do this. As a child,' Miran added, with a smile for me. 'When I was about your age, Borna, I would come and watch the sunsets every night. You can never see enough sunsets.'

I said nothing. My wife's skin was golden in the falling light. She was treasure. She was mine.

We turned a corner. Miran gasped.

To the west the sun hung over the valley.

'It's beautiful…'

Something stirred in me then. Something that had been growing within me for months.

I reached into my tunic, and lifted my father's golden disc from around my neck. 'Borna,' I said. 'I want you to have this.'

'What is it?'

'It belonged to my father, Perigrinus. It was an award for his bravery in battle.'

The lad's almond eyes were large as I placed it over his head. He gripped the precious metal, and would not let go.

'You deserve it,' I said, 'because you have been brave, too, and I am proud of you, Borna.'

Miran was smiling. 'I love you,' she whispered to me.

I put my arm around her, and she rested her head against me. Borna came to my left side, and I placed a fatherly hand on his shoulder. So we stood, silent and beloved, until the red had run from the skies.

'That was beautiful,' my wife said.

I kissed her. It was a perfect moment.

And now I would ruin it.

'If anything bad ever happens,' I failed to say gently, 'and we are split, then this is the spot where we will meet.'

Miran said nothing.

'I will have Ranko and Zoran find ropes,' I told her. 'We will put them in the kitchen, and you are to bring them here if the town falls. Together, we can make it down the cliffs and to safety.'

I expected Miran to react badly. To chastise me for bringing war into dreams.

'We will be ready,' she said instead. 'Won't we, Borna?'

I still had a lot to learn about my wife.

—

When we returned to the house I placed my arms and armour on the table, and began the business of preparing for battle.

Ranko and Zoran had sensed that the time for jokes with me had passed, and instead bantered with each other on the dusk-filled street.

My only company was Borna, who watched wide-eyed as I worked the edge of my sword with a whetstone. I looked at the golden medal hanging about his neck, and could not have been more proud: from my father's hands, to my son's.

'Come,' I told the lad. 'Sit down.'

'Why are you cleaning it?' he asked, looking at my equipment. 'Was it dirty?'

I shook my head. In truth, the weapons and kit were already immaculate.

'A soldier is only as good as his equipment,' I told him. 'Above all else, you must keep your blade sharp.'

'I don't have a blade,' my son replied with some disappointment.

'You will,' I promised. 'And then we can clean them together.'

Borna's eyes shone, and a surge of pride welled up within me: I'd said the right thing.

'Can I tell you a secret?' I asked him.

His young eyes went a little wider. 'A secret?'

'A secret.' I laid the blade down on the table.

'What is it?'

'The secret is that I have never been happier.'

'Because you like cleaning?'

'No.' I laughed. 'You know that I love you very much, don't you?'

The boy nodded shyly.

'And you know that I love your mother?'

He nodded again.

He didn't understand what I was saying, not truly. What I was saying was as much for my own ears as his.

'If I weren't in the house, and something were to happen, you would protect her, wouldn't you?'

'I would,' he said proudly.

'I know you would.' I tousled his hair. 'But I'll always come for you both. You understand?'

'I understand.'

He did not, of course. He was a child, and I was an adult waffling in worry. I caught the rest of my words before they left me, and pushed them back down inside my chest.

'I'll look after you,' I promised him.

I saw movement from an interior door, then: Miran.

'How long have you been standing there?' I asked her.

She said nothing. Her eyes said everything.

I left my weapons on the table and followed my wife to bed.

—

After we had made love I fell asleep for a little time, but I woke hours before the dawn.

Miran was already awake.

'You haven't slept?' I asked her in the darkness.

'I have not.'

'Why?'

'Because of what's going to happen today, of course.'

I sat up in the bed. 'You know? Who told you?'

'You did. You're like a trapped wolf, my love. That can only mean one thing.'

'I'm sorry.' I sighed. 'I didn't want you to worry.'

Miran kissed me on the cheek. 'I know. And there's something else on your mind.'

How could she read me like one of Cynbel's scrolls?

'Bato,' I admitted. 'I think he likes me.' And that fact bothered me – was I being used? Was Bato's seeming friendship a ruse? Would he betray me to the Romans?

I told Miran as much, and she laughed. 'I don't know if Bato *likes* you, darling, but he certainly values you. So did King Pinnes. So did Prince Arminius. Is it so hard to believe that Bato has also recognised what you are capable of?'

'That's just it,' I admitted. 'Arminius, Pinnes, Bato. They trusted me. Why?'

Her hand took mine. 'Because you are the most trust-worthy of people, Corvus. Who else has left his home because he did not agree with the war his legion was fighting? You gave up everything for truth. *That* is why people trust you.' She kissed me again. 'And it is why I love you.'

I took my wife in my arms, and prayed that someone would knock on the door, and bring me the news that the war was over, or that the Romans had left. Instead, my eyes on the open window, I watched as the black of night gave way to charcoal greys of dawn.

I opened my mouth to speak.

Miran put her hand across it to kill my words.

'Don't say anything, my love. Do what you must, and come back to us.'

I left our bed, and dressed for war.

Chapter 31

There was a stink of fear on the hillside.

It was in the air. Indescribable, yet undeniable. Dawn had come and gone. At first there had been no sight of mass movement in the Roman camps, but then trumpets had blared, and the red snake had uncoiled itself from the valley floor, and turned its hungry fangs towards the nest of the rebellion.

The scales of the massive serpent now writhed as it slid from its camp, the shields of ten thousand killers.

'Just two legions?' Agron asked me.

Together we stood on the walls. More soldiers were pouring onto them, the bravest of Bato's army. Men who would not stand back while others did their fighting. There are many roles in war, but there is only one front line, and those who flock to it are a special breed of soldier.

I could see the pride in Agron that such men existed, and were his to command. Fear was not welcome in my friend's heart.

'How's your arm?' I asked him, worried about the wound he had taken at Raetinum.

'Good enough to hold a shield,' he promised me. 'I'll fight left-handed.'

'You did badly enough with your right.'

He laughed at that. 'Don't worry, Corvus. The Romans aren't getting onto the walls today.'

There was nothing but confidence in his voice. I wished I could echo it, but the sight of two legions forming up was a formidable one, and rivalled the majesty of the sunset I had witnessed from the clifftops.

'Beautiful, aren't they?' Agron said. 'I would have gladly fought beside these bastards if it had been as equals.'

But the Empire recognised no such thing. Rome was above all, and now she would carry vengeance to the walls of those who had defied her.

'The approach isn't wide enough for both legions,' I said, looking at the ground ahead of us. 'One of those legions is a reserve.'

Agron nodded. 'How wide will their front be?'

'A thousand men at most. We can do this,' I added, and I believed it. Though Tiberius commanded a staggering amount of elite infantry, thanks to the position of the town with its high cliffs and narrow peninsula, only a fraction of that force would be able to attack us at once.

I felt a hand on my shoulder, and turned.

It was Danek, the young, promising warrior of Agron's tribe.

'It will be an honour to fight with you again.' His hand was out.

I took it. 'The honour is mine.'

'Where would you like me, lord?' the young man asked of Agron.

'By my side, once again,' Agron smiled, and I could see Danek blink hard at the glory given to him. 'Make our tribe proud.'

'I will, lord.'

Danek was so choked on honour that he could barely speak. He took up a position at Agron's left side, while from his right I looked out over the forming Roman ranks.

Which legion would come?

I knew there was little chance of me coming face to face with Marcus, but what of the rest of the Eighth? My closest brothers were dead, but the others I had called friend, and comrade? Would I be called to end the lives of those men? For there was no doubt in my mind that I *would* kill them, and without hesitation. In the town behind me were Miran and Borna.

For them, my sword would sing.

A blare of trumpets rang mournfully through the valley.

'Here they come,' Agron said.

The Romans advanced.

–

Since the beginning of the rebellion, the people of Arduba had sown the approach to their town with death, and now the sweat of their labour was repaid with the blood of their enemy.

Entire files of the enemy ranks disappeared, swallowed by the ground and the bear traps that had been dug into the slope. Roman engineers had no doubt scouted the hillside, but the traps were camouflaged, over a year old, and looked no different to any other part of the approach to our walls.

Other Romans screamed and clutched at their feet as rusty nails drove into them. All across their advance, Roman soldiers staggered, and bled.

But still they came.

That did not stop the rebels from cheering. Every time the ground opened up to swallow their foe, the men on the walls roared in delight. Between each of these great cheers they threw insults towards the enemy. Many spat. Some even waved their cocks, or showed their arses.

'They're ready for this,' Agron said of his men. He was smiling, full of pride for their spirit. There was no doubt that they were eager to kill, some almost foaming at the mouth.

Beware the man who is fighting with his family at his back.

Beware the man who knows that this is the final stand of his cause.

'Roman bastards!' Danek was yelling. 'I will fuck all of your mothers!'

That was the sentiment of the thousands of men who stood shouting and waiting for the advancing legions. It was too loud to think, and so instead I watched.

The rippling lines of red shields.

The roaring threats of rebels.

The open gate.

'Agron!' I pointed – a huge gap in our defences. *How?*

'Don't worry!' My friend shouted to be heard. 'It's a gift for our Roman friends!'

I heard it, then. A rumble, followed by a cheer. I looked back out over the wall, and saw something tearing towards the Roman ranks.

A cart.

A cart full of stone.

My stomach turned as a memory struck me. A remembrance of the time when I had fought with the legions, and we had advanced upon a hill fort far smaller than this one. The rebels had released boulders down the hillside, and they had left bloody smears through our ranks. I had seen a cart used once before in an ambush, but these wagons were far bigger, and far more heavily laden. I almost felt a moment of sympathy for the men who would receive death in this manner, but the thought of Miran and Borna in danger drove all mercy from my mind, and so it was with a smile that I watched the first cart tear through the Roman ranks, tossing men in the air as though they were toys, and leaving others as nothing but puddles of guts.

I thought there had been cheering before.

I'd been wrong.

The sound around me became deafening as a second cart ripped a gaping wound in the Roman force.

Then a third.

Then a fourth.

The cheering of the rebels was a storm of hate and bloodlust.

'Kill them!' Danek was spitting. 'Kill them all!'

And then he ran.

They all ran.

'No!' Agron shouted, because he had seen where they were going, and why.

'Back!' he called desperately. 'All of you back!'

But there was no stopping them. The rebels had seen Roman death and smelled human weakness, and now they poured towards it, out of the open gates to drive into the wounds of the Roman ranks.

'*Back!*'

But they would not come back.

The bravest fighters had come to the walls to fight, and brave men seize opportunity. They saw such fortune now, and flocked behind men like Danek – young, well-meaning idiots who could not see that our victory lay in staying behind our walls.

'Come back!' Agron shouted.

They charged instead.

'Agron!' I gripped my friend. 'What should we do?'

It was the first time I'd ever seen worry in his eyes. 'Call up more men to the walls,' he told me. 'I'll go and get them back.'

'Not a chance. Your arm's still injured. You take care of the walls, I'll go get the others.'

'I'm going out!' Agron said, but I ran before he could convince me otherwise.

Bato was at the open gate.

'Back inside, you fools!' he roared. 'Back inside!'

The rush of men slowed, but did not stop.

'They're winning, lord!' rebels were shouting. 'Our men are pushing them back!'

I saw Bato's expression change in an instant. Anger fled. Hope came in its place.

'We're pushing them back!' more men were shouting, 'We're winning!' and I could see the rebel leader on the verge of a disastrous decision.

'You can't fight them on the slope, Bato!' I shouted quickly, risking his fists. 'They have four more legions behind this first one! *Four!*'

My words were few, but they were loud, they were true, and they did enough.

Four legions.

'Back!' Bato began to shout again. 'Get back inside, you bastards, or I'll lock you out!'

I had no doubt that he meant it. We could not afford to leave an open invitation in our defences for ever, nor could we afford to lose the thousands of men who had streamed out to take the fight to Rome.

'I'll go get them!' I shouted to Bato.

'They're lost, you fool! Help me close the gate!'

And perhaps I was a fool, but those men on the slopes were my comrades, and they were dying for the safety of their families, and mine.

I could not let them fight alone.

'I'll get them back inside!'

'Corvus!' Bato yelled. 'Corvus, come back!'

Instead I drew my blade, and charged the Roman ranks.

Chapter 32

Danek and the other rebels had seen the huge gashes torn into the Roman ranks by the loaded carts, and into these gaps they poured like burning oil. The Roman war machine relied on well-disciplined formations. Once those formations were broken, they could be exploited. The Roman soldiers didn't know which way to turn, who to cover with their shield, where to drive their blade, and so it was that in the moments following the furious charge, the men of Rome died in droves.

They were shocked to their core. They had climbed the hill expecting blood, and death, and the traps had unnerved many. The carts were a terrible sight to behold, but none had expected a mass of screaming rebels to pour forth from behind their walls, and throw themselves with glee at the men of the legion.

I could see that shock on the face of the first man that I killed. His skin was darker even than mine. I was not against the Eighth. This legion had been raised in the east of Rome's empire, and pulled back to the interior to put this rebellion down.

We put them down instead.

I came with such force that I knocked the man clean off his feet, shield on shield. He was helpless on the ground, and I stamped his skull into a bloody ruin, feeling the bone give way beneath my feet. A second soldier rushed me, but his feint did not fool me, and I took his second stroke easily on my shield, and drove my blade through his thigh. He screamed as he fell to the ground, and I left him there to bleed to death.

'Back to the walls! Back to the walls!' I shouted, though the truth was that I made no effort to leave the fight myself. These bastards had come to rape and enslave my family, and so I killed them with brutal dispassion. I was a machine of death, and the product of my labour was blood. I killed men with my fists. I killed men with my sword. I killed men with my shield.

A blade thrust towards my face. I ducked it, and drove my own up and through the man's jaw. It lifted the helmet from his head, blood cascading from his mouth, a gruesome waterfall.

'Back to the walls! Back to the walls!'

I saw true horror, then.

My eyes were drawn to a pit in the ground. Romans had fallen into it and lay impaled on sharpened stakes. Some were dead. Some were not. They gripped the shafts that protruded from their chests and stomachs. Their eyes were as wide as cattle with the stink of blood in their nostrils.

The terrible sight nearly cost me my own life. I was hit from my blindside, and stumbled backwards. I couldn't see my attacker. I could only hold my shield up, and defend myself against his furious blows, then the shoves of his own shield. Too late I realised what was on my enemy's mind.

He wasn't trying to kill me with his sword.

He was driving me into the pit.

I tried to dig my heels into the ground, but the earth was wet and slippery with blood.

I could not hold.

Momentum was his. The pit yawned like the mouth of some terrible beast, and I knew that one way or another it would consume me.

And so I made my choice.

I gave up my fight.

A mighty shove, and the Roman sent me backwards to my end.

I felt my feet slip over the edge, and then, with all my strength, I twisted and pulled my shield beneath me.

I heard it splinter.

I heard it crack.

I found myself lying atop a dying Roman, his bloody breath hot in my ear as he begged his gods for a mercy that would not come.

I was alive, but for how long? I expected a javelin in my back at any moment. There was no time to apologise as I braced myself against the skewered Roman, and looked up at the lip of the pit.

For the first time I saw the soldier who had pushed me into the hole. He was a big man.

'Javelin!' he was shouting. 'Someone bring me a javelin!'

I wouldn't give him that chance.

I reached down into the pit and felt my fingertips touch the top of the dying soldier's weapon.

The Roman at the pit's lip turned. He saw what I was doing. It was a race now. He could run, but could he live with the shame?

My fingers gripped the shaft of a javelin. I hoisted the weapon. The dying Roman – my perch – screamed as I braced myself against him.

Too late the soldier on the lip saw that the tables had turned.

He tried to run.

I found his back.

He went down with a yelp, but a battle of thousands still raged above me. I had to get out. Every second counted, and yet I could not bring myself to abandon that pit while the men within it screamed with a torment that no man should know. I did not see gratitude in their eyes as I slit their throats – they were too lost to pain – but I hoped that they would know peace.

There was no such hope for me. With the dead Roman beneath my feet I reached up and gripped the ankles of the soldier I had struck with the javelin. He was a heavy man, now my ladder, and I clung to the greaves of his shins as I hauled myself up out of the pit. It was hard work, and sense told me to abandon my armour, but I would not give up the precious metal of Agron's tribe, and Borna's late father.

Hand over hand I came, a terrible chthonic spawn. The ground gave birth to me, a child of nightmare, slick with blood, and wet with the gore.

And then I saw him.

The transverse crest. A centurion's helmet. *Marcus.* He cut and thrust his blade with precision, and my heart lurched as I saw the man that I would be too late to save.

Danek.

'Lift your shield!' I shouted. 'Danek, protect yourself!'

But the young man wanted glory, not safety. He could have weathered the storm, but there was no honour in that, and so he counter-attacked instead, and Marcus let him. It was boy against man, and the ending was written.

Danek overstepped, and Marcus drove his sword through his chest.

'No!'

Three heartbeats later I reached them. I hit Marcus from the back. We went to the ground, his blade lost and trapped in young Danek's ribs.

'*No!*'

Only then did I see the snarling face of the man I was about to kill.

A stranger. My mind had betrayed me, and the shock of that almost cost me my life. The Roman drew his dagger, and I felt the tip of it pierce the chainmail and the skin of my back.

I yelled out in anger. The craftsmanship of the metal had slowed the blade, and bought me seconds. I would not waste it, and brought my helmet down onto the Roman's face.

Again and again he brought the dagger down onto my back.

Again and again I brought my helmet down onto his face.

My chainmail held.

His skull did not.

I pushed myself backwards, and wiped blood from my eyes. All around me was chaos, shouting, screaming, crying, cheering. My battle sense was gone. If we were winning or losing, I could not tell, but I knew well what the blares of trumpets were signalling: relief in place; reinforcements.

Tiberius was rotating the legions.

'We have to go now!' I shouted to everyone and no one. 'We have to go now!'

I looked down at Danek. There was no hope. His eyes were open, glassy, and stared with the empty look of the dead.

'Back to the walls! Back to the walls!'

I grabbed some men. Shoved others. There was no denying the tide of battle now. The Romans were surging, and many of Bato's men had realised as much, and were running back up the hillside. I stared in open-mouthed horror as some were swallowed by the earth, victims of the traps as yet uncovered by the Romans.

'Back to the walls!' I yelled.

And then I ran with the others.

I ran for my life.

I expected at any moment to fall through the soil, and find myself impaled on sharpened stakes. I expected at any moment to gasp in agony as a Roman javelin found my back.

Instead, with scorching lungs and racking breaths, I made it to the gate.

There were hundreds of other men there, bloodied from battle, and heaving for air.

One of them saw the brilliance of my armour and mistook me for a nobleman.

'Lord!' he begged, and then I saw why there was true fear in his eyes. 'They've locked us out!'

Chapter 33

The gate was closed. I turned and looked back down the hill. Any resistance against the Romans was over, and now fresh ranks of the enemy marched slowly across the carpet of dead that we had left in our wake.

'Open the gates!' I shouted with the others. 'Open the gates!'

Men were banging at the wood. Calling for their leader.

He appeared on the walls, as impassive as the stone.

'Lord!' Bato's men called to him. 'Open the gates.'

He said nothing. The rebel seemed oblivious to the coming Romans, his eyes fixed instead on the nuisance that his men had caused.

And then he disappeared.

The trapped men wailed to see him go. 'Lord!' they cried. 'Lord, let us in!'

I looked at the wall, and quickly dismissed the thought that I could climb it. The stone was high, and smooth.

We needed ladders.

'We've got to attack the Romans!' I shouted at the men, thumping some to get their attention. 'Listen to me! We've got to attack the Romans!'

Many turned to face me, and listen. These were some of the bravest men in Bato's army, and brave men seized opportunity.

'What are you suggesting?' one of them called.

'The Romans will be bringing ladders for the walls!' I shouted as loud as I could for every man to hear against the din. 'We need to take them from them, and use them ourselves.'

Gods help me, but I swear that I saw a few of them smile.

'He's right,' several of them chorused. 'We've gotta get those fucking ladders, lads!'

'They'll open the gates!' Someone spoke up with optimism, but he was quickly silenced by a vicious-looking man. It was impossible to guess his age, only that he had been born with a sword in his hand.

'They're not opening the gates!' he snapped. 'And nor should they! Our families come first. Corvus,' he said to me, and I still felt some surprise that these rebels knew me by name. 'Will you lead us?'

Had there been any other choice I would have said no. I did not want command, but more than anything I wanted to see my family, and so I spoke the two words that every leader must know:

'Follow me!'

‒

Hundreds of rebel soldiers followed me back down the hillside. Hundreds of men stood by my side as I carried my sword against Rome.

There was no surprise in my heart when I saw the insignia on my enemy's shield. Fate is cruel, and it would demand that in order to save my life, and the lives of these rebels, I must draw the blood of those I had once called comrades.

'Form a wedge!' I shouted, my eyes fixed on the soldiers of the Eighth Legion.

The vicious-looking man was beside me. There was no time to learn his name. Often we know no more of our brothers of the battlefields than their deeds that day, but that is enough.

'Let's kill the bastards,' he told me. 'What are you looking for?' he asked then, seeing my eyes scanning along the ranks.

'Young ones,' I told him. The legion's newest soldiers. Not only did they have the least experience, but it was likely that their older comrades would have told them to bear the burden of carrying the cumbersome ladders. 'That's where we'll attack,' I said. And then I saw them, fresh-faced, and wide-eyed. Once I would have died for these lads, but this was not that time.

'Prepare to charge!' I shouted back through the ranks, and men echoed my words as they sought to buy courage with yells, and chants. The battlefield is a noisy place — a place of insults and cheers — and now we raised our own voices as we plunged downwards towards the Roman ranks.

I knew what was coming before I saw it, but still I felt my stomach turn to lead as the javelins arced through the sky and stung down like hornets' tails. How many men they struck I could only guess from the screams, but these were brave men, and they did not falter.

Ahead of us, the Roman ranks braced behind their shields to receive our charge. Our speed had denied them the chance for a second wave of javelins. And now, as my old friend Brutus had been fond of saying, shields would meet, and blades would eat.

'For Dalmatia!'

I had a second to see the terror in the young men's eyes before me, and then I was killing them.

—

We did not hit the Roman ranks like a wave. Rather, we drove into them as a nail is hammered through the palms of a man on the cross. We were an incision, but a brutal one. Sheer weight and force of will carried us through the legion's first rank, and into the second. Our front was not wide, but we had driven deep, and there, in the hands of the young soldiers, were the ladders.

Rarely have I taken pleasure in battle. Certainly there was none of it to be had in my slaughter of these youths. As I had expected, the youngest and the newest had been given the task of carrying the unwieldy burdens, and they were no match for the best killers in Bato's army.

I killed quickly. I killed cleanly.

The vicious man on my flank had no such mercy. 'Bleed, you bastards! Bleed!'

He did not drive and thrust his blade, instead swinging his sword in wild blows that opened the necks and faces of the young soldiers that he struck. It was gruesome work, but work that may have saved our lives.

'We've got ladders!' men were shouting. 'We've got ladders!'

'Back!' I ordered immediately. The longer we lingered, the worse our chances of escape. 'Back!' I shouted at the vicious man.

'You go!' he said. 'I'm killing Romans!'

His eyes told me that there would be no persuading him otherwise, nor the other few dozen men who refused to back out of the enemy ranks for a second time.

So be it. Their blood would pay for the lives of others.

'To the walls!' I shouted. 'Get the ladders up! Go!'

Men began to stream back up the hill. There was no order to it now. I saw that two groups of men carried ladders, and ran to join one, dropping my shield so that I could lift it with them. Suddenly a javelin arced over my head and took the life of a man in front of me, his body sending me stumbling to the ground.

'More men on the ladders!' I shouted as I regained my footing. 'Don't stop! Run! We can do this!'

And so we did. Others fell to the javelins that cut through the air, but we made it to the wall, and slammed the wood against the stone.

I looked to my right, and saw the other ladder erect, men already at its top, the rungs thick with more.

'Two at a time!' I shouted across to them as I saw the wood strain beneath their weight. 'Two at a time!'

But they would not listen.

They crammed the rungs.

The wood splintered.

Men crashed to the ground.

I looked at our ladder, the only one remaining. Our only means of escape.

The Romans were coming up the hill, an irrepressible tide of red.

I shoved the men back from the rungs.

'We go one at a time!' I called to all, raising my sword. 'Or we do not go at all!'

My meaning was clear. Men would wait their turn, or fight me.

No challenge came. 'Go!' I told the next man. 'Go!' I told the man after him, and one after another they went, though never so many as to overload the wood.

I looked down the hillside. There were thousands of Romans, and now fewer than a hundred of us on this side of the wall.

If they charged, we would die.

I looked up at the walls for Bato, or Agron. I wanted them to promise me that they would protect Miran, but I saw neither. Instead, a cheer echoed along the wall like rolling thunder.

There was only one thing that could mean.

I looked back down the hill, and saw a vision made for dreams.

Despite my pride I dropped to my knees, and gave thanks to all the gods.

The Romans were withdrawing.

Chapter 34

The approach to Arduba had once been a pleasant, green hillside. Now it was death's domain. A butcher's yard. Across the gradual slope that ran up to the walls, thousands of bodies lay beneath the beating sun. The grass was red. The smell was overpowering. Blood. Guts. Shit. Death.

And then there were the screams...

Men called for mothers and mercy in Latin, Thracian, German and Dalmatian. The language of misery was universal. The tongue of pain was spoken by all.

'How many did we lose?' I asked Agron. I stood with him on walls that had been thick with men. They had been the bravest and best of Bato's army, and without orders they had flooded from the town's open gate to plunge into the Roman ranks. They had wrought great carnage on their hated foe, and tore the first legion to shreds, but Tiberius had four more to funnel into the fight, and the Eighth Legion had steadied the line.

'More than two thousand,' Agron told me, and that news made me sick. I had feared as much – I could see the evidence of it before my eyes – but still, to hear it confirmed rocked me to my core. Two thousand gone. Two thousand of Bato's best.

'They were the equal of the legions,' my friend said, and the truth of that was on the slope. Thousands of Roman bodies littered the approach to our walls. The sons of rebellion had sold their lives dearly, but at best, we had deprived Tiberius of just one of his five legions.

'We still have men,' Agron said, but his tone suggested he knew the truth of the matter – many of the rebellion's born warriors were gone. By raiding the Roman ranks for their ladders I had saved perhaps two hundred, but the rest of the garrison was made up of soldiers who had been pressed to fight, rather than those who were born with steel in their hearts. Walls or not, they would not be able to stand against Rome's professionals. Every army needs its born killers. The men who will lead a charge. The men who will rally when all hope is lost. Without them, an army is nothing but dead men walking.

'You did well,' Agron told me then. There was fatherly pride in his eyes, and I felt lifted to see it. War had taken much from me, but it had been generous too. I loved this man as though he were my own family, and I had no doubt that he saw me as the son that life had denied him.

'Not well enough,' I replied, and that was the truth.

Agron shook his head, and looked down the slope at the bodies of the men who had charged from our walls. 'You're not responsible for their decisions, Corvus. I suppose it's fitting in a way.'

'I don't understand.'

'We broke from Rome because we wanted to die on our own terms, and not when Rome demanded our blood.' The noble warrior looked at the bodies of the fallen. 'If *that* is not dying on your own terms, then I do not know what is.'

'We needed them on the walls,' I said, and Agron did not disagree with me.

'We will make do.' He shrugged after a moment, but I sensed the hollowness of his words.

'It's over, isn't it,' I said as fact.

'It's never over,' my friend lied. 'We have the walls, and we have a lot of men to hold them.'

I held his eyes. I saw the pain in his. The pain, the pride, and the acceptance.

He could not lie to me.

He would not.

'Gods, but we gave them a good run, didn't we?'

There. The admission. The fact. The truth.

'We did.' I was too numb from battle for the weight of that to choke me. Covered in gore, and bone-tired, I felt as though I were watching a play, and my words belonged to an actor. Anyone but me.

Agron put his arm over my shoulder. I wondered which of us it was meant to steady.

There were tears in his eyes. Tears for the dead. Tears for the missing. Tears for those yet to fall. 'We gave them a good run,' he said again, the words drenched in the pride of a born warrior. 'Years of war against the mightiest empire, and yet here we stand. *Here we stand*, Corvus.'

His words were hard and faithful. Agron's mind knew that the odds were insurmountable, but his heart refused to give up belief.

'Here we stand,' I told him.

There was nothing else to say.

—

I watched from the walls in a near daze as a Roman officer rode towards our gate. The man was proud and dignified, and everything about his decorum said that he had been born to wealth and privilege.

'Lord Bato!' he called in a strong voice.

'Speak,' came from further along the battlements.

'We offer a truce to collect wounded and dead. Do you agree?'

There was a moment of silence. 'Until when?'

'Sundown,' the tribune replied. 'Once the sun is behind those mountains, the truce is lifted.'

'I agree,' Bato rumbled. 'See to your dead.'

Agron had listened in silence. 'Come with me,' he said then, and I followed behind him, and into Bato's presence.

It was a shock to see the rebel leader. He had always had the look of a grim man, but it had been tempered by humour, and the love of battle. There was no sight of joy, now. Bato was as daunting as a mountain peak surrounded by storm clouds.

'Agron,' he said, 'take some men and recover our wounded.'

'What of the dead, lord?' Agron replied, his use of 'lord' a clear indication that he recognised that Bato was on the edge of some precipice.

'Put them in the pits,' Bato replied without passion. 'The bastard Romans aren't stupid. They expect we will bring our dead in here, so the families can mourn, but they will not give us the chance to take them back out for burial, you mark my words. We'd either have to put them over the cliffs, or suffer them rotting here.'

I said nothing. It was something I could well imagine. There were no rules in war. No price too high, no tactic too low, for victory.

Agron was also silent. Bato registered the fact, and spat. 'Well? Speak what's on your mind, Agron.'

'Is this wise, lord?' the noble asked gently. 'As much as I want decency for our dead, they are already gone. There are thousands of bodies out there, ours and theirs. If we allow the Romans to clear the slopes, we give them a free approach to our walls.'

'I have considered that,' Bato nodded. 'And you are right to point it out to me, Agron, but let me ask you this. What mercy can we expect from the Romans, if we show none ourselves?'

Many times since meeting him I had been physically hit by Bato, but those quiet words struck me with more force than his fists or swords had ever done.

He knew it was over.

'Corvus,' he said to me then, 'when Agron has gathered the men, you will oversee the removal of the dead, understood?'

'Understood, lord.' I was too stunned to say more.

'And what of me?' Agron asked.

Bato looked out over the carpet of dead. It was a long moment before he spoke the words that placed Rome's blade against his neck.

'You will go to Tiberius, my friend, and you will tell him that in return for the lives of my followers, I offer him my full surrender, and my head.'

—

The stink of blood and guts was overpowering as the fallen cooked in the heat of a summer afternoon. I was as numb as the dead that I carried. One after another we dropped them into the pits atop of the skewered Roman soldiers. Enemies would lie together in the dirt.

I was too tired to care about the flies that crawled over dead eyes, innards, and my own face. I was too shaken to feel nauseous as one man's arm came away in my hands. In death there is often comedy – a release for the soldiers who fear their own ends – but this graveyard was silent. The end was too near for us all. We had been stunned into silence. There was no talk. There was not even reverence. There was simply the mechanical movement of the damned.

The first sign I saw that things had changed came when a group of Dalmatians laid down the bodies they were carrying, and began to spit. Their eyes had been empty, but suddenly they were hate filled, and I followed them down the slope.

The Romans were coming. They carried no shields. They wore no helmets. There were swords on their hips, but none in their hands.

'It's just their burial party,' I said to the men around me. 'Come on, let's get this done, and then we can go and have a drink.'

I had hoped the mention of alcohol would inspire the rebels back to action, but my hollow words were ignored, and instead, their eyes burned holes in the advancing Romans.

With a sigh, I lay down my own burden, and stood.

Earlier, thousands of Romans and Dalmatians had faced each other in ranks, and killed. Now, without shields or drawn weapons, hundreds of enemies faced each other across the tide mark of bodies.

No one spoke. No one cursed.

Everyone stared.

It was a look behind the curtain. A curiosity. For the first time in a war that had dragged on for years, and taken the lives of tens of thousands, the soldiers of each army stood and faced their foe with no immediate fear for their lives, and I wondered how many of them were thinking the same thing that I was: *they look just like me.*

Without shield, without snarls, without swords, without shouts, the faces of Dalmatian and Roman were more alike than they were different. A narrow sea was all that separated our homes. A narrow choice was all that had made them enemies, and not the allies they were meant to be.

'Come on,' a Roman said to his comrades. 'You shouldn't stare that long at someone unless you plan on fucking them. Let's get this done so we can have a drink.'

The Romans began to move. The Dalmatians fell from their own trance, and then:

'*I know you.*'

Words meant for me.

They were as flat and hard as sword iron, and they came from the mouth of a man from another life.

I recognised him at once. In the first days of the rebellion, fires had spread in our garrison town of Siscia. I had been a section commander then, and the guard commander had ordered me to take my men to fight the fires.

He had been grizzled and hard-looking then. War had not eased his features, nor his words.

'You're the fucking traitor.'

Curiosity fell away. Hate came in its place. Where there had been two groups of men recovering their dead, now there were two lines of enemies on a battlefield.

'That's him!' one of the Romans repeated. 'That's Corvus!'

I suppose that I should have felt pride that the rebels began to move closer to me, stood ready at my back. I had wanted their acceptance, and here it was, but I could not tear my eyes or thoughts from the grizzled centurion whose stare burned into me.

And then he said it.

'How's your father?'

My throat closed. My heart thumped. There was humour in his eyes. Humour and hate.

A question fell from my mouth like rocks. 'What's your name?'

Four had been given to me by Ziva.

Marcus.

Longus.

Lucius…

'My name is Clodius, *traitor*.'

He smiled.

I charged.

—

There was a second to register the delight on Clodius's face, and then he ran to meet me. Amidst the dead we struck each other like bulls, and men cheered at the two warriors who wrestled in the spilled blood of their armies.

I grasped for the bastard's face and eyes. He pulled at my hair, and tried to hammer my throat. I got a hand free and drove my elbow hard across his face. I felt something break beneath it, but the man had no room for pain.

'Traitor!' he kept saying. 'I'll kill you!'

I could taste other men's blood in my mouth as we struggled on the ground, desperate to get my arm around his thick neck so that I could choke the life from him, but Clodius was no less desperate to end my own life's road. He drove my face into the bloody mud, and his fists into my side.

'Traitor!'

Barely was I aware of the ring that had formed around us. Romans cheered their man. Dalmatians cheered for me.

'Kill the traitor!'

'Kill him, Corvus!'

'Do it for Rome!'

'Do it for Dalmatia!'

I tried to grip the bastard's skull but it was slick with blood and he slipped my grasp. He was a wide man but fast, and now he was on top of me, his angry fists crashing into my head. The world spun. I fought by instinct. I gripped the fucker's ears and wrenched his face down onto the bone of my shoulder. Once. Twice. Three times.

Then I heard a scream, and he reeled backwards.

I still held one of his ears in my hand.

Blood poured down Clodius's head. Hate filled his eyes.

He prepared to charge me again.

'I'll fucking kill you!' I screamed, but then I saw a horse, and a boot.

And then I saw nothing at all.

Chapter 35

I woke in my bed. For a blissful second I hoped that the battle and its aftermath had been nothing but a nightmare.

Then I felt the ache in my limbs.

Then I felt the ruin of my nose.

'Don't touch it,' Miran said from the other side of the room. 'I've reset it. Don't ruin my great work.'

She was washing something in a bowl of water. I sat up, and saw the red – my wife had been cleaning the blood from me.

'What happened?' I asked her.

'You don't remember?'

I shrugged. 'I was fighting.'

'That's as much as I know,' Miran said, and I saw the pain of a soldier's wife in her eyes. 'Bato's men brought you here. There's six of them outside the house.'

'What? Why?'

'You're not to leave.'

The words stunned me. 'I'm under arrest?'

'They didn't say that.'

Despite the pain all through my body I stood. 'If I can't leave the house then I'm under arrest.' I could only think of one reason why that would be so. 'I broke the truce...'

Miran's look told me that she did not understand, and so I told her about the truce that Bato had made for the recovery of the dead and wounded.

For a second she put her face into her hands. 'Did you kill anyone?' she asked then. 'During the truce?'

'No. But… I ripped his ear off.'

'Corvus!'

I should have been more careful with my words, but I was still drunk on battle, and fatigue. 'I'm sorry, my love.'

'Why did you do it?' Her anger began to boil. 'Why would you put people in danger by breaking a truce?'

I sat back on the bed, then. The weight of it all was too much.

'Corvus, why would you do such a thing? Why?' my wife shouted, then she recognised my manner, and came gently to my side. 'Corvus…' she took my hand in hers, 'who was it?'

I struggled as the reality of it settled like poison in my stomach. 'He was… he was one of the men that killed my father.'

For a moment Miran said nothing. 'And you ripped his ear off?' she asked quietly.

I nodded.

'Good,' she smiled. 'Then he will remember daily that he must fear you.'

Her words were savage. I looked at her. There was no mercy in my wife's eyes. 'There is righteous war, and there is righteous violence, Corvus. You did what you did for your father, and I am proud of you.'

'You are?'

'Of course.' She kissed my killer's hands. 'You don't enjoy death, my love, but you do not shy from it either. There is nothing noble about a man who refuses to fight when he has to. Nobility and honour come from having the ability to fight and win, but only using it against those who would prey on those weaker than themselves.'

I almost smiled. 'That sounds like something Cynbel would have said.'

'Caesar's weren't the only scrolls in that box, Corvus.'

My eyes went wild. My heart broke. That box, and all it contained, were ash within Raetinum's dead walls. 'I should have read them…'

'You had other things on your mind.' She kissed me. 'And I have a good memory, my love. When all this is done, we will sit down together, and rewrite them.'

I kissed her back. Hours ago I had been deep in battle. I had ended lives. I had fought for my own.

Here was the reason why.

'I'd like a cow,' I told her then.

'Excuse me?'

The words caught me by surprise as much as my wife. 'When this is over,' I said, bringing her into my daydreams. 'When this is over we can rewrite Cynbel's scrolls, and we can have a cow.'

Miran understood, then. Thumper had been fond of his cattle. Rome had taken them from him, but I could raise one in his memory.

'We'll call it Thumper,' I told her.

My wife pulled a face. 'You want to milk a cow while thinking of Thumper?'

I laughed at that. 'Well, not now that you've said it like that.'

Miran smiled.

I kissed her.

A moment of bliss after battle.

It could never last.

Someone hammered on the door.

I was summoned to Bato.

Chapter 36

Bato's men were banging on the door of the house. There were six of them, grim-looking men all. Miran said nothing, but I felt her worry all the same.

'If they'd come to kill me they'd have drawn their blades,' I tried to comfort her. The words did something to ease her mind, but not my own – this could be a trap to lead me quietly to slaughter.

I left willingly all the same. Swinging blades do not distinguish between those they have come to kill, and those who get in the way, and I would not place Miran and Borna in danger. If I was to answer for breaking the truce between Bato and Tiberius, then I would do so out of sight of my family.

I ruffled my son's hair. Kissed my wife.

'Look after them,' I told Ranko and Zoran.

'We're coming with you,' Zoran said. Both brothers had swords on their hips. Neither were smiling.

'Stay and watch my wife,' I said quietly, but Ranko shook his head.

'Who do you think told us to go with you?' he replied quietly. 'Sorry, Corvus, but she scares us more than you do.'

I looked at my wife. She knew what I was discussing with the brothers, and her firm eyes left no doubt that her order was to be followed.

'Stay inside the house,' I told her. 'Please.'

And then I closed the door on my family.

–

As we walked through Arduba's narrow streets, I expected to be attacked at any moment. Would I be seized and executed, or would I be killed in a gutter, out of sight?

No doubt Bato's six men sensed my mood, and that of the brothers. We were tense, and coiled.

'You have nothing to fear from us, sir,' one of the Dalmatians spoke up. 'I was over the wall with you today. Your quick thinking saved my life.'

'But is he safe from Bato?' Ranko spoke up.

For a moment the soldiers said nothing. 'Bato is Bato,' one of them said at last. 'No one is safe from him.'

The words hung ominously on my shoulders as we walked through Arduba's small square. Despite orders of a curfew, the inns were full of sullen men. There was no laughter. No banter. Men looked into their cups as though they hoped the wine would swallow them.

I felt the gathering inside Bato's headquarters before I saw it. Heard the low murmur of voices. The shifting of feet. When we entered I felt the heat come from dozens of bodies packed inside on a summer's night.

Bato's leaders.

None of them was smiling.

The men who had escorted me stopped inside the door. I walked on. When Ranko and Zoran tried to do the same, Bato's soldiers held up their arms to keep them by the entrance. I met the brothers' eyes, my look telling them not to argue. I had my own sword at my hip, though it would be of no use in a room full of warriors.

'Corvus,' Bato greeted me with all the warmth of winter. The man was seated, and I felt a pang of sympathy for the furniture that must bear his massive weight. Bato had never loomed so large, and I wondered if my punishment would be meted out by his brick-like hands.

I came to a stop out of sword's reach. 'Lord,' I said.

For a moment Bato said nothing. Instead he seemed to survey the lines of my face. The scars on my arms. The room was lit by candles that cast long shadows, and no doubt I looked a tired and sorry sight, my eyes cast into darkness, my limbs corded from war.

'You broke the truce,' Bato said.

I did not deny it.

'The Roman broke it too, lord,' someone spoke up, and I recognised the voice of the soldier who had brought me here.

Bato waved a hand to quiet him. 'It is the conduct of my own army that concerns me,' Bato told the room. 'Do you know why a man's word is important, Corvus?'

I felt as though I was supposed to stay silent, and so I did.

'The entire world rests on men's word. Alliances. Marriages. Money. Wealth. What is it all?' Bato asked the room, still sitting. Still quiet, and firm. 'Nothing but a man's *word*,' he told me. 'Nothing but *trust*. Without it, there can be nothing. Without trust, without our word, we would live like animals.'

Bato sighed. The war had come to his heart, and heavily. 'When I gave my word of truce to Tiberius, I spoke for every man in the army. When you broke that truce, you did not only break your word, but you broke *mine*.'

Now I smelled danger. Now I felt fear.

'I should have killed you,' Bato said as fact. 'Do you know it was me who kicked you to the ground?'

He waited for an answer. 'I did not, lord.'

'I would have been within my rights to kill you then,' he said. There was no sign of regret in his voice – no disappointment that he had not taken my life – and I dared to hope.

'Why did you do it?' he asked me simply. 'Why did you break my word?'

I saw no reason to lie, or hesitate. Not when the lives of my family might depend on it. Still, the words clung with barbs to my throat. Simply speaking them made me wish to spit blood.

'He was… he was one of the men who killed my father, lord.'

Bato's eyes widened. A murmur spread through the room.

The rebel leader's stare crept into my eyes. My mind. My spirit.

'Truthfully?'

'Yes, lord.'

He held my eyes.

He held them longer still.

And then he sighed again.

Bato was enjoying this about as much as I was. This was not a performance for his own pleasure, but the duty of a leader. The duty of a man holding his army together on a precipice.

'You broke my truce, Corvus. How can I trust your word that it is because he killed your father?'

I needed to gamble, and so I rolled the dice of honesty. 'Because I would do it again, lord. I'd break your truce and saw his head from his shoulders if I had the chance again.'

Silence fell like winter. Every man held his breath as they waited for the explosion from the man who had an anger like no other.

Instead, Bato stood quietly.

I looked up at his face. His scars. He was a mountain made flesh, and I expected to die in a landslide of fists.

Instead he placed a hand on my shoulder. 'You did the right thing,' he told me, and then he looked to the men in the room.

'Corvus attacked a Roman for the death of his father. Is that not what we have all done? When Tiberius ordered this army to be raised, he asked for the blood and sacrifice of men whose uncles and fathers had been lost to Roman blades, and sold into Roman slavery. *I* did not honour Rome's peace, not when they had taken so much from my family. *Corvus* did not honour their peace, not when they had taken so much from him, and so I find no blame in his action today.'

He hit my shoulder, then. 'Only that you should have killed the bastard before I got there.'

Laughter ripped through the room. There was relief in it, and with pride I realised that these men of Dalmatia had not wanted to see me punished.

I was one of them.

I was home.

And Bato was not finished with me.

'We lost a lot of good men today,' he said with sadness. 'They died with great valiance, but they died nonetheless. Closing the gates was the hardest decision of my life,' Bato addressed the room, 'and I have made dozens of decisions that meant the death of great men. Today was no different.

If any man harbours ill will towards me then let him speak, but hear this first.

'I did not bar the gates for my safety, or for yours. I did it for our families. I did it for the women, children and elderly of our tribes. If the gates were open, we might never have been able to shut them, and we would be having this conversation in afterlife, or worse, Roman chains. If any man thinks differently, speak now, and freely.'

No one spoke.

No one moved.

'Speak!' Bato ordered. 'If you have something to say, now is the time to say it! You are free men here. Act like it!'

'They died with honour,' a nobleman said at last. 'That is all there is to be said, lord.'

Others quickly muttered their agreement.

Bato looked into my dark eyes. 'You were on the other side of the wall, Corvus. What do you think?'

'You made the right decision, lord,' I said truthfully. 'The men were dead the moment they left the gate.'

'Not all of them,' he said with pride. 'Thanks to your quick thinking to steal the Romans' ladders, Corvus, hundreds of my men are still in the fight.'

Bato looked down on me with fondness. What was he thinking? That I had once stood against him, and now by his side? That he had once wanted my death – called for my death – but now he had spared it, and willingly?

'Corvus,' Rome's enemy spoke with pride, 'you have done the rebellion great service. You stole treasure from the legions. It was your idea to trap them at Raetinum. And today, your quick thinking and courage saved the lives of hundreds of my men.'

I waited.

He spoke.

'You have fought with nobility for Dalmatia, and so it is only right that I make you a *noble* of Dalmatia. Corvus, I grant you lands of my own, and title in my tribe. Do you accept?'

My mouth opened to speak, but no words came out. On the edge of defeat, with Bato's lands under the heel of Rome, it was a symbolic gesture and nothing more, and yet…

'I am honoured, lord.'

And I was. Honoured beyond words. My only regret was that Miran, Borna and Agron were not present to hear Bato's words.

'You're a good lad,' Bato said fondly. 'I am proud to be your leader. All of you!' he shouted to the room. 'Leading you in this war has been the greatest honour of my life! You might be an ugly bunch of bastards, but you fight like bears, and I would die for every single one of you!'

And he would. I knew it. Agron had taken that offer to Tiberius, and perhaps I alone recognised the melancholy behind Bato's words. Would this be the last time he addressed his leaders? Would this be the last time he stood in the company of those who had followed him into rebellion and war?

'We slaughtered the bastards today!' Bato told them, and men cheered. None needed telling that the Romans had exacted a heavy price of their own. There was no man in this room who had not lost friends and comrades.

'Let us speak of courageous fellows!' Bato shouted then. 'Let us honour their battlefield deeds! Who will speak for the dead?'

'I will speak,' I heard myself say, and Bato thumped me on the shoulder.

'Lord Corvus will speak!' he announced to a cheer. 'And of whom will you speak, Lord Corvus?'

Lord Corvus? The words were so alien to me that I almost stammered over my words.

'I will speak of Danek, lord.'

'He fell?'

'He did, lord, but he took many of the enemy with him.'

Bato's eyes told me to go on.

'He was a young lad, but courageous. We used to train together. He always wanted to get better. He wanted to prove himself against Rome.'

'And he did that,' Bato spoke proudly. 'How did he die?'

'He was cut down by a centurion, lord.'

'Did you kill him?'

'I did!'

'Then Danek is avenged!' And men cheered. 'We will remember Danek!' Bato shouted. 'We will remember them all! Who will speak next?' our leader asked us, and a man answered from the door.

'Lord,' he said.

I recognised the voice at once.

Agron.

And he came with grave news.

—

The room was as silent as a tomb as we waited for my friend to speak. Agron's face, usually so alive with friendship and mischief, was now as flat and as grey as slate.

'Speak,' Bato commanded him.

There was no tremble in the rebel leader's voice. No hint of fear. He had offered his own life to save the lives of his followers, and now he would hear his fate.

'Tiberius rejects your offer, lord.' Agron spoke of that secret term. 'However, he is willing to accept the surrender of the Dalmatian rebels, and spare their lives, on one condition.'

Dalmatian rebels...

My stomach churned. I knew what Tiberius's term would be before I heard it.

'There will be no mercy for the Thracian, German and...' he looked at me, '...Roman deserters.'

For a long moment, no one said anything.

'We should accept his terms, lord.' A young commander spoke up at last, and all eyes snapped to him. 'The tribes must come first,' he said stiffly. 'It is unfortunate, but the needs of the many must come before those of the few.'

Bato snorted. 'If you believe that then give your lands and wealth to your followers. It is the needs of the rebellion I am concerned with, and that includes all who fight for her.'

'But, lord,' the young commander tried again, 'there will be no rebellion if we do not accept Tiberius's terms. There will be no army, and there will be no Dalmatia... We cannot win this fight, lord.'

There. Out in the open.

I expected Bato to yell. I expected him to rage.

Instead he stood silent, and fuming. Bato was no fool. He knew that he'd lost most of his best fighters today. He knew that the Romans had more than four legions at his door, and that they could call for more.

'Agron,' he said. 'Do you believe that Tiberius would stand by his word?'

'I do, lord.'

'Why?'

'He wants to expand Rome's borders, lord. He says there is a place for Dalmatians by his side as he does so.'

'By his side.' Bato snorted. 'He means on the end of his whip.'

'Perhaps, lord,' Agron allowed. 'But when Tiberius says that we have proved our worth as fighters, I am inclined to believe him. We have proved our courage time and time again. Why wouldn't he want to make use of us?'

Bato's face flushed with anger that he fought to control. 'And you would be at peace with such an arrangement, Agron?'

At this, Agron shook his head. 'No, lord. I would rather die than sweat for Rome.'

Muttered agreement passed around the room. 'When we rebelled,' Agron went on, 'we did so knowing that it could cost us our lives, but if we were to die then we would choose to do so as free men, and on the soil of our homeland. You gave us the option to die for Rome, or for our tribes. We chose Dalmatia, lord, and I choose it still.'

Men shouted their agreement, clapped their hands, and stamped their feet.

Bato said nothing. The scar on his head throbbed in the candlelight.

'I hate Rome with all of my being,' he said at last, 'and my natural desire is to tell Tiberius to eat his own shit, but Arduba is not only a home to warriors. We have families here. Children. For their sake we will discuss this proposal, and let no man say that Bato the Daesitiate was a tyrant.'

Men mumbled agreement. I crossed to the door, where Ranko and Zoran waited. 'Wait for me at the house,' I told them, but both brothers shook their heads.

'We'll stay close,' Ranko said. They had heard every word, and were more worried about the safety of this deserter than his family.

'Miran will kill us if we abandon you,' Zoran insisted.

I could see that arguing with them would be futile, and pointed to the closest inn. 'All right. Wait for me there and I'll see you when this is done.'

Both brothers offered me their hands. In the decades that I had known them, I had never seen either look so grim.

I said a silent goodbye to both, then walked back into the room.

Bato's men shut the heavy doors behind me.

'Now,' our leader spoke, 'let us decide this like men.'

—

I stood beside my friend Agron. I was still sore from battle, and my head was beginning to throb after Bato's boot earlier in the day, but my life was in the balance, and that had a way of drawing a man's attention.

'We could surrender, lord.' A nobleman was speaking. 'And then resume the rebellion from a more favourable position.'

Bato snorted at that. 'You think Tiberius will let us keep this army intact, or anything close to it? We'll be broken up and scattered to the winds, spread out through Roman garrisons. They won't make the same mistake they made when they allowed us to gather as one at the marshalling grounds.'

Such debate had been going on for an hour. Bato encouraged his men to voice their opinions, but there was no doubt that he'd made his mind up that there would be no surrender – not when it meant the lives of his Thracian, German and Roman deserters.

So far as I knew, I was the only example of the latter. The only one to choose rebellion over legion. There were hundreds of Thracians and Germans in the rebel ranks, but still, they made up a fraction of Bato's army.

I knew the fact that Bato had made me a lord and title holder meant nothing in the face of Roman justice. To them I would only ever be Corvus the Traitor, and nothing would protect me save – perhaps – an amnesty for all soldiers. I did not doubt there would still be blades in the night, and I must be forever on my guard, but at least a painful public execution would not be my fate, should Tiberius grant clemency to all in Arduba.

I almost laughed at myself for the sudden impulse to tell Agron of my new title. I knew he'd be proud, and I wanted him to be proud, but there was no room here for anything but the discussion of surrender.

'We fought this war for honour, and so that we wouldn't have to live and die on Rome's terms.' An older nobleman was now speaking. 'What does it say of our tribes if we hand over those who came to fight by our side? Our gods would spit on us. Our ancestors would be ashamed, and rightly so.'

To this there was a chorus of agreement. The Dalmatian people were proud, and martial. The talk of surrender stuck in their throats, and the thought of dishonour threatened to choke them.

'Have we fought as single tribes?' the older man went on, 'or have we fought as one army? What does it matter if a man was born in Dalmatia, or Thrace? He has fought and bled with us. He has sacrificed. Look at Lord Corvus,' the man pointed at me, 'who in this room can say that they have done more for the rebellion than him?'

I felt Agron's eyes. '*Lord?*' he asked silently.

There was no time to answer. The old man was still speaking. 'How dare we even think about giving up men of this army who have done more than we. I am a Dalmatian, not Roman, and I will not act as some pampered senator who sends others to die in his name! I am Dalmatian, and I will die as a Dalmatian!'

I did not expect the cheer, I did not expect the applause, but the old man's words had struck the hearts of these men, and any thought of surrender died with his words. These were honourable men, and they would die as honourable men.

'Then it is settled!' Bato decided. 'There must be clemency for all, or clemency for none.'

'I will take word to Tiberius at dawn, lord,' Agron told him, but Bato shook his head.

'No, my friend. This time I will go myself.'

Unease swept the room – an unwillingness for their leader to place his head in a trap – but before Agron could speak, a fist hammered against the door.

'Open it!' Bato ordered at once, and as the doors parted, I heard the sound of chaos pour into the room.

'Lord!' Bato's bloodied guard shouted. 'There's fighting in the square!'

Any man who was sitting moved straight to his feet. Dozens of hands went to the pommels of swords.

I saw Bato master his face, and his tone. 'The Romans have breached the walls?'

'No, lord,' the guard gasped. 'It's our men. Lord, they're fighting with the Thracians and Germans.

'*Lord, they're killing each other.*'

Chapter 37

It struck me in an instant. As the bloodied guard gave his breathless report, I knew what madness had taken hold in Arduba, and why.

It was not because Tiberius wanted revenge against Thracians and Germans that he had refused to offer them the clemency he would grant to the Dalmatians. It was because he knew that there would be enough rebels wanting to save their own skins that they would be willing to give up the lives of their comrades. Inside this room had been a couple of dozen of the rebellion's wiser leaders, but many of the men in the town had no such interest in honour. Their guiding star was survival, and so they fell on the men who stood in the way of it.

There was no time to wonder how the word of Tiberius's offer had reached them. That it had was danger enough.

'Lord!' I shouted to Bato. 'This was Tiberius's plan! He knew this would happen! We must get men onto the walls, now! The Romans will be ready to attack!'

Bato grasped what I was saying, and why. 'That bastard,' he growled. 'Follow me!' he told his men. 'Let's break this up! Break up the fight, and get everybody to the walls! Prepare for a Roman attack!'

'This is my fault,' Agron said quietly. Somehow Bato caught the words, and took a second to place his hand on Agron's shoulder.

'You did your duty, my friend,' he assured him. 'It was your responsibility to carry the words. It is not your responsibility what men do with them.'

Agron nodded, but I could see that he was shaken. 'Agron.' I squeezed his arm. 'Agron, snap out of it. Tiberius is going to launch an assault, I know it. We've got to get this fight broken up, and get men on the walls.'

Something of the old Agron floated to the surface, and he did not hesitate in following Bato out of the open doors. I was behind him, and though the big man partly obscured my vision, there was no hiding what had become of the town square.

'Gods…'

Men were pouring into the square from the side streets, and they did not come to break up the fight, but to join it. Hundreds of rebels were punching, kicking and stabbing those who they had once called comrades. Knots of tall Germans and stern-faced Thracians fought off their attackers with fists, knives, even stools. They did not fight alone, however, and many Dalmatians stood bruised and bleeding by their side.

Ranko and Zoran were among them.

I gripped one rebel by the shoulder, and threw him backwards out of my way. I dropped another with a punch. Then another. I did not touch my blade in its scabbard.

'Stop!' Bato was roaring. 'All of you, stop!'

But they would not stop. The flock was wild and panicked, and when I reached my old friends from Iadar, I understood why.

'I'm sorry!' Ranko sobbed, and his eyes were thick with tears. 'Corvus, we're sorry!'

I didn't understand. 'Sorry for what?'

They said nothing. The guilt in their eyes said everything.

No.

'*You told them what Tiberius had said?*'

'We didn't know they'd react this way!' Zoran pleaded. 'We were just making conversation!'

I felt sick. *They* had been the ones to bring word of Tiberius's offer into the ranks, and *I* had sent them.

'Get to the house,' I told them. 'Bar the door, and do not leave Miran's side, do you understand me?'

They understood. I saw the terror in their eyes. 'Go!' I shouted, and the brothers fled.

I turned and looked around me. There was no end to the chaos in the square. As some men were calmed, more arrived from the side streets, their blood up as they sought to save their own lives, and the lives of their families.

'Stop!' Bato was shouting. 'Calm yourselves!'

But stools and fists and words were flying.

'They're not Dalmatian!'

'I won't die for them!'

'We've had enough!'

I saw Agron push one man back, then another. His face was stern and hard, a patron at the end of his tether with his wards. 'You are soldiers, not children!' he chided them. 'Act as men!'

And they heeded his words. They heeded them too well.

I saw it happen. Every second. There was nothing I could do but watch, and shout, and feel my heart shatter in two.

'Act as men!'

And there is nothing men do better than kill.

A blade was drawn. I saw it plunge towards my friend's back. I saw his mouth twist, and his eyes bulge. I saw the shock of it rip his spirit free from his body, and not because he feared the end, or was afraid of death, but because he knew that the rebellion was over, and that he had died at the hands of those that he loved.

'Agron!'

I drew my own blade. I was not trying to keep the peace, now. I had lost one father, and now a second fell, his strings cut. I had not been able to avenge the death in Iadar, but here Agron's killers stood. They had taken my friend's life. I took theirs, and any who dared defend them. Four bodies lay beside him before I dropped to Agron's side.

I clutched his hand. I looked into his eyes.

I wanted to tell him that he was my friend. I wanted to tell him that, in the short time I had known him, he had been a father to me.

There was blood on his lips. Barely a glimmer of life in his eyes.

'*Lord Corvus...*' he managed to smile.

And then he died.

I felt a hand on my shoulder. It was a light touch, and I turned.

It was the old nobleman. The man had spoken in defence of honour. 'Go to your family,' he told me. 'Get out while you can.'

I would not let go of Agron's hand. I would not let go of his dream.

'We need to stand on the walls. We can still win.'

But the old man shook his head.

'It's too late for that lad,' he said calmly, and I saw that he too had accepted death.

Why?

And then he told me.

'They're already in the town.'

Chapter 38

I had assumed that the people flooding into the town square had done so because they had been roused by the fight, and wanted to join it.

I was wrong.

'Romans!' they were calling now. 'Romans! They've come up the cliffs! Romans!'

My stomach lurched. My hands shook.

I looked to the old nobleman. 'They knew we'd fight each other...' I said almost to myself. 'They knew our sentries would be looking in, not out...'

The old man nodded. 'You're a survivor, lad. Get your family. Get out.'

I hesitated.

'I will wait with Agron.' The man smiled. 'He was a good friend in life. There is no man I would rather die beside.'

I accepted that with a nod. I did not want to leave my friend, but I needed to be with my family. 'Where is Bato?' I asked. There was no sign of the massive man, and the old man had no answer for me.

'Go,' he said instead. '*Survive.*'

–

The first challenge to that survival came in escaping the town's square. As wolves circle sheep, so the threat of the Romans coming had driven people into the town's centre.

There was no getting through the torrent of panic.

If I couldn't go out I must go up, but there were no ladders to retrieve this time. If I was to get to the top of the buildings I would have to do it with my body alone – a body that had already been pushed to its limits in battle this same day.

Still, the scent of death does wonders for a man's energy, and the thought of his loved ones suffering can drive him even harder still. It would not be grace that carried me above the crowd but sheer determination, and so I chose a barred window as my target, then attacked the nearest wall with the will of a man who knows that to fail is to die.

I gripped the bars and hauled myself up, looking for my next foothold. There was an awning to my left, but I did not trust it to hold my weight. Above me was an open window, but despite straining and stretching I was still a foot short of the sill.

I chanced to look into the square, and the press of humanity that could no longer fit within it. Screams rose as people were trampled. Agron and the old nobleman had been lost to sight, and I prayed that his end had been painless.

But it was a quick prayer. I needed to be on the rooftops, and so I used one hand to brace against the bars, and used the other to undo my belts, and the sword that they held. Then, with my sheathed blade acting as a weight on the end of my leather 'rope', I threw the sword up towards the open window, swearing as the blade and scabbard came back down with a painful strike across my head.

I tossed it again. It fell and struck me again. And again. And again.

But on the fifth throw the sword disappeared through the window, and I pulled gently, my heart surging as I felt the blade catch against the corners of the window frame.

I had to keep the 'rope' tight and began climbing immediately, my feet braced against the wall, my sweating hands gripping the leather for all that I was worth. Hand over hand I went, and after a yard I realised that should the hook fail me, or I lose my grip, then the fall would be enough to guarantee that I would never see my family again.

And so I would not fall.

I would not fail.

Hand over hand.

Inch by inch.

And then I was at the sill.

I pulled myself through the window with little grace, but a heart full of gratitude.

I was still alive.

Below me, people were screaming.

As I tied my belts back around my armour, I looked out of the window, and heard the unmistakable shout of Roman orders.

I ran out of the room and saw a ladder to the rooftop. I cleared it in the blink of an eye. Somewhere below me, I heard the door shatter open as others broke through to seek refuge within. No matter, I was ahead of them, and I gave silent thanks to the architects of Arduba. The town was small, the buildings tightly packed, and by starlight I ran across the rooftops, leaping from one to the other.

At times I peered down into the streets, and once I saw one that was not clotted with frightened faces, I prised a trapdoor open with my hand, and dropped into the building below.

The cowering family screamed to see me. I ran down their staircase, threw open their door, and found myself in an empty street.

It was familiar to me. I had walked every street of Arduba for just this reason. I knew how long it would take me to get to my family. I knew we had a chance, and yet...

And yet, far down the slope, beyond the walls, I heard the blare of Roman trumpets, and the cheer of a legion as it began its ascent to Arduba. I would have forced them from my mind had I not looked down the street, and saw something that turned my stomach in horror.

The town gate was open.

Chapter 39

I had two heartbeats to decide if I should run to my family, or the open gate.

One.

Two.

I chose the gate.

Arduba was Miran's home. It was Borna's home, and the people within its walls were Miran's people. *My* people. There was a chance for us if we could keep the Roman force on the other side of the wall. We could still surrender. They had come up the cliffs. They would have to be lightly armed, without armour. We could beat them, but we could not drive a legion back through an open gate.

And so I ran. My chest heaved against my mail, and I pulled my sword from its sheath.

Hope flared in me as I saw the silhouette of men on the walls, but why were they standing by an open gate? How could they expect to defend the town with such a hole in its defences?

And then I saw the reason.

Large, and looming, and ominous in the starlight.

'Lord Bato!' I panted. 'Lord, we must close the gates!'

Instead Bato stood still and silent as he watched the Romans advance. In the night, they came upwards as a dark and creeping tide that glittered like waves beneath the moon. They were a sea of death that would drown us all.

'Where is Agron?' Bato asked me with the calm of a man at peace with his decisions.

'Agron's dead! Lord, we need to close the gates!'

Bato's chin dropped to hear the news of his old friend, but then he shook his head. 'I've sent men to the Romans to offer unconditional surrender, Corvus. I must save who I can.'

His sad words struck me with such force that my own were knocked from me, and I choked on the enormity of what the man was saying.

'Lord…'

'I'm sorry, Corvus.' He turned to face me then. The man who defied an empire. 'It's over,' Bato told me. 'Go. Go to your family.'

I wanted to scream. I wanted to be sick.

Instead, I ran.

—

I was halfway up one of the town's hills when I spoke a silent apology to Miran's fallen husband, and dumped his armour in the street. I had no time to waste on retying my belts and so I left them and my sword's scabbard on the ground. I needed speed.

I ran on, cursing aloud as I tripped over something in the darkness of the street.

A woman.

A child.

Leaking, and butchered.

My eyes adjusted to the gloom and I recognised the boy's face, or what was left of it. I had seen him playing with Borna, but I had no time to mourn their death – only to worry about such an end for my own family. There were clashes in the streets. The screams of the raped are different to those of the wounded, and both rang out across the rebellion's last stand. Knots of rebels were rushing into buildings to seek refuge. Some carried the injured. Some carried loot. All carried fear.

I ran on, and turned into the street that had given another home to my family. I could smell smoke on the breeze, and gave praise to gods when I saw no sign of flame here. Though we had not prepared these houses to burn as we had done at Raetinum, a blaze could spread quickly in any circumstance, let alone when there were no organised groups to fight it. Perhaps the Romans were lighting buildings to spread fear. Perhaps rebels were doing it to sow confusion to escape. Perhaps a torch had simply been dropped in the wrong place. Whatever the reason, the hiss, crackle and pop of flame were notes added to Arduba's lament.

As I hammered my fist against the door of my home I thought of Raetinum. We had barely escaped with our lives, even with the courage of Ziva and his men, and a plan to trap the Romans – how would we ever do it here?

'Open up! It's Corvus!'

The cliffs. They were our only chance.

'Open up!'

The door swung open on its hinges. For a second relief flooded through me, but then:

'Where's Miran?' I asked the brothers. 'Where's Borna?'

'They weren't here when we got back,' Ranko finally managed to speak. In his eyes I was no longer Corvus, his childhood friend. I was the man who had saved an eagle.

The man who had raided the Roman camp. The man who had saved Bato's finest soldiers. I was a warrior, he was not, and he feared me.

And so he should. 'I told you to come back here!' I raged at him. 'I told you to come back!'

I wanted to hit them both, but the thought of my wife and Borna in danger cut through the rage. 'We need to search every inch of this house.'

'We've already checked—'

'We will check again!'

And so it went, casting furniture aside as though it weighed no more than Cynbel's scrolls. 'Miran! Borna!'

And then it hit me:

The ropes.

Panic had knocked sense from me. My mind had been soiled by terror, and I had not thought to look in the first and most obvious place.

I ran back into the kitchen.

The ropes were gone.

'They've gone to the cliffs!' I shouted at the brothers. 'Let's go!'

I burst through the doorway, and outside. The brothers were on my shoulder, but my eyes were drawn to four men standing in the deep shadow of the street. Their features were lost to me, but I saw enough to be certain of two things.

Three were Romans.

They held a prisoner, a rebel soldier. He pointed towards me, and the home in which I lived, and then a gladius was drawn across his neck, and the man fell down in the gutter.

And then I heard it.

'Corvus!'

My heart stopped.

My tongue dried.

'*Corvus!*'

There was no doubting the man behind the words. No escaping the recognition of my greatest betrayer.

Behind him a building was catching light in the growing fires, the shadow of Marcus falling across me like an executioner's sword.

His face was flame-lit, and ugly. Where was the handsome boy that I had known? Where was the dreamer? Where was the young man who had promised to be my greatest friend?

Dead.

The one who walked in his place was a killer's corpse. His tongue moved, but his eyes were dead and poisoned.

'Don't run,' Marcus said, his words as lifeless as the ash that began falling around us. 'We end this. *Here.*'

He did not recognise or acknowledge the two brothers that stood beside me. If Marcus had ever possessed the heart of a caring man, then he had left it in the mountains.

I chanced to look at the two soldiers behind him. They were both tall men, with smiles like scythes.

'You are Longus,' I knew in my heart, 'and Lucius.'

By silence they admitted their part in the murder of my father.

Rage stirred in me. Pride boiled. The call of revenge was loud in my ear.

'Where's Clodius?' I sneered. 'Scared of the dark?'

'Clodius is busy.' One of the tall men spoke. 'We can deal with traitors well enough on our own.'

They were coming forwards by inches, their blades hanging by their sides. The climb up the cliffs meant that they had come without shields and armour, but I had dropped my own too, and so was at no advantage.

'Let's get them,' Ranko hissed next to me. 'Corvus, we can do this.'

I was angry at the brothers, and said nothing. It was their loose lips that had allowed Tiberius's poisoned offer of truce to spread in the first place.

The boys knew as much. They knew that they had cost the lives of hundreds, maybe thousands, and so I should not have been surprised when a look passed between them, and the brothers charged.

'For Iadar!'

The Romans held the slope. The Romans had the training. Both were to their advantage, but pride was not. They had never expected that these amateurs of war would take the fight to them, much as Rome had never believed that the tribes would rise up as one. The surprise bought the brothers seconds, and the clash of steel rang out as Longus and Lucius parried their furious blows.

Marcus had not moved.

His dead eyes had not left me.

'I should have killed you on that hill,' he said at last. 'I saw the weakness in you then, but never did I believe that you would become a traitor.'

I looked past him. The two Romans had quickly turned the tables, and were now pressing the brothers back down the slope. It was professionals against amateurs. Killers against conscripts.

I wanted to rush to their side, but Marcus tracked my every move with the ease of a coiled snake.

'Marcus…' I tried. 'That is Ranko. That is Zoran. Call off your men. Marcus! You know them! Call them off!'

But he would not, and Zoran yelped in pain as the first cut found his flesh.

'If you want to settle things with me, then settle them!' I shouted. 'Leave them out of it!'

But Marcus said nothing.

And so I moved.

His blade struck out at me with such speed that it grazed my throat before I could jump back. I felt the skin break, and a trickle of hot blood run down my front.

'Marcus! Stop this madness!'

He was sick, but I could heal him.

I could save them all.

'Marcus, we don't need to do this!'

I tried to move past him again. His blade shot out. I jumped back.

And then Ranko screamed.

'No!'

Ranko fell to his knees. The blow was a bad one.

'*No!*'

I moved. Marcus struck. I parried.

'Ranko, get up!'

But he could not.

'Are you watching, Corvus?' One of the Romans smiled to me before he loomed over Ranko, and spoke to my childhood friend. 'Tell his father that Longus sent you.'

He swung the blade. Ranko's head fell from his shoulders.

'*No!*'

I screamed, I attacked. Marcus blocked it all with ease.

'Ranko!' Zoran moaned, and his brother's death was the making of his own. Shock held him in an iron grip. He could not – would not – parry Lucius's blows.

I saw the tip of the blade appear out of Zoran's back. It had driven through his heart, and through my own. My friend was dead before he hit the floor.

Life had no such mercy for me.

'I'll kill you all!' I raged. 'I'll kill you all!' Somewhere in this town was my wife, and child, but they could not be safe when such men as these drew breath. I wanted peace, I yearned for peace, but life had given me war instead. Life had given me killers, and decreed that moments of bliss must be bought with buckets of blood.

So be it.

I attacked.

Longus. Lucius. *Marcus.*

For my family, I would kill them all.

I waded towards my enemies. Never had my sword been faster. Never had my strokes been stronger. Never had I so freely given myself over to the desire to kill.

And all for naught.

I was good. Marcus was great. So too were his accomplices, and within the first ten strokes of my blade I realised that I was going to die, and that I would never see Miran again.

I would not let it end like this.

The fury of my attack had led these men to believe that I had committed myself to revenge, or death in the pursuit of it, and so they were surprised when I broke off from my blows, and leapt backwards out of sword's reach. My crazed attack had bought me inches, and in battle, inches are enough.

I ran.

'Coward!' Marcus spat and gave chase, but he wouldn't catch me.

None of them would.

'He's going to jump!' Lucius shouted, and he was right.

I leapt over the street's low wall, vanishing into the blackness beneath me, and towards the only hope that I had left.

Chapter 40

I did not land with the grace of the cat that had once shown me these rooftops, and I felt my weaker shoulder scream in pain as I hit the house, but Arduba's tiered streets had saved me, if only for a moment. I had taken my own life into my hands, jumping into the flame-lit night. Would the Romans do the same?

Yes.

A black shape fell down through the dark. I moaned with pain as I tested my shoulder. I moaned again as the flames lit the face of the brother I had loved above all others.

'Marcus, please, this has to end!'

He drew his sword from the scabbard. I fumbled beside me for my own blade, but I had lost it in the fall.

Marcus tutted, and sneered. With his free hand he drew his long legionary dagger and tossed it to me. 'Here. I won't have men say that I did not beat you fairly.'

'You don't need to beat me at all, you fool! What's wrong with you, Marcus? What sickness has taken you?'

He prowled the rooftop. He was a predator, and it had been a long hunt that had led him to his prey. I could see his hatred of me. Feel it.

'Marcus,' I tried, 'you're *sick*. Just say it! Tell me that you didn't want to do these things! Tell me that other people made you do it! Do you hear voices? Do the gods talk to you? Do they make you commit such acts? Marcus, brother, talk to me! We can heal you!'

I could not desert him. I could not have been so wrong about him. This was not *Marcus* that carried his blade.

It was his sickness.

'Marcus, just tell me that it wasn't you that did those things! Tell me what you want to get better! You are still my brother, and I can forgive you! Just tell me! Tell me that you're sick! Tell me what you want to get better!'

Marcus stopped pacing:

'You could… forgive me?'

For a second there was something of my brother in his tone, and hope flared within me. If we could beat his sickness, Marcus could help me save my family, he could…

'You could forgive… *me*,' he said again, but this time there was nothing but contempt in his voice.

'Forgive *me*?' His anger rose. 'FORGIVE ME? It is *you* who should be begging for *my* forgiveness, *brother*. *You* are the one who abandoned me for a slave girl! *You* are the one who let me join the legions alone! *You* are the one who failed the test of war! *You* are the one who turned traitor and deserted your brothers! *You* are the one who stole from them! *You* are the one who has killed Romans instead of answering for your own crimes! Forgive *me*? I am the only true friend you ever had! The only one who did what was necessary so that you could be a great man, the hero you were born to be! A hero of Rome!'

His words burned hotter than the buildings around us. Flame was spreading.

'That's not true!' I beseeched him, desperate to bring him back to my side. To save him. 'Marcus, that's not true.

Something has corrupted you. Something has changed you. Let me help you change it back!'

He laughed.

Cold, and hard and bitter.

'I am who I always was, Corvus,' he said at last. 'I was born to kill for Rome, and that is what I will do.'

He raised his blade.

'Defend yourself.'

I dropped my dagger instead. 'I will not.'

I could save him.

The flames were growing higher. I could see the scars on my brother's face. See the bottomless wells of hate in his eyes.

'All you have ever done is abandon the people that love you,' his words rasped like a frozen blade drawn free from its sheath. 'You are a plague, Corvus, and now I will end you. *Pick up that dagger.*'

'I will not.'

I would not.

I could save him.

'Very well,' he leered. 'Beatha and your father weren't armed either.'

The bastard knew me, and the hateful words sent me down to snatch up the blade. It was in my hand with a heartbeat to spare, and I parried his first thrust to the side, and stepped back across the rooftop. Around us, the town of Arduba screamed in its death throes.

'I heard about your new family,' Marcus laughed darkly. 'We have spies in the rebel camp, and I paid them well for news of you.'

He lunged. His sword came hungrily for my neck. I pulled my shoulder back, and twisted from its bite.

'When we find them, I've given orders that they are not to be harmed. I want them unspoiled when I rape them, Corvus. I don't want anyone else to have the pleasure of skinning your family alive.'

'Bastard!' I came at him with the dagger. Marcus sneered as he easily knocked it aside.

'I wonder if Miran will beg as loudly as Beatha did.'

He braced for my next attack.

But it did not come.

I saw the look of disappointment on his face. Registered his surprise.

And then he saw why.

I was standing on my sword. Fortune had guided me to the blade that I had lost in my fall, and too late Marcus attacked to stop me recovering the gladius. I stepped, I span, and I came up with it in one hand, and a dagger in the other.

'*Say it again*,' I told him. '*Tell me what you did.*'

Marcus spat. 'I cut your woman's throat.' He smiled. 'And then I fucked her into the afterlife.'

Mercy died.

I attacked.

Marcus had trained in swordsmanship for years. He was a natural at it, always had been, but my blades took on a mind of their own. Revenge controlled them, and the sword song was loud across the burning rooftops.

All around us the flames were climbing. People were screaming. The rebellion had made its last stand in this town, and now it was dying on its knees.

'You are a plague!' Marcus shouted at me again. 'You are a traitor!'

I had no words for him, only steel. I parried his counter-attack with my sword, and counter-attacked with the dagger. I had no space to think, only to kill, and the animal in me cried triumphant when I felt the blade strike meat, and Marcus stumbled backwards.

Beatha's murderer stumbled backwards.

My father's killer sank to one knee.

A surge of vengeful pride rushed through me as I stepped forwards to strike a final blow.

And then Marcus looked up...

His eyes were enough to stop me.

His face did everything to send me backwards.

Marcus's jaw had been severed on one side. It flapped below his face. His tongue rasped. His breath moaned.

Tears filled my eyes.

I had done this to my brother.

'Marcus...' I tried, but as I stepped forwards his blade came up towards me. He would not surrender. 'Marcus, this is madness!'

The madness of brothers.

The madness of war.

The madness of Rome.

Marcus staggered to his feet. The wound was an affront to my senses. A brutal insult. The wet meat shone in the firelight. The handsome boy was a vision of hell.

'Marcus... brother... drop your sword.'

He lunged with it instead.

I stepped, parried, and ended it.

I ended it all.

Chapter 41

I knelt in my brother's blood. My blade was in his chest, but I dared not pull it out and let more rush from his body.

Marcus couldn't speak. His face was a ruin, but his eyes could talk, and they told me that I was hated still. They told me that I should be the one dying on this rooftop. *The traitor.*

His wasn't the only life ending in Arduba. Fires were spreading through the town. Screams clawed at the sky. The rebellion's last stand was at a bloody end.

'You took so much from me,' I told him. 'But not everything.'

I had Miran.

I had Borna.

I had that thing that we are told will make us feel righteous:

Revenge.

But it didn't look as I had expected it would. It didn't feel as I had hoped.

Marcus's tongue flapped as he tried to speak. He was struggling to breathe. I was struggling not to cry.

'It didn't have to be this way…'

His acts.

The war.

Man makes misery for himself. We had a home. We had friends. We had love.

Why couldn't that be enough?

Marcus choked.

Marcus shuddered.

Marcus took his last gasp, and then he stilled.

I didn't shout.

I didn't scream.

I left his body on the rooftop, and ran to the only family I had left.

—

There were Romans raping. Romans looting. Romans killing rebels. Rebels killing Romans. Arduba was awash with blood and fire, a boiling cauldron of hate and pain. At points I saw centurions try and rally their men. Try and hold them back from the orgy of sin. 'Back to the walls!' they shouted. 'Tiberius has accepted their surrender! Back to the walls!' But the legions' blood was up. They wanted to plunder. They wanted to loot. It had been a long war – a hard war – and now they would take their spoils.

I ran across rooftops until a burning building forced me into the streets. I had stripped Marcus of his belts, and carried his blades on my hip, and my own in my hand. I was wild-eyed and blood splattered, and those few soldiers who noticed me turned their backs and went for easier sport. My feet were my only ally now, and I ran for all I was worth until I reached the clifftops, and my heart near burst with joy.

Miran.

Borna.

I could see them, standing where we had watched a sunset. Standing where we had shared the greatest moment as a family. As loved ones.

'Miran!' I yelled. 'Miran!'

She did not turn at first. I ran closer. 'Miran!'

Movement stopped me. A movement that seemed so unnatural that it drew my eye and halted my feet.

'No...' I gasped as, by the light of the fires, I saw a half dozen women and their children run to the cliff's edge, and throw themselves over the edge of it. I had seen death in all its forms, but this suicide gripped my heart in an iron vice. I wanted to call to them, to help them...

But I had my own family to save.

'Miran!' I stepped closer, and finally she heard me, finally she turned.

I was looking at a stranger.

'Stay back, Corvus.'

She was holding a blade, but it was her words that cut me.

'Back?'

She held the knife out towards me in a trembling hand. Behind me, Arduba burned. Women screamed. All was chaos.

'Miran...' I pleaded, 'it's me, my love. It's Corvus.'

'I know who you are!' she snapped. 'Look behind you! It's over!'

I dropped my sword, held up my hands, and inched towards my family. 'It's not over, my love. We can escape. Did you bring the ropes?'

My eyes were on the dagger in her hand – why was she so threatened?

'The ropes are gone,' Miran near-whimpered. 'Someone took them.'

I swallowed at the news. The cliffs were steep, and deadly. But still...

'We can do this, Miran. We can escape.'

But she shook her head, and the blade shook in her hand.

'It's over, Corvus...'

'It's not over!' I stepped forwards. 'We can save our family! We can save our child!'

Instead, Miran put the dagger to his neck. 'He is *my* child. I am his mother. *I am his mother!*'

I looked at Borna's flame-lit eyes. They were listless. Fear had emptied his mind.

'Put down the blade,' I tried. 'My darling, why would you fear me?'

'Because you want to save us!' she yelled. 'And there is no saving us, Corvus! I won't be raped! I won't have Borna sold as a slave! I won't do it!'

'Put down the knife! We can escape!'

Tears streamed from my wife's cheeks. Tears streamed from my own.

'We can escape the Romans...' Miran said softly, 'but we cannot escape death...'

Hope died.

Fear came.

'Miran... Miran, don't...'

She pulled Borna tight. I looked into his terrified eyes. He was holding something. Clutching it to his chest.

My father's medal.

My body shook with racks of fear. 'Miran, please...' I whimpered.

'I love you,' she said.

I ran.

She jumped.

I reached for my family, and snatched air instead.

'*Miran!*'

They fell to darkness.
They fell to death.
There was nothing else for me to do, but join them.

Epilogue

In the bend of a river, on top of its cliffs, a man's limits were reached, torn and broken.

His heart beat, his lungs drew breath, but what made the man who he was, and who he wished to be, was no more.

There was only pain. There was only suffering. The man needed nothing now but oblivion, and so he followed his family into death, and ran and leapt from the clifftops.

He fell through the air.

He begged for death's embrace.

But death would not take him.

The river swallowed him instead. He opened his mouth. Water filled his throat and lungs. The end was near.

And then the river spat him out.

On the bank he lay gasping. There was a shape beside him. A boy's body. There was something around his neck. A golden disc that caught the light of a burning town.

The man did not think about taking it. He was beyond reasonable thought. The man's heart and mind had been hollowed. He was numb, a vessel for nothing but darkness.

He belonged nowhere.

He was alone everywhere.

Only one thought remained. A memory that rose through the fog of his misery. Climbed out of the sea of his pain.

The man pushed himself to his feet, and ran for the white cliffs.

Author's Note

Well, here we are. We've driven poor Corvus to breaking point, and sent him on the journey that will lead to him being discovered in a German forest – a *Blood Forest*, to be exact, which was my first publication as an author. (The book has since been retitled as *Ambush*.)

Corvus, and the majority of characters in *Rebel*, are works of fiction. Tiberius and Germanicus are historical figures, as is Bato the Desitiate, who led the Dalmatian rebels. Little is known of his life, and so I've used artistic licence with his character, though I think it's in keeping with what we do know of his nature: Bato was a rebellious warrior, who dragged Rome through one of her most painful wars.

It was not a war that saw great pitched battles in open fields. Rather, the Romans were forced to dig the rebels out of their mountain bastions and walled towns. There were many such assaults, and so I have combined some with others for the sake of the story. The events of Splonum and Raetinum I have merged into one. So too Adetrium and Arduba.

Cassius Dio tells us that Germanicus captured Splonum despite it being well protected by walls, and nature. The rebels repelled the first attacks but then Pusio, a German horseman, threw a stone at the wall, and a section of it collapsed. Splonum's rebels were so shocked – so terrified of witchcraft – that they surrendered.

Germanicus then marched on Raetinum. He soon overwhelmed its defenders, but the rebels had set a trap: the walls and outer houses were set on fire, encircling the Romans that had poured into the town. The rebels escaped the flames by hiding in tunnels beneath the town. Many Roman soldiers perished in the blaze.

Despite that setback, the war was going in Rome's favour, albeit slowly. There was famine in Italy, largely due to the rebellion, and the men of the legions were eager to end the war. According to Dio, the soldiers were so impatient that Tiberius worried they might mutiny, and so he split his force into three columns. Tiberius dispatched two of his commanders with forces to attack rebel towns and tribes, and took Germanicus with him in pursuit of Bato and the main rebel force.

Considering that Germanicus had had independent command up until that point, I wonder if Tiberius was keeping him close so that the younger man didn't gain too much glory on his own. Regardless, they finally caught up with Bato at Adetrium, which was a fort close to modern-day Solin, in Croatia. Tiberius and his men could not overcome the fort's natural and man-made defences, and according to Dio, they were themselves besieged – Dalmatian rebels, operating in their homeland, made the resupply of Tiberius's force extremely difficult, and dangerous.

Honour forbade that Tiberius retreat, and believing the battle to be one he could not win, Bato eventually sought terms. His rebels would not accept them, however, and so Bato left these men – presumably a different tribe to his own – to carry on the fight elsewhere.

Tiberius launched an assault, sending his soldiers in a dense square that was eventually broken up by the terrain. The rebels let loose carts filled with stone, which caused bloody mayhem in the Roman ranks. Tiberius's men came close to breaking, and he was forced to continually send reserves up the slope to stop them from retreating. Many of the rebels had left their fort to fight, but they found themselves cut off by a flanking force that Tiberius had sent through the most difficult terrain (young soldiers, take note: there is no such thing as a flank secured by a natural obstacle. Expect the unexpected).

Abandoning their weapons and armour, the Dalmatians ran for the walls. Though they did keep the Romans out, they soon capitulated to Tiberius.

The battle was a pivotal one, but the Romans still had other pockets of resistance to put down before the flames of the rebellion were fanned again. The town of Arduba was one such place. Strongly fortified, with a swift river flowing all around its base, it was a formidable place.

It was Germanicus who offered clemency to the Dalmatians within the town, but none to the hundreds of Thracian and German deserters that had joined the rebellion. Though there is no record of it, I believe this was a deliberate tactic of Germanicus to create a wedge between the different nationalities in the rebel ranks. Apparently it worked, because fighting broke out inside Arduba. The women of the rebellion sided with the deserters, one group fearing rape and enslavement, and the other certain death as traitors. In a war that was nothing if not brutal and tragic, the end of these rebel families is particularly gut-wrenching. Certain that there was no escape, women took their children in their arms and jumped from Arduba's cliffs, or threw themselves into its flaming buildings.

Soon after, Bato sent his son to Tiberius to offer his unconditional surrender. A tribunal was established, where Bato asked no mercy for himself, even putting his neck forwards to take a blade. However, he made a case for clemency for his followers, saying, 'You Romans are to blame for this; for you send as guardians of your flocks, not dogs or shepherds, but wolves.'

After three years of battles and bloody campaigns, the rebellion was at an end, and for Rome, it was not a moment too soon. Mere days after Bato's final surrender, word reached Tiberius that three of Rome's legions had been ambushed and wiped out in Germany – the events that Corvus will become involved in in *Ambush*.

Of course, it would take Corvus more than a few days to walk from Croatia to Germany, and so I'm stretching the timeline in this series – but this is historical fiction, after all, and we wouldn't want him missing out on the great events of his time, would we?

And imagine… What if Bato had held out for another few months? A few weeks, even? On hearing the news that Varus had lost his three legions to Arminius, Tiberius immediately marched with the legions to secure the German frontier. He could not have done this unless the rebellion was put down. Something would have had to give. Would that have been in Germania, or Dalmatia? Bato and his followers were so close to forcing Rome's hand – how might that have changed the future of Europe?

Of course, we'll never know, nor will we know if Bato and Arminius had any idea of the other's intentions. I believe a case can be made that they did – they both had the same enemy – and also that they did not – alliances shifted quickly, and either could have sold out the other for their own gain.

It's been a lot of fun writing this series. As I mentioned above, it is historical fiction, so please take what I write with a grain of salt. I won't be giving Rome's soldiers AK-47s, but I will take artistic licence at times, including with the way that our characters talk. We're not reading this story in Latin and Illyrian, and so I try and find a point where the speech is familiar enough that we don't get taken out of the story. That means that this novel won't be for everyone, but so be it – no book is. For those of you who do enjoy it, and keep coming back, my heartfelt thanks. I love writing about Corvus and his friends, and I'm very excited to bring you the next one.

Oh yes, there's a next one, my friends.

As we know from *Ambush* and *Siege*, Corvus survives the first phases of Arminius's war against Rome. The survivors of those battles have escaped with their lives, for now, but reinforcements are coming with Tiberius, and they include the Eighth Legion.

The men who killed Corvus's father are coming to Germany, and with Arminius and the tribes risen against Rome, there's still a lot more blood to shed.

Acknowledgements

Writing and publishing a novel is a team effort. Thank you to Canelo, and Craig in particular, for championing this series.

Thank you to my friends, family, and agent, Rowan, for the usual support.

And final thanks belong to you, the reader. Thank you for joining me on this adventure. There would be no Corvus without you.